CHAMPAGNE TOAST, MURDER CHASER

JONI FOLGER

OLIVER HEBER BOOKS

ACKNOWLEDGMENTS

Each of us have those people in our lives who we know we can always count on, those who are there for us through thick and thin—and in area of my books—especially through edits, revisions, counseling, and support. (She said with a giggle) I have a few of those incredible folks that I'd like to thank, so bear with me...

First and foremost (as always) is agent extraordinaire, GDC—Christine Witthohn. I know that when needed, you're only a phone call away, though we don't get to chat as often as I'd like. Thank you for sharing your experience, wisdom, and support. You are a delight and a blessing, my friend.

Much love and gratitude goes to my long-time friend and sista, Natalie Bellissimo. Nat, no matter how far away you are, I know that I can always count on you. Your enthusiasm for what I write (no matter what I write) fills me with joy. And of course, your editing and grammar skills are an extraordinary thing to behold and very much appreciated. I've said it before, and I will say it again, you are and always will be... family.

And finally, a very special thanks to my editing pals Val 'Valine' Braun and Kelli McMellon. You guys are awesome—thanks for all that you do. Love you guys.

1

—————

Elise Beckett stepped through one of the elegant sets of French doors and out onto the wide wraparound veranda on the south side of Lodge Merlot—the event center for River Bend Winery and Vineyard—and into the warmth of a glorious April evening. Behind her, the building was lit up, decked out in its finery, and filled with humming conversation and flowing libations. She placed her glass of champagne on the railing and gazed out at the surrounding land with its row upon row of grapevines, now just silhouettes under the cover of twilight.

The 1,200 acres of fertile farmland that the vineyard now occupied had been in Elise's family for over a century, though the vineyard itself was only about 40 years old. With her degree in horticulture, and for more than a decade of that time, she'd helped to expand and shape the vineyard, caring for the original vines while adding the drought and disease-resistant hybrids which now flourished here.

Pride swelled in her chest and emotion swamped her. Like her father before her—God rest his soul—she'd always felt a keen connection to the land and the river beyond. The vineyard sat along the banks of the Colorado that flowed through Delphine, Texas. The river then meandered lazily from there through the county seat of Bastrop followed by Smithville and a myriad of other towns as it flowed southeasterly before emptying into the Gulf of Mexico.

River Bend was a big part of Delphine's history, and the entire Beckett family was involved in its operation. While Elise got to play in the dirt on a daily basis, her mother, Laura, along with Elise's older brother Ross, managed the operational and financial end of the business. Her younger sister, Madison, with her amazing creativity and attention to detail, was in charge of Lodge Merlot and all the fabulous events held there. And finally, her grandmother and matriarch of the Beckett family, Abigail DeVries—Miss Abby to just about everyone in the county—ran the Wine Barrel, the vineyards retail outlet.

Yes, River Bend was definitely a family affair all the way around and would continue to be so going forward.

They'd had lovely mid-April weather in the area for the last week or so with sunshine and delightfully cooler-than-normal temperatures in the upper seventies. Thankfully, the forecast showed more of the same for the next ten days. However, with summer right around the corner and the way the temps had been rising year after year, Elise was trying to enjoy the weather now and not worry about what may come in the next month or two and how that would affect the grapes.

Earlier today, as the Thursday afternoon had started to wane, car after car began to arrive at the vineyard, slowly filling Lodge Merlot's generous parking lot. By the time the big, golden orb had slipped over the horizon, the lodge had been filled to the brim with family and friends. This was the rehearsal dinner followed by a splashy party in anticipation of one of the biggest events of the season come Saturday: a Beckett family wedding.

My wedding, Elise thought with a smile.

She turned, and through the crystal-clear windows, her gaze swept over the full tables, the dance floor, her friends and loved ones, and finally, her fiancé. She still couldn't quite believe that on Saturday she would be marrying Sheriff's Deputy Jackson Landry right here on the vineyard.

It would be an outdoor wedding, and most of the preparations for that part of the event were already in place. Madison had really outdone herself, writing everything down in her big binder, every detail meticulously noted. The chairs for the attendees on the generous lawn and the arbor that she and Jackson would be married under were all set. They would begin prepping Lodge Merlot with the tables for the reception and dinner afterward first thing in the morning, and the rest of the countless decorations would be completed over the next two days. It was going to be lovely—her dream wedding come true—and an event to remember.

Jackson's parents, Sharee and Victor Landry, were archaeologists and had arrived the previous evening from South America where they'd been working on a dig for several years. They'd been gone for large portions of Jackson's early life, so Elise's grandmother had practically raised him. Along with Ross and Madison, Jackson had been part of the family for as long as Elise could remember. He'd been Ross' best friend—still was—and she'd always thought of him as another sibling... until she hadn't.

She didn't know exactly when her feelings for Jackson had changed, but boy had they. Unfortunately, their timing had never been good in the past. While she'd been involved in one relationship or another, Jackson had been unattached. And visa-versa on quite a few occasions. Happily, over the last few years they'd finally found their stride and, after Saturday, they would start their life together as Mr. and Mrs. Jackson Landry.

Mrs. Jackson Landry.

The butterflies in her belly fluttered their wings at the thought, and she couldn't keep the smile from her face.

At the sound of the French doors opening at her back, her smile grew. She didn't need to turn around to know that Jackson had come looking for her. She seemed to have a perfect radar for him lately and him for her.

"Whatcha doin' out here all by your lonesome, little lady?" he asked as he slipped an arm around her waist and pulled her back against his hard chest. "The party's inside, and I have it on good authority that your fiancé is looking for you to bail him out of all the uncomfortable situations happening in there."

Leaning back, she sighed. "I know exactly what you mean. I just needed a breather from all the questions ... and friendly advice. I tell ya, if one more well-meaning individual asks me when you and I are gonna start a family, I think I may have a meltdown."

His deep chuckle rumbled. "Yeah, you've got a point there. I got cornered by Elvira Hauser and her sister, Gladys, when I made the mistake of heading into the kitchen for another one of Ross' hidden beers. And now that I think about it, I do believe that was one of their questions." He sighed. "That there is a precious twenty minutes I will never get back."

Elise turned in his arms then and studied him. Jackson Landry was tall with a toned, athletic frame, a shock of sandy-brown hair, and dreamy deep-green eyes.

Just yummy, she thought. "Well, I'm sure you handled the Hauser sisters with your usual charming ways and had them eating out of your hand with that handsome face and rugged allure," she teased before sliding her arms around his waist.

He gave her a lazy grin. "Well, o'course, darlin'. They're both sweet on me, for sure. But then again, all the older ladies just drool over me, don't ya know? They all love said rugged allure."

Elise laughed out loud. "Yeah, well, they aren't the only ones, Deputy."

"Well now, I do like the sound of that." He leaned in for a quick kiss.

She took her time kissing him back before glancing over his shoulder to where she could see her brother in deep conversation with his wife at their table. And Caroline didn't look too happy.

"What's up with Ross and Caro?" she asked with a frown. "He'd better not cause a scene or make her mad. I'll have no choice but to whoop his butt in front of everyone."

"Too late for that, bruiser. I think you may have to get in line. After my twenty minutes with the Hauser ladies in the kitchen, I got back to the table to find him griping about how the evening was dragging on."

"I beg your pardon? There is a full blown party going on all around him in there."

Jackson chuckled. "Don't I know it. In any case, he seemed to think that I had some control over the event and complained that rehearsal dinners were a big waste of time and money."

"Please don't tell me that Caro heard that. As I recall, their rehearsal dinner was a spectacular event held right here at the Lodge a little over a decade ago," she replied, watching the two through the window. "I mean, I love my brother, but if she kills him at *our* rehearsal dinner, I will testify on her behalf at the trial."

"That would be why I'm out here with my beautiful fiancé and not in there where the smoke was beginning to billow. I tried to tell him that this rehearsal dinner wasn't really for us. That it was a time-honored tradition and money well spent."

She tilted her head and studied him. "What do you mean?"

"Well, El, come on. While Saturday is absolutely all about you and me, I'm of a mind that tonight is more like giving a select slice of family and friends a sneak peek at the coming event. Kind of a tease like a movie trailer. They get a preview as we walk it though." He nodded toward the party in full swing inside. "Then they get a nice meal and party to boot. Plus, it puts 'em all in a good mood for the main event on Saturday." He winked at her. "Know what I mean?"

She giggled and shook her head at his logic then leaned in to kiss his cheek. Really, he was just too adorable. And smart as a whip. "And tell me, Deputy, how did my idiot brother take that explanation?"

"Oh, he was having none of it." Jackson smirked. "He didn't even notice when Caro walked up behind him as he was pontificatin' on the whole thing. I tell ya, that boy never seems to learn. Caro can be quite stealthy, you know."

"Well, sounds like you did all you could by trying to talk some sense into him. Sometimes I just don't understand what my sister-in-law was thinking when she married him. It's just baffling to me." She glanced back through the window again where Caroline was now poking her finger into Ross' chest— a bad sign— as he was obviously trying to pacify her. "Still, you think we should go in there and rescue him? Or maybe at least separate 'em."

Jackson took a quick look over his shoulder then shook his head. "Nah, let's just give it a few more minutes. Caro will have him jerked up straight in a bit."

With a sigh, Elise turned and picked up her glass of champagne from the railing. Taking a sip, she gave him a sideways glance as he stepped to the railing next to her. "So, what do you have left to do tomorrow?"

He shook his head. "Not much. About all I have left on my list is to show up out here on Saturday and say 'I do', darlin'. Got the tickets for our flight to Napa Valley and then on to the Great Pacific Northwest via train ready to go. The rental car and hotel reservations are confirmed as well. All we have to do is get ourselves to Austin-Bergstrom airport on Sunday morning."

"Wait. Are you all packed?" she asked in shock as she stared at him over the rim of her glass.

"Well, mostly. I suspect there will probably be a few odds and ends pop up that I'll need to add between now and go time. How about you?"

Elise gave him a pained look. "You know how I hate packing, Jax. And to make matters worse, Maddy is already finished with her packing."

Jackson frowned. "Maddy?"

It was a bit unconventional, but Madison, along with Elise's best friend and bridesmaid, C.C. Duncan, bridesmaid Tina Babcock, as well as Tina's significant other and Jackson's deputy partner, Jim Stockton, were all joining them in the northwest in ten days. Miranda Rollins—who had more money than she'd ever spend in her lifetime, thanks to her late husband's investments—was footing the bill for the entire group to accompany her as she checked out the vineyard that he'd purchased a controlling interest in before he'd died.

Elise huffed out a breath. "Yes, Jax, Maddy. Have you forgotten about the group meeting up with us? Miranda, Madison, C.C., and Tina, as well as your partner, Jim?"

He gave a beleaguered sigh. "No, El, I haven't forgotten about them. Believe it or not, I still do have most of my mental faculties in place even after living through this whole wedding hullabaloo. I just don't get why Maddy's already packed and ready to go. I mean, they're not meetin' up with us for another two weeks."

She shook her head. "I'm sorry. I was under the impression that you'd met my sister Madison."

"Okay, okay, don't be a smart-ass. I guess after all these years I'm still baffled by the differences between the two of you, is all."

"Differences between us? Is that some kind of dig?"

Jackson laughed and pulled her into his arms. "Nope, just a statement of facts. You each have your own unique gifts and odd quirks, which I might add, makes you both adorable."

Elise probably would have taken umbrage at his comment but for that last bit. Still, she narrowed her eyes at him for good measure. "All right. Nice save, buddy." After a moment, she frowned. "Jax, you don't mind that we're meeting up with them on our honeymoon, do you?"

"Me? No, darlin'. We're gonna have two full weeks in Napa jam-packed with romance, wine tasting, good food, and so much more." He wiggled his eyebrows and leered at her.

"Very funny."

"Spoil Sport. Anyway, spending another week with friends for more fun and frivolity is fine by me."

"Fun and frivolity? Right." She gave him a speculative look. "But you don't mind all the wine stuff? I mean, our lives kind of revolve around River Bend here already."

"Nope. I'm actually looking forward to our two weeks in wine country, especially checking out that famous Napa Wine Train and the castle winery tour thing we've signed up for."

"Me too. I'm also excited to visit Miranda's Bella Luna winery in Oregon as well. It's a small vineyard, but the winery is a castle similar to the one in Napa built with stone shipped over from Italy." She shook her head. "I don't think she's even been there yet, but it sounds like she and one of the other shareholders have gotten off to a rocky long-distance start. So, in true Miranda style, I guess she's going to make herself known in person, being the majority shareholder and all."

Jackson grinned. "Well, that ought to be fun to watch. Miranda is anything but subtle, but then again, she can be pretty charming when she wants to be. She'll probably have them wrapped around her little finger before it's all said and done."

"Probably, knowing Miranda. Anyway, the vineyard is only a little over an hour from Pelican Point on the coast where David and RJ have taken over David's aunt's theater company. It will be nice to have a visit with them in a pleasant environment after the death and mayhem at the Delphine Opera House a few years ago. The murder mystery the two had put together for the restoration debut would have been spectacular without the whole 'real murder' thing on opening night."

David Marchant and his partner RJ Taylor had moved to the Oregon coast to take over David's aunt's theater company right after the whole murder debacle at the newly remodeled historic Opera House in downtown Delphine. The murder had happened on stage in front of a full house on opening night. The two men had already planned their move to Pelican Point long before that terrible night, but it had left a sad mark on what would have been a lovely end to their time in Delphine. Still, Elise was looking forward to seeing them again.

"Yeah, that show got off to an interesting start but ended pretty abruptly, I will say that," Jackson agreed. "After that investigation, I'm good with no death and mayhem for a while. Plus, I don't even want to think about how that could have ended, as I'm not keen on losing you anytime soon. And that there was too close for my comfort."

"Absolutely. I'm with you on that. It was way too close."

Shaking off the murder vibe and the uncomfortable memories, Elise sought to lighten the mood. "Seems like Sharee and Victor are doing well and don't look any worse for wear after traveling all the way from South America and getting in late last night. I would be wiped out traveling that far the night before an event like this, but they both look unfazed."

Jackson looked through the windows to the dance floor where his dad was dancing with Miss Abby and his mother was cutting the rug with Neil Paige, the vineyard's foreman and Laura Beckett's not-so-secret beau. "Yeah, living the outdoor life in remote areas of the planet and diggin' in the dirt seems to work for them."

She could hear the touch of sadness in his voice, feel his longing for the parents that were always gone. "You know they love you very much, right, Jax?"

"Oh, I know, El. They love me as much as they're able to love anything other than the next dig, and I'm glad they could take time to be here. I'm fond of them as well, in my own way, but let's be honest here, Sharee and Victor Landry should never have had a child. I think they just figured that out a bit too late."

"Jax— "

"No, El, don't give me those sorrowful eyes. It's true and you know it. I came to accept that fact a long time ago. Miss Abby raised me out here on this vineyard with y'all. That's just plain fact. And I thank the Big Guy upstairs for her every single day."

"I love you, Jackson Landry," Elise murmured with misty eyes. "We've always been your family, and come Saturday, it's you and me, love."

"And that's enough for me, darlin'."

Just as he leaned in for another kiss, the second set of French doors farther down the veranda opened and Miranda Rollins stepped out, cell phone to her ear. And it was obvious that the woman was fighting mad. Elise and Jackson couldn't help but hear her angry words from where they stood in the shadows twenty-five feet away. Whether Miranda knew they were there or not, or just didn't care who overheard, she fired off her words in sharp, no uncertain terms.

"Now you listen to me, you ugly little man. You don't know me or anything about me, but I will tell you this. Insulting my intelligence or disparaging my late husband will get you nothing but trouble. I have already made my position on this topic well known over the last few weeks, and I haven't changed my mind."

With wide eyes, Elise held her breath as she and Jackson listened to Miranda's side of the heated conversation.

"*Really*?" Miranda asked with sarcasm and a raised eyebrow before laughing out loud. "Oh, sweetie, you really have no idea who you're talking to, do you? You may think you can sucker the other two owners into selling to you for a pittance but you're wrong. I've already spoken to both of them, and that's never going to happen for you. Besides, even if you could somehow talk them into taking your pathetic offer, you do realize that it would do you no good, correct? I own controlling interest in Bella Luna, and even with their shares, you would still fall woefully short."

Something must have caught the woman's attention as she listened to the man on the other end of the line because she turned slightly and her eyes widen for an instant when she saw Elise and Jackson. Then, with a heavy sigh, she went back to her conversation.

"Look, you can bluster all you want, but I'm pretty sure my attorney made the situation crystal clear to you. I will not allow you to tear Bella Luna apart no matter what you say. I'm going to be there in two weeks' time, and if you go against my wishes, if you do *anything* in the meantime, trust me when I say that you will regret it with every fiber of your being. I will do whatever I have to do to take you down. Do you understand me?" Miranda shook her head and smiled. "No, that's not a threat, you idiot. That's a promise."

With that, she ended the call and turned to Elise and Jackson with a pained look. "Sorry you two had to hear that."

"Is everything okay, Miranda?" Elise asked.

Miranda laughed out loud. "Did it sound okay, El?" Before Elise could respond, the woman waved a hand in the air and shook her head. "Sorry, I didn't mean that. Thanks for the concern, but it's nothing I can't handle, and my attorney is already on it."

"More problems at Bella Luna?"

Miranda nodded and her brandy-colored eyes sparked with her anger. "That man is the most underhanded little pissant that I've come across in quite a while. He wants to buy out everyone on the cheap, break up the vineyard, and sell the land for a huge price. Like we wouldn't see what he was doing. So stupid. Anyway, it's not going to happen, and I will make sure of that one way or another. Everything's gonna be fine by the time y'all get there. Promise." Looking around, she ran a hand through her honey-blonde hair. "Well, I think I deserve another glass of River Bend's fine champagne. I'll see y'all back inside."

Elise watched her friend head back into the building before turning to Jackson. "Well, that was uncomfortable."

Jackson chuckled. "That's a bit of an understatement, pal."

"I hope she can smooth it all out. I was looking forward to seeing Bella Luna but not if it's going to be in turmoil."

Jackson tucked a strand of hair behind her ear and smiled. "Let's not borrow trouble, okay? We're gettin' hitched in two days' time. How about we just bask in the pre-wedding glory for now."

Elise giggled. "The 'pre-wedding glory?' Boy, you really are in a mood, Deputy Landry."

"I am feeling quite festive, darlin'," he replied as he leaned in for another kiss.

In the next moment, the French doors at their backs blew open and Ross' voice boomed across the veranda at them, "There you two are. What the hell are you doing out here? You're gonna have plenty of time for that mushy crap over the next few weeks while we're all here slavin' away. Get your butts in here. Gram wants to say a few words."

Elise turned to Jackson as her brother went back to the party. "I've said it before and I will say it again. My sister-in-law is *such* a lucky woman," she said tongue-in-cheek.

Jackson rolled his eyes. "Guess we'd better get a move on before he has a meltdown. Plus, we don't want to keep Miss Abby waiting."

He held out his arm, and as she took it, they strolled back into the lights and sound of the party. But though she tried, Elise couldn't get Miranda's ominous words out of her head.

I will do whatever I have to do to take you down.

"Ouch! For the love of mud, Wanda. Careful with those pins, okay?" Elise winced. "I'd like to get through this day without having to call for a medic or stem the flow of blood from a head wound. I'm wearing white today, you know."

"Sorry, Elise." Holding out her hands, Wanda Haverty laughed and shook her head. "Would you look at that? My hands are shaking so bad that you'd think I was the one tying the knot in the next forty-five minutes or so, and not you."

"It's okay. Trust me. I'm right there with you." Elise laughed along with the hairdresser. "You've done a beautiful job. It's perfect. Really."

She watched in the mirror as Wanda put the finishing touch, and hopefully, the last bobby pin into place in the elegant chignon she'd created for Elise's wedding day.

Her wedding day.

The very thought just about robbed her of breath and had her pulse picking up speed.

The morning had begun with a non-stop flood of activity that, at a quarter after one, showed little sign of slowing until the two o'clock festivities concluded and the reception began. She was starting to worry that she wouldn't be able to catch a normal breath and relax until then. Looking in the vanity mirror, her eyes strayed to her wedding dress and veil hanging on the armoire door behind her.

The sleeveless, trumpet-style dress with its lace-edged court train had a square neckline and lace back with a zipper hidden by lovely satin-covered buttons down the back to the waist. The matching lace veil would be the last touch put in place with a comb, covering the exquisite chignon that Wanda had just finished. The veil was long and would trail to the floor behind her.

Staring at the veil, her heart began to pound. She felt her nervousness start to grow, but before her mind could get really amped up and go any further down the anxiety rabbit hole, her sister entered the bedroom, a striking vision in ice-blue chiffon. The bridesmaid's trumpet-style, floor-length gown held a similar silhouette to Elise's wedding dress and complemented Madison's dark blond hair and cornflower blue eyes perfectly. The sleek, backless gown with its crisscrossing spaghetti straps, boned bodice, and leg slit from knee to ankle on one side was both simple and elegant. The nosegays that the three brides-maids would carry also reflected Elise's cascading bouquet with its lavender roses, white lilies, pale blue delphiniums, and baby's breath. The color scheme was carried throughout the wedding party, the table decorations for the reception, and the arbor for the ceremony.

"So, everything is set and looks amazing down at the Lodge. I'm telling y'all, that wedding cake is a work of art. Cheryl Taylor is a genius. The caterer arrived about an hour ago and is already set up and ready to go. We're right on schedule," Madison told her in a voice that was cool as a spring breeze as she crossed to where Elise sat at the vanity to inspect Wanda's handiwork. "The wedding guests have started to arrive and the parking lot is halfway full already." She frowned at Elise and then raised an eyebrow. "Why are you grinning at me like that?"

Elise reached for her sister's hand and blinked back her misty sentiment. "*You* are the genius. There are a gazillion moving parts to this thing. I don't know how you've pulled it all together. And you look so beautiful, Maddy. It just fills me with joy, that's all."

Madison squeezed her hand briefly before rolling her eyes. "Have you gotten into the champagne early? Let's not get too gooey yet, okay? I've just spent an hour on my makeup, and you can't ruin yours before the ceremony." She cleared the emotion from her throat and turned to the hairdresser with a thumbs up and a nod of approval. "That chignon is spot on, Wanda. Really lovely work."

"Thanks, Madison. I just told Elise that I think I'm more nervous than she is."

"Not possible," Elise replied. "I'm just really good at internalizing."

"Internalizing what?" Laura Beckett asked as she entered the room followed by Miss Abby, C.C., and Tina.

"Only my terror," Elise said with a laugh.

"Oh, pooh," her grandmother replied with a wave of her hand. She leaned down and hugged Elise from behind, meeting her gaze in the vanity mirror. "You and Jax were made for each other, little girl. So, you just let go of any anxiety you may have about this day. Nothing but joy today. You hear me?"

Elise blinked back tears that threatened again. She really had to get a grip. "Yes, ma'am. I love you, Gram."

"Ditto, moon pie. Now, come on, let's get you into that beautiful dress. We're on the countdown. We've got a little over half an hour until showtime, and we're sticking to the schedule."

As Elise stood, Laura pulled her into her arms and spoke quietly into her ear. "I'm so proud of you and Jax, sweetheart." Then she leaned back and cupped Elise's cheek. "And I know that your daddy is looking down from heaven right now and beaming with joy for the both of you."

Elise cleared her throat. "Thanks, Mom."

"Okay, okay, save the waterworks for the main event. Let's get a move on," Miss Abby prodded. "Times a'wastin'."

Laura frowned. "Geez, Mom, take a breath. The wedding can't start without the bride, and I reserve my right to say my piece before we walk my girl down that aisle."

"Fine, fine. Whatever. Just make it snappy."

Laura grinned at Elise and shook her head. "That said, let's get you into that dress. Neil has the open horse-drawn carriage ready and waiting out front."

"Ross will text me when everyone's seated and he, Jax, Jim, and Wes are about to take their places," Madison added. "We'll head down then."

Between her mom and grandmother, they helped Elise into the stunning gown. Madison zipped it up the back and helped C.C and Tina to fluff and smooth out the train of the skirt. As Elise turned toward the mirror, her breath caught at the vision she saw there.

Laura stood back with Miss Abby and put a hand over her heart. "Oh, my beautiful girl, you are going to take Jackson's breath away the minute he sets eyes on you."

Miss Abby took out her lace handkerchief and dabbed at her own eyes. "I can't wait for that boy to see you, darlin', to watch him take your hand."

"Okay, now y'all have to stop that right this minute," Madison said. "Or we're never going to make it. We'll all have a meltdown right here and now."

Laura took a deep breath and slowly let it out with a nod. "You're absolutely right, Maddy. I'm counting on you to keep us on schedule. We'll just have to suck it up." She addressed Elise as she turned to them. "So, let's go down the checklist, El. Something old, something new, something borrowed, something blue. All covered?"

Elise nodded. "Yes, ma'am. I've got a blue garter as well as blue flowers in my bouquet. The garter is also new, so two birds, one stone. Gram gave me a beautiful lace handkerchief to borrow for the day, and you gave me the lovely antique necklace I'm wearing as a wedding gift. So, I think we've got it all covered."

"Excellent."

About that time, Madison's phone chimed. "It's Ross," she confirmed, looking at the incoming text. "He says that the last of the guests are being seated now. Pastor Miller will address the congregation, and then she'll give Jax and the groomsmen the sign to get into place. So, we should get going."

Elise again tried to catch her breath as Wanda finished attaching her veil and C.C. handed her the spectacular cascading bouquet, but her pulse raced and she couldn't quite settle her nerves. In a flurry, they headed downstairs and out the front door to where Neil stood waiting and ready to help them all into the carriage.

Then they were on the move again. She didn't know if it was the gentle sway of the carriage, the soothing clip-clop of the horses' hooves on the driveway, or the excited chatter of her brides-maids, but she gradually felt a sense of calm begin to settle over her. By the time the horse came to a halt down the driveway at Lodge Merlot and they'd all stepped down out of the carriage, her nerves had finally steadied a bit.

As Madison's phone chimed again, she looked up with a smile when they heard the beginning strains of Pachelbel's Cannon in D major. "That's our cue." She gave Elise a quick hug. "See you on the other side, Sis."

From her vantage point on the walkway at the side of the Lodge, Elise watched her bridesmaids turn the corner one by one and begin their walk down the long, grassy aisle. After a few moments, Pachelbel slowly diminished and the chords changed to the traditional Wedding March.

"Ready?" Laura asked quietly.

"I am," she replied with a nod. With her mother on one side and her grandmother on the other, they followed the bridesmaids around the corner and began their walk toward the arbor where Jackson waited, tall and handsome. As the smile spread across his face and their eyes met, every fear, every bit of anxiety she'd had up to this point simply vanished like so much mist. A sense of rightness settled over her and, as they neared, she smiled back at him, incredible joy blossoming in her chest.

When they reached the arbor, both her mother and grandmother kissed her on each cheek, and Jackson took her hand as she stepped up next to him.

"Hey, pal," he murmured. "You ready for this?"

"Hey, yourself," she answered. "I'm absolutely ready."

And then Pastor Miller began, "Dearly beloved ... "

It was mostly a traditional ceremony until they got to the vows.

At that point, Pastor Miller gave them both a radiant smile. "I understand y'all have written your own vows," she said. "Jackson, would you please begin?"

Elise handed Madison her bouquet and turned to face Jackson as he cleared his throat, took her hands in his, and looked deep into her eyes.

"Elise Brianna Beckett, we've known each other since we were kids. I'm not sure why it took me so long to realize that I've loved you for most of that time, but I guess everything happens when it's supposed to. What I do know for certain is that going forward, no matter what life throws at us, my love for you will only strengthen, because I'm gonna love you for the rest of my life, darlin'. We've laughed together, fought together. You challenge me, frustrate me, make me laugh, and give me comfort. You constantly surprise me, and I've found that I need you beside me like I need my next breath." He turned and took her wedding ring from Ross. Sliding it onto her finger, his bright green eyes sparkled. "So, here in front of family and friends, with this ring I entrust you with my heart and vow to safeguard yours with all that I possess. I promise fidelity and devotion to honor and cherish you for all the days I'm given."

Elise felt a rush of tears rise but blinked them back as best she could before taking a deep breath and letting it out slowly. "Jackson Christopher Landry, I feel deep down that you've been a part of my life forever. We've had our triumphs and our struggles, we've fought and made up, we've given each other comfort when needed, space when required. I believe a soulmate is someone who has the keys to your locks. You have the key to make me calm when I'm anxious. Motivated, when I am uninspired. Passionate, when I am downcast. You have the keys that make me a better person in every way. You unlock every aspect of me that's good. You are all that I need, and I love you with every fiber of my being."

She turned and took his wedding band from Madison. Sliding it onto his finger, she beamed up at him with all the love in her heart. "So, here in front of family and friends, with this ring I entrust you with my heart and vow to safeguard yours with all that I possess. I promise fidelity and devotion to honor and cherish you for all the days I'm given."

As they stood gazing at each other with all the emotions running through them, Pastor Miller laid her hand over their clasped hands, raising the other into the air in blessing. "And now, by the power vested in me, it is my honor and delight to declare you married. Go forth on your journey together and live each day to the fullest. You may seal this declaration with a kiss."

Grinning from ear to ear, Jackson pulled her into his arms and kissed her good and proper to the hoots and hollers of the congregation.

And the celebration commenced...

. . .

ELISE SURFACED SLOWLY the next morning, as she always did, and flung a hand out to Jackson's side of the bed. Her eyes popped open when she found his side empty. Of course, Jackson was usually up at the crack of dawn, and she was definitely not an early riser, but on their first morning as a married couple, she would have preferred to wake up with him next to her. Even Chunk, her sixteen pound Snowshoe Siamese was nowhere to be seen, though that was no surprise. The persnickety feline had always been partial to Jackson, for sure. However, since moving into Jackson's sprawling ranch-style home on the outskirts of Delphine less than a month ago— now *their* home— Chunk had acclimated at the speed of sound and taken to constantly following Jackson around when he was home. Chunk was fickle that way.

The wedding reception and dinner had raged on for close to four hours after the ceremony, and it was almost seven p.m. by the time the last of the guests had driven away. The immediate family had adjourned to the manor house for a couple hours to wind down and spend the last of the evening together while the cleaning crew began the process of setting the Lodge to rights for the next engagement. Still, she and Jackson had gotten back to the house just after ten, putting all the wedding gifts into the spare room for opening when they returned from their honeymoon. Elise made sure that door was closed good and tight. She wasn't about to have Chunk getting into their wedding gifts, which he would absolutely do, given an opportunity.

Today, they would go back to the vineyard for a family brunch at eleven o'clock before getting ready to head to the airport for their flight to California later in the afternoon.

Casting an eyeball at the clock on the bedstand—at just after eight, and earlier than she'd expected—she finally dragged herself out of bed, threw on a robe, and went looking for her two guys. She found them both in the living room. Jackson was lounging on the sofa with the Sunday newspaper and a cup of coffee in hand while Chunk was snuggled up close and pawing at said newspaper every so often to get Jackson's attention.

She stood watching from the doorway for a moment with a smile on her face before Jackson finally looked up.

"Well, are you just gonna stand there grinning at us? Or are you gonna get your morning cola and join us on the sofa?" he asked with a wink. "Chunk has been wondering where you were."

"Ha! Now, that's a crock." She pointed to the lazy fat-cat and shook her head. "That big tub of lard has preferred you right from the start, but now that we're living here with you, I don't think I even exist for him anymore."

"Oh, come on. That's not true. Just depends on who's filling the food dish, that's all."

Elise slapped a hand on her hip. "Is that a swipe at me for not being a morning person? Because he was fine and dandy with having his breakfast mid-morning when we lived at the apartment. That he gets up with you before the sun has even approached the horizon, just goes to show how fickle he is and how low he'll stoop for a full dish."

"Whoa, whoa, whoa," Jackson said, putting up a hand. "Take it down a notch, darlin'. That was just a statement of fact, not an accusation of any kind. It also was an acknowledgement of your last sentence, because I am well aware of his propensity for manipulation. He and I have had that conversation."

Chunk had been watching their exchange like a tennis spectator, but at Jackson's last comment—as if he understood exactly what was being said—he gave them both a bored look. Jumping down from the sofa, he crossed to his papasan chair, nestled in on the seat with his back to them, and began to bathe.

"Now, see what you've done?" Jackson asked with a sad look. "You've hurt the poor boy's feelings."

"Yeah, like he's got any feelings to hurt."

With a chuckle, Jackson shook his head. "Did you talk to your mom about taking care of him while we're gone?"

"I did. She's going to come over every couple of days to check on him, scoop his boxes, make sure that he has food and water. Lord knows, I would never ask Ross to do it. We'd have an emaciated fur-baby living in squalor by the time we came home."

"Probably an accurate assessment."

After retrieving a cold diet cola from the refrigerator, Elise joined him on the sofa. "So, since we're going directly to the airport after brunch, what all do we have to do before heading over to the vineyard?"

Jackson folded the newspaper and set it aside. "Nothing for the trip. I've already loaded our bags into the rig. Ross is gonna go with us to the airport. He'll drop us off and then leave my truck at the vineyard so we won't have to pay for parking while we're gone."

"That's convenient. But what if I find something else that I wanna pack?"

He raised an eyebrow at her. "Sugar, I'm not sure there's anything left in this house for you *to* pack, so I'm not all that worried about it. You could barely get the roller bag zipped, remember? I have visions of buying you a whole new wardrobe in California when that bag explodes in the aircraft bin from the pressure."

"Ha-ha. Very funny. It wasn't that bad ... after I took a few things out," she muttered under her breath.

"There you go."

Setting her can of diet cola on the coffee table, she sighed.

He tilted his head then and gave her a curious look. "So, what's with the frown?"

"What? Oh, I was just thinking about Miranda."

"Miranda? That's kinda out of the blue. What about her?"

"You know how we overheard that tense phone conversation she had on the Lodge veranda on Thursday night at the rehearsal dinner? The one with the other shareholder that she's having problems with?"

"Yeah," he replied hesitantly. "And?"

"Well, I think it happened again yesterday at the reception."

Jackson gave her a narrowed look. "You *think*?"

"Okay, don't look at me like that. I just sort of overheard bits and pieces of it."

"El ... "

"No, really, listen to me. It wasn't like I was eavesdropping. I'm telling you that it got pretty heated again, Jax. She threatened legal action, which is her business, I know, but she's paying for Maddy, C.C., Tina, and Jim to come out and meet us at that same vineyard in two weeks. If this disagreement becomes an all-out war between shareholders, I'd hate to see her spend all that money and then have it be a mess and uncomfortable for everyone when we all get there."

Jackson ran a hand over his face. "Look, again, let's not borrow trouble. This is not our circus, El, not our monkeys." He put up a hand when she would have argued and spoke in a stern tone. "Miranda Rollins is perfectly capable of taking care of herself *and* has the money and attorneys to do so. If the situation is not resolved by the time we all get up to the northwest, then I say that we just continue on to Pelican Point for a visit with David and RJ."

"But—"

"No buts. Listen, if the circumstances get worse, and she doesn't cancel the whole thing, then in my mind, that's on her. But either way, it's her business, darlin'. However, knowing Miranda, if that's the way this goes, and we end up bypassing that stop, she'll understand."

"I guess."

"Now ... " he began, and before she could form her next thought, Jackson snaked an arm around her waist and pulled her onto his lap.

"Hey. You're taking your life into your hands, mister. I haven't sucked down but a quarter of my cola requirement yet this morning."

He grinned. "I'll take my chances as *I* haven't gotten a proper good morning from my wife yet."

"Your wife. I do like the sound of that." She leaned in and ran a hand over the stubble of his jawline. "I suppose we should rectify that discrepancy."

Then he was kissing her almost before the words were out of her mouth.

TWO HOURS LATER, they'd both showered, dressed, said their goodbyes to the fat-cat, and arrived at the vineyard with Madison pulling her car in beside them.

"Good morning, newlyweds," she called as she got out of her SUV hybrid and walked toward them.

"Morning, Sis," Elise replied. "How's the apartment?"

"So far, so good." Madison nodded as they walked up the steps to the front door of the manor house. "Still unpacking and organizing. I will say, two weeks in, it's still kinda weird. I mean, not living out here at the vineyard anymore, but I suppose I'll get used to it. I really did need a place of my own. I'd just been putting it off, and Mr. and Mrs. Powers are really the best landlords you could have."

"They really are," Elise agreed. "I loved living in that little apartment over their pharmacy. And having them right downstairs is a plus you'll come to appreciate if and when things go wrong."

"Well, thanks for putting in a good word, El."

"Please. They know you, Maddy. They were really just glad to have a smooth transition to someone they knew and not to have to go through the advertising and vetting process for a new renter."

"It's still appreciated, El. Made it really easy on me."

As they entered the house, the scent of bacon filled the air and had Elise's stomach growling. Laura came out of her office as they started down the hallway toward the kitchen.

"Hey, there they are, the newlyweds." She gave Elise a hug, then Jackson.

"Really? So, what am I? Chopped liver?" Madison asked with a faux pout. "I tell ya, you move out, and two weeks later, nobody knows your name."

"Oh, stop." Laura laughed and gave Madison a hug as well. "I miss you gobs ... what was your name again?"

"OMG, you're so funny, Mom."

They all headed to the dining room where Ross was already seated at the table and scrolling on his phone.

"Hey, big brother," Elise greeted him with a hug from behind and a kiss on the cheek.

"Wow. What did Jax put in your diet cola? You're never nice to me, especially not at ... " He made a show of looking at his watch. "Ten-twenty in the morning."

"That is so not true, and don't be a jerk." Elise shook her head and took a seat opposite him at the table.

Jackson sat down next to her. "And don't bring me into this, buddy."

"So, where's Caro?" Madison asked.

"She'll be along in a bit with the boys."

Elise smirked at him. "She still mad at you?"

Ross glared at her. "She's not mad at me, El."

"The look on her face Thursday evening said differently." She laughed and gave him a dubious look.

"Yeah, well, we've talked that out since then. It's fine."

Jackson grinned. "You do know what *fine* means, don'cha?"

"Shut up, Jax."

"Alright, alright, that's enough," Laura intervened. "I'm gonna go see if Mom needs any help. Play nice, children."

In the lull, Madison sat down next to Elise with a cautious look. "Hey, El. Have you heard from Miranda?"

Elise slipped a quick glance to Jackson who narrowed his eyes. "Uh, not today. Why?"

"Well, I think she's been having some kind of trouble with someone in the northwest, maybe at the vineyard where we're meeting you. She seemed to be on the phone a lot toward the end of the reception yesterday. I heard bits and pieces of one of the calls. And she left a little early." Madison shook her head. "I mean, we all have the tickets for our flight out in ten days, but I just wanted to make sure everything was okay. I'll try calling later."

Elise turned and pointed a finger at Jackson. "See, it's not just me."

"What do you mean, El?" Madison asked.

"It's nothing, Maddy," Jackson answered before giving Elise a meaningful stare. "It's Miranda's business. We need to leave it be. If she needs anything from us, which I have no idea what that would possibly be, she'll say so. Like I said, not our circus."

In the next moment, Laura came through from the kitchen with a platter of crisp bacon in one hand and a basket of piping-hot biscuits in the other, followed by Miss Abby carrying a huge breakfast casserole. Orange juice and coffee were already sitting on the buffet along the far wall. It looked like they were getting a breakfast feast for their send-off this morning.

"Let it go, El," Jackson murmured quietly. "It'll all work itself out."

She nodded, but a bad feeling was starting to take hold, and she could only hope he was right.

3

B y two thirty, they'd finished brunch. Jackson's parents had left early to start their trek back down to South America and their beloved dig, and he and Elise had said their goodbyes to her family. Ross rode with them to the airport, and he'd surprised Elise with a bear hug right there on the curb at departures, which was completely out of character for him. It was actually sort of sweet the way he'd mumbled his way through a quasi-congratulations speech before climbing into the truck cab and driving away.

They'd slogged their way through security to their departure gate, and after a three-hour flight, landed in Los Angeles at the tail end of rush hour; though Elise was unsure if there was actually ever an end to rush hour traffic in Los Angeles. They'd spent a lovely evening in Malibu with a couple of Jackson's old friends before heading toward Napa the next morning.

Their reservation at the huge craftsman-style bed and breakfast in the heart of Napa was outstanding and a perfect location to see the sights in town. The famous Wine Train was a delight that they'd indulged in twice—once for lunch with tours and tastings at two separate wineries, and once for an incredibly romantic dinner at the end of their first week. They'd spent much of their ten days in Napa just driving around the vineyard-covered landscape, taking photos, shopping, and visiting various wineries.

Each vineyard they'd visited had given Elise a different perspective on the propagation and cultivation of several new grape varieties that were proving heartier and more resilient in the face of changing weather patterns. Like her family's vineyard during the Bastrop County Fire all those years ago, Napa Valley's vineyards had endured their own wildfires a handful of years after that. However, also like River Bend, they now seemed to be flourishing again.

Their last day in the Napa area had been highlighted with a lovely and informative afternoon at Castello di Amorosa just outside of Calistoga. At the remarkable castle winery, they'd enjoyed more tastings and spent several hours on a guided tour of the massive 14th century Tuscan-style castle winery. From what she'd heard, Bella Luna, the vineyard and winery in the Pacific Northwest that Miranda's late husband had invested in, had been based on Castello di Amorosa over a decade ago. Though on a much smaller scale, the original owners had built the castle winery itself in much the same manner with stone shipped over from Italy. Elise couldn't wait to get a look at Bella Luna after touring Castello di Amorosa.

Considering that she had grown up on a vineyard, as well as the time spent at River Bend cultivating and tending the grapes, it was hard for Elise to say that she'd ever had too much wine. That said, by the time they'd dropped off the rental car on Thursday morning and caught the bus from downtown Napa to Martinez Amtrak Station for their sleeper car to the Pacific Northwest, she'd come close to her limit. Of course, that didn't mean that they couldn't send a couple of cases of outstanding vino home to be waiting for them when they returned.

Neither of them had ever had the opportunity to travel by train and were pleasantly surprised by the experience. Their sleeper car was small but comfortable and provided a lovely break from the hubbub of the previous few weeks. The overnight trip up the west coast had been peaceful and unhurried, so by the time they arrived at their destination late Friday afternoon and picked up yet another rental car, instead of being travel-weary, Elise felt energized and ready for the next leg of their trip.

Miranda had made reservations for them at the same bed and breakfast as the rest of the gang, so as they followed the GPS directions, Elise gave Madison a call.

"Hey, Sis," Madison answered. "You guys on your way?"

"Yep. GPS says another twenty-five minutes should do it. Everything okay there?"

"I guess," Madison said after a slight pause. "Miranda met us here when we got in this afternoon. Seems she's been here for a couple of days dealing with some business things at the winery. Anyway, Meadowview, the small town where we're staying, is really pretty, El. It's so green and lush, and the weather has been beautiful, though sixty-five degrees is a bit cool for my Texas blood."

Elise laughed. "Throw on a sweater, little sister. I can't wait to see it all."

"Bella Luna is only about ten miles out of town, and Miranda's going to give us a short tour of some of the common areas of the winery itself after dinner. I suppose we'll get the full deal tomorrow during daylight hours. I told her that I'd call her when you guys got in. She made the dinner reservation for six-thirty, so that should give you and Jax an hour or so to check in and freshen up from your trip beforehand."

Elise breathed a sigh of relief. It sounded as though Miranda had possibly resolved at least some of the problems she'd been having with one of the other Bella Luna shareholders. Hopefully, they would all have a pleasant stay without the stress of that conflict hanging over their trip. "That sounds good, Maddy. I'm actually starting to get hungry, so the timing will be perfect. We'll see you in a bit."

"Everything okay?" Jackson asked when she hung up.

"Seems like. Dinner reservations are at six thirty, and afterwards Miranda's going to give us a short tour out at Bella Luna. We'll get the full tour tomorrow. Since we're staying here for the rest of the week, and Pelican Point is only about an hour away, maybe we can take a run over to the coast the day after tomorrow for our visit with David and RJ."

"Good plan."

"I'll give them a call when I know more about our schedule here. I'm really looking forward to seeing what the guys have accomplished with David's aunt's theater."

Jackson nodded. "While that theater stuff isn't really my thing, they did a pretty good job with the renovation of the Opera House in Delphine, for sure. So, if that's any indication, my guess is that the theater in Pelican Point will be another job well done."

Twenty minutes later, they pulled into the gravel parking lot of Riverside Manor, a large, farmhouse-style bed and breakfast set on the banks of the small stream that cut through the heart of

Meadowview. Once they'd checked in and freshened up, Elise and Jackson met up with the rest of the group in the small room off the parlor that served as a cubby bar while they waited for Miranda.

"How's your room?" Tina asked as they got seated in the comfortable over-sized chairs. "Ours is so great, really comfy and pretty."

"Yeah, really pretty," Jim echoed with wide eyes and a sarcastic tone. "That's the important part."

Tina narrowed her eyes at him. "Be very careful with that tone, Jim Stockton. If you want to make fun of me, you are more than welcome to find another room better suited to your manly tastes."

Jim sighed. "Now, darlin', I wasn't making fun of you, just jokin' around a bit."

Tina harrumphed but relented some when Jim reached over and took her hand.

"Our room is lovely as well and overlooks the river," Elise said as she studied the memorabilia on the cubby walls. "And I love the old world feel of this place."

C.C. nodded. "Me too. From the little I've seen so far, the whole town gives off that old world vibe you're talking about. It's so cool. Like something out of a bygone era."

"So, how was the honeymoon? Did y'all have a good time in Napa?" Tina asked, wiggling her eyebrows suggestively. "I bet you drank a ton of vino."

Jackson chuckled. "Yeah, I'm pretty wined out." He held up his beer glass. "Hence the brew."

"We did have a couple cases shipped home," Elise added. "But I'm with Jax. I think I tasted, sipped, and drank more wine in the last two weeks than I have in the last six months at home. Which is definitely saying something."

"Well, you'll just have to suck it up," Miranda said as she came into the room on the heels of Elise's comment. "Because I've set up a tasting tomorrow after a full tour of the vineyard and winery. There's a small tasting room in the basement of the castle just off the cask room. So, we'll take a ride around the vineyard—which I know you're jonesing for, Elise—then tour the castle and finish off with the tasting."

Madison laughed. "I'm sure we'll all put on a brave face and muscle through the inconvenience, Miranda. I, for one, am so looking forward to it, as I'm not wined out quite yet."

Miranda looked at her watch. "Okay, well, let's head out. The restaurant is within walking distance and our dinner reservation is in twenty minutes. Gives us plenty of time to get there and get seated."

Dinner was a lively affair at the little Italian restaurant, with the gang peppering Elise and Jackson with questions about Napa and their honeymoon. Miranda seemed like her old self, so although Elise was curious about how her friend's problem out at Bella Luna with the other shareholder had been resolved, she hesitated to mention it. Like Jackson had said before they'd left River Bend, it really wasn't their business, anyway. By the time they'd finished dinner an hour and a half later, the sun had set and darkness had settled over the landscape.

"Miranda, are you sure you want to head over to Bella Luna this late?" Jackson asked as they all walked back to Riverside Manor. "I mean, if we're gonna be coming out tomorrow for a full tour, we'll have daylight to see the grounds and we can see the winery in operation."

Miranda waved a hand in the air. "It's only a short drive away, and I really want y'all to experience the castle after dark. It's got a real medieval vibe to it. We'll keep it short, an hour tops." She tilted her head and gave him a considering look. "Of course, if you're too tired, we could scrap it. I know you've had both an overnight and full day of travel."

"No, no, that's not it. The train trip was actually really comfortable and relaxing," he assured her. "I just don't want to put you out. Plus, I don't see how we'll all fit into one vehicle."

"Oh, don't worry about that, Jax," Madison put in. "Miranda rented a good-sized van. We'll all fit into that pretty easily."

"Correct," Miranda agreed. "So, no worries. We'll be back at a decent hour, early enough for you to get your beauty sleep, Deputy."

Jackson grinned at her. "Good deal. But it's not a 'deputy' here, you know. Jim and I are *way* out of our jurisdiction. We're just regular folks here, so mind your p's and q's," he added in jest with a point of his finger.

"In that case, I suppose we'd better all be on our best behavior. Who knows what kind of pokey they have here in this rural wilderness."

Back at the bed and breakfast, they all climbed into the rented van—in which they all indeed did fit—and hit the road for the short trip to Bella Luna. Elise's first glimpse of the castle winery was just as Miranda had described it: Medieval. The large stone castle wasn't as massive as Castello di Amorosa, but it was just as impressive with its towers spearing up into the night and lit up against the darkened sky, making it seem all the more imposing.

"Geez, Miranda," Madison exclaimed as they all piled out of the van. "This is incredible."

"It is, isn't it?" Miranda drawled. "It's pretty spectacular during the day, but this is why I wanted y'all to see it after dark first."

"It sure does make an impression, I'll give you that," Jim said. "You almost expect armored knights to be posted at the entrance."

"Is there a skeleton crew at night?" C.C. asked.

Miranda shook her head. "No, not that I know of. Why?"

"Well, whose car is that?" She pointed to the other side of the lot where a dark-colored sports car was parked beneath the boughs of a large fir tree, so easily missed although there were no other cars around.

"Oh, That's Nicola Ricci's," Miranda replied with a nod. "Nico's the winemaker for Bella Luna. He's a delicious Italian whose family has been making wine for generations. He sometimes works in the evenings depending on the time of year and where he is in any given process."

They all crossed the lot to the walkway and the wide stone steps that led to the massive, intricately carved oak doors at the entrance and followed Miranda in as she entered the open lobby area.

"Hello? Anyone here?" Miranda called out.

When there was no prompt answer, Miranda shrugged. "This place is so big that if someone's not in the immediate area, they'd never hear you."

No sooner were the words out of her mouth, when a man came out of an alcove to their left. This, Elise assumed, was the 'delicious Italian' to which Miranda had referenced. Nicola Ricci looked to be in his late thirties and had to be a good six feet tall with a well-toned physique and the handsome good looks of his heritage. He filled out the stone-washed jeans and casual, white button-down shirt very nicely. And with his thick dark hair, warm brown eyes, and smooth olive skin, he was indeed quite delish.

"Oh, Nico, it is you," Miranda said. "I figured as much."

"Good evening, Miranda. Are these your friends from Texas?"

"Yes. I wanted them to see the castle after dark before the full tour tomorrow."

The Italian's smile was dazzling white. "It does make an impression, doesn't it?"

"That's just what I said," Jim replied. "Very Medieval."

Nico's rich laughter echoed around the room. "Quite."

"Let me introduce you to the group," Miranda said, and proceeded to go around the room with the introductions. However, when she got to Madison, Elise noticed that Nico's interest seemed to perk right up, and he held her sister's gaze just a little longer than anyone else's.

"It's a pleasure to meet you, Madison," he murmured with a sensual smile.

"Nice to meet you, too," Madison replied. "Will you be here for the tour tomorrow as well?"

"Oh, I wouldn't miss it for the world."

Miranda cleared her throat, interrupting the moment the two were clearly having. "Why are you here tonight, Nico? What have you been up to?"

The man sighed. "I was just cleaning up a few things downstairs." A distasteful look crossed his handsome face and colored his tone. "That idiot Thompsen was here when I arrived earlier. He'd made a mess downstairs, which I must say, bordered on sabotage, in my opinion. Though there was no permanent damage, we had words, I'm afraid. You and I need to talk."

"Oh, for the love of— That man is a menace." Miranda glanced at Elise. "Roger Thompsen is the shareholder who's been causing such havoc. I'd thought that my attorney had shut that whole thing down."

Nico laughed again, this time without humor. "Don't let him fool you, Miranda. There's no question that he's far from done causing problems. That's what we need to talk about." The man's eyes flared with his anger. "I'll admit that I came close to doing him physical harm earlier. Pathetic little man. Don't worry, I did restrain myself. However, nobody tells me how to make wine or comes into my fermentation room and starts moving things around without my expressed consent, especially someone who knows nothing about the process."

"I agree. That's definitely your purview, darling. Furthermore, he has no business making any changes at all without speaking to the other shareholders first. I'll call my attorney tomorrow, but I'd like to discuss what happened with you beforehand."

"Of course." Nico paused and seemed to realize that everyone was listening to the exchange with avid interest. His smile returned, and he put up a hand with a sheepish look. "I do apologize for monopolizing your time with business. I'll let you get on with your tour." He glanced at Miranda. "Let me know when you'd like to meet. I'm available later this evening or in the morning. Just give me a shout."

"Thanks, Nico."

Elise watched him go as a little kernel of concern began to grow. She'd hoped that the situation had been somewhat resolved, and clearly, Miranda had thought so as well. Obviously, that was not the case, and if this Roger Thompsen was not above sneaky acts of attempted sabotage, she worried for Miranda and the other shareholders.

Miranda ran a hand through her hair. "Okay, so let's just forget about all that nonsense for now. Follow me, ladies and gents. I want to show y'all a couple of the rooms on this floor before we head back to the B and B." Miranda started through the alcove that Nico had come from. "Down this passageway is the Grand Hall and the Chapel room. They're both quite exquisite."

They stayed to rooms on the main floor, and the rest of the short tour went smoothly. Thoughts of concern for Miranda and the other Bella Luna shareholders slipped from Elise's mind to be replaced by the stunning architecture of the castle winery. Unfortunately, that reprieve didn't last long. When they got back to Riverside Manor, they found Roger Thompsen himself waiting for Miranda, his wife sitting meekly by his side.

"I want to talk to you, Mrs. Rollins. Right now!" the man shouted at Miranda the minute they walked into the building. He jumped up and stalked toward her. "I've been waiting here for thirty damn minutes."

The man was at least half a foot shorter than Miranda, and she stared down at him for a moment in stunned silence before a deceptively sweet smile eased across her features. "As we didn't have an appointment, and since you have been instructed to speak only to my attorney, the time you've spent waiting here is not my concern, *Mr.* Thompsen."

"I don't care what your crooked suit says. You've cost me time and money, lady, with your obstruction and bullheaded ways. I'm trying to help us all prosper, can't you see that?"

"Oh, that's rich. You can't whitewash the fact that you're trying to line your own pockets by destroying Bella Luna. To be honest, I find your disregard for the other shareholders to be obscene." She stepped right into the short man's bubble and leaned down into his face. "And let me be perfectly clear, I've spoken to Nico, and he's told me about your attempt to deliberately hamper production at the winery. As the major shareholder, I will not stand for that. If it continues, I will make very certain that you will regret it with every fiber of your being for the rest of your short, little life. Do you understand me, Mr. Thompsen?"

The man's face turned a mottled shade of red, and Elise thought that at any moment she would see steam coming out of his ears. She held her breath as he stood toe-to-toe with Miranda.

"Yeah?" he sneered. "Well, I've got a lawyer of my own now, missy, and I will not be bullied by a ... a loose woman like you."

"Loose woman? Really?" She threw back her head and laughed. "You don't even know me. However, it's obvious that your greed seems to know no bounds. Rest assured that I won't be bullied by a misogynistic scam artist like you. Anything further you have to say to me can be said through my attorney. Good evening, Mr. Thompsen."

As Miranda turned away from the man, he reached out and grabbed her by the arm.

"Don't you dare turn your back on me," he shouted, pulling her back around to face him. "I am not through with you yet."

"Roger!" his wife gasped.

"Hey!" Jackson shouted. "What the hell's wrong with you? Let go of her."

Miranda simply put up her free hand toward Jackson while she stared at the man with an icy glare, then pointedly looked down at his hand still gripping her arm. "Take your hand off of me ... right now," she demanded in a lethally quiet tone.

The man swallowed hard, his Adam's apple bobbing up and down. He dropped her arm as if it was on fire and quickly took several steps backward, but Miranda followed him. "You know, I've met numerous men like you in my lifetime. Men who think that they know what's best for everyone else. Men who seek to dominate others—especially women—and will use all kinds of underhanded tactics to do so. You do not scare me, Mr. Thompsen. Not in the least. Now, I suggest you scamper on back to whatever hole you crawled out of before this situation gets dangerously out of hand and someone gets hurt."

Elise watched as Roger Thompsen, confronted by a strong-willed woman, folded like a house of cards.

"You haven't heard the last of this," he muttered as he backed toward the door and, incredibly, snapped his fingers at his wife to follow him.

"Is that so?" Miranda drawled, never taking her eyes from the man.

"My lawyer will be in touch. Just you wait and see." Then he turned and fled from the building, leaving his poor, cowed spouse to scurry after him.

Taking a deep breath, Miranda turned to the group with an edgy smile. "Well now, wasn't that quite a show? I think I'll head into the cubby bar for a chaser. Anyone care to join me?"

With that, she turned on her heel and headed in that direction.

And they all followed.

Fortunately, after a couple of rounds, the mood lifted, and the scene Roger Thompsen had made took a back seat to a discussion about their short tour of Bella Luna earlier.

Thirty minutes later, Miranda got a phone call and excused herself.

The group finished up and then went their separate ways to their rooms soon after. As Elise and Jackson climbed the stairs, she caught sight of Miranda heading out the front door and figured she was going to meet Nico. Her heart went out to her friend. Miranda was probably the strongest woman she knew, but the kind of stress that Roger Thompsen brought could take a toll on anyone. Hopefully, the next day's festivities wouldn't be marred by yet another episode.

ELISE WAS NOT an early riser by any stretch of the imagination, as Jackson and the rest of her family would attest, but she opened her eyes the next morning at just after seven, wide awake and ready to go.

"I know, I know," she told Jackson when his surprise was evident. "I can't explain it, so don't say a word. I'm going to take a shower and get ready to meet everyone downstairs for breakfast." As she headed for the bathroom, she grinned over her shoulder. "I'm really hoping to see that same look on Maddy's face when I beat her to breakfast. That'll make my day."

They did, indeed, beat everyone to the dining room and were already filling their plates when the others began to trickle in at half-past eight.

"What the—" Maddy exclaimed as she caught sight of Elise.

"Close your mouth, Sis," Elise told her, as the look on her sister's face gave her a chuckle. "I am on time once in a while. Sometimes I'm even early."

"Okay, Jax. What did you do with my sister?"

"Hey, don't look at me. She woke up on her own about twenty minutes after me with a song in her heart."

Madison rolled her eyes. "That's just so weird. The Earth may be off its axis or something."

"Oh my gosh! You're so funny," Elise replied with sarcasm. "You're killing me, here."

Miranda came in a bit late and went directly to the coffee bar just as the proprietor, Mrs. Dearborn, was replenishing the coffee urn.

"Oh, Mrs. Rollins, here, let me pour you a fresh cup."

"Thanks. Give it to me in a to-go cup, if you would."

"Of course." The woman gave Miranda a sideways glance as she went about the task. "You know, I want to apologize for Mr. Thompsen's behavior last night. If I would've known what he was up to, I would have asked him to leave long before you got back."

"Well now, that's not your fault. His bad behavior is all on him."

"True, but that man is so unpleasant. I should have known better. It seems like he causes trouble wherever he goes. I just feel awful for his poor wife. Everyone in town knows how he treats her." The woman stopped and gazed around the small dining room with a guilty look. "Oh, listen to me. I do apologize. That was unkind."

Miranda gave Mrs. Dearborn a warm smile. "No worries, Mrs. D. We're all entitled from time to time. Besides, I'm pretty sure we won't be having any issues with Mr. Thompsen going forward." Giving the woman a pat on the shoulder, she took the to-go cup offered and turned to the rest of the group at the table. "Okay, y'all have thirty minutes to finish up breakfast, grab your things, and park yourselves in the van. I've got another call to make and then this party is hittin' the road for Bella Luna." With that, she sauntered out of the room.

Forty minutes later, they were on the road.

Nico was waiting for them in the parking lot when they arrived, and he squeezed in next to Madison for the vineyard tour. He gave a continuous commentary as they drove around the fields, which Elise found interesting. Unfortunately, they only spent about an hour on that part of the tour, though she could have spent several hours listening to Nico talk about hybrids, irrigation, cultivation, and more. However, she couldn't complain as she knew that portion of the trip was basically for her, anyway.

Back at the winery, they began the part of the tour that everyone else was looking forward to—the castle itself. Since they'd seen part of the main floor the previous night, they moved on to the upper levels before heading down into the bowels of the castle where the more fascinating rooms could be found. Again, for Elise, they started with the fermentation room where Nico ran through his process and answered her rapid-fire questions before they continued down the hall toward the tasting room.

"There are so many hidden alcoves and secret passageways in this place," Miranda told them. She waved a hand toward one such hallway. "But my absolute favorite is the Torture Chamber off the Armory. It's just up ahead, and it's crazy."

"Uh, torture room?" C.C. repeated. "Are you kidding?"

Miranda's throaty laughter echoed through the dank hallway. "Not at all. When they built this place, they added all the bells and whistles to give it a real medieval feel." She stopped at the next door way. "Check this out."

They followed her into the Armory, a room with walls covered in shields and all sorts of weaponry. Swords, daggers, bows. There were brackets that held spears and helmets of all shapes and sizes. However, the real showstopper was just through the archway at the back wall. Here was the Torture Chamber that seemed to hold all manner of devices designed to inflict pain and agony.

Elise's mouth dropped open as they all shuffled into the large room behind Miranda. "Good Lord, Miranda. This *is* crazy."

Her friend grinned. "I know, right? Some of it is pretty gruesome."

She waved a hand toward the large piece in the center of the room. "There's the rack, and then the iron chair covered in spikes in the corner." She pointed to the left. "That's fairly creepy."

"I'll say," Tina said with a shudder and moved closer to Jim.

"There's a pillory along the wall." Jim nodded in that direction. "Not all that gruesome. That was more for humiliation than torture."

"Ah, yes, but my favorite is over here. The Iron Maiden. It's really quite horrific." Miranda started around the rack toward the tall, human-shaped cabinet along the back wall but stopped short. "What the—"

C.C. stepped up beside her and made a face. "Geez, that's a bit much, Miranda. Although it does seem pretty realistic."

"What are y'all talking about?" Elise said as she crowded in between them. "Oh, dear Lord, is that blood?"

There was a wide swath of it leading up to the Iron Maiden and a pool of it around the foot of the cabinet.

"That's not real, right?" C.C. asked in horror.

Miranda shoved a hand through her hair and the color drained from her face. Turning, she took a deep breath "Uh, Jax?"

He stepped up next to Elise, and when he saw the blood, shook his head. "Okay, I'm gonna need y'all to move back into the Armory right now." He turned to Ricci. "And Nico, I'm gonna need you to call 911."

4

After moving the rest of the group back to the fermentation room, and though they were way out of their jurisdiction, Jackson and Jim carefully surveyed and secured the scene in the Torture Chamber. Neither of them were strangers to a bloody crime scene and there was a good amount of blood here, but what kind of blood it would turn out to be was for an investigative team to establish. However, both Miranda and Nico had assured Jackson that no fake blood or blood of any kind had ever been used for effect on the tours that they knew of, so perhaps that at least could be ruled out.

Of course, once the Iron Maiden was opened, it would undoubtedly be apparent where all that blood had come from. Jackson knew it was unlikely, given the amount of blood at the scene, but he was still harboring a tiny spark of hope for a simple, innocent answer.

While they waited for the local authorities, which Nico had confirmed would be the County Sheriff and his crew, Jackson took photos of the area with his cell phone, more for his own peace of mind than anything else, as he wasn't about to step on any local toes. After that, he and Jim headed out into the hallway to wait.

They didn't have to wait long.

Shiloh County was fairly small and it only took about twenty minutes for the sheriff to arrive from the county seat, which was in the town of Murphey fifteen miles to the south. As the Sheriff and one of his deputies followed Nico down the hallway to where Jackson and Jim stood outside the Armory, Jackson studied the man. He looked to be in his mid-fifties, and Jackson estimated him at just shy of six feet tall, with a stocky build, sharp gray eyes, and short, brown hair graying at the temples.

"Sheriff, this is Jackson Landry," Nico said as they approached. "He's the one I told you about. Jackson, this is Sheriff Dillon Masters."

"Mr. Ricci here tells me you're in law enforcement, Mr. Landry," Sheriff Masters said, those sharp gray eyes narrowing slightly. "That true?"

"It is, Sheriff. This is my partner, Jim Stockton. We're from Delphine, Texas, and we're both deputies with the Bastrop County Sheriff's department."

They both handed the sheriff their IDs for his perusal. After he'd looked them over, he handed them back with a brisk nod. "Long way from home, gentlemen."

"You could say that," Jackson replied as he slipped his ID back into his wallet. "We were just taking a tour of the winery when this was discovered. I had Nico call it in and then we made sure the scene was secured."

"I see."

"It's at the back of the Torture Chamber, which is just through the Armory there." Jackson gestured toward the doorway.

Masters nodded again. "Yes, I know where the Torture Chamber is. I'm more of a beer man, but my wife is a fan of Bella Luna's vino. She's dragged me through a couple of tours out here, although, we've never stumbled across this type of a situation."

"Wasn't the Saturday excursion we were expecting, either," Jim replied. "I was really just looking forward to the wine tasting, which we never even got to do. This was pretty surprising, for sure."

"I'll bet." The sheriff hooked a thumb over his shoulder to the tall, lanky deputy standing behind him. "This is one of my deputies, Jesse Navaro. He'll take statements from the rest of the group while you two accompany me to the scene. I would be interested in your initial thoughts and assessment of what you found."

With the air of a man expecting his will to be done, Masters turned without another word and headed into the Armory. Jackson raised an eyebrow and exchanged a look with Jim before shrugging and following the man into the room with his partner close behind.

Masters stood in the middle of the Armory and shook his head. "I just don't get it. I don't go in for this kind of thing. I mean, sure, history is interesting and all, but this stuff?" He shook his head again. "All these weapons are from another era, another country, even. I don't get recreating it. But that's just me." He turned and ran a hand over his face. "Different strokes for different folks, I guess. Come on, let's get this over with."

They followed him into the Torture Chamber where he stopped

and took in the room with its collection of tortuous devices. "Okay. Where is this bloody scene?"

Jackson stepped around him and crossed to the end of the rack to where the Iron Maiden stood against the far wall. "It's over here, Sheriff." He pointed to the bloody swath leading up the human-shaped cabinet and the drying pool of blood around its footing. "Looks like somebody dragged someone or something over to the Iron Maiden. The pool around its base suggests that whatever it was may have been left inside."

The sheriff frowned and pulled out his phone. "Looks like we're gonna need a proper sweeper team." As he punched out a number and put the phone to his ear, he glanced at Jackson with a knowing look. "I have a feeling that you've already gotten some photos of this whole mess, but we'll need *official* photos before we can open that thing up."

"Sheriff—" Jackson began, intending to tell him what he'd done and why, but Masters lifted a finger and cut him off as someone on the other end of the line answered his call.

"Richards, this is Sheriff Masters. I need a sweeper team out here at Bella Luna Winery ASAP. Looks like we may have ourselves a crime scene." He paused and closed his eyes briefly. "Yes, that's what I said, so make it snappy." Hanging up and pocketing his cell phone, he turned to them with a roll of his eyes, then gave Jackson a 'gimme' motion.

Jackson pulled out his own phone and brought up the photos he'd taken for the Sheriff to peruse. "You know, Sheriff. I didn't mean to step on any toes by taking these," he said as he handed over his cell. "It's just that Jim and I have dealt with some crazy scenes, so it's just kinda engrained, you know?"

Masters waved away his concerns as he looked through the photos. "I'm not worried about that, Landry," he said when he'd finished. "Truth be told, I would have done the same."

"Good to know. And call me Jackson."

The sheriff took a card from his pocket and handed it to Jackson along with his phone. "That's my cell number. I would appreciate it if you would send me those photos."

"You bet." As the man continued to stare at him, Jackson tilted his head. "Is there something else?"

"Well, you seem to be fairly comfortable with this kind of thing," he replied slowly. "You said you've seen some crazy scenes. You see a lot of this in the Lone Star State, do ya?"

Jim smirked. "We're about an hour out of Austin and still a bit rural in the Delphine area, but like Jax said, we've had our share of weird murder scenarios over the last few years."

"Is that so?"

"Yeah, but if there's a body in that Iron Maiden, it would be a first for us," Jackson added. "Why do you ask?"

"Just thinkin'," Masters said vaguely. He started for the door but stopped and turned back with a frown. "So, are you two on a group vacation or something?"

Jim burst out laughing. "This is actually the last half of Jackson's honeymoon, Sheriff. He and Elise spent a couple of weeks in Napa Valley before meeting up with us here in the Northwest. The 'group' out in the fermentation room was the wedding party."

Masters grinned. "Well, well. That's interesting."

Jackson shook his head. "You have no idea. Miranda Rollins is the majority shareholder in Bella Luna. Her late husband bought the shares prior to his death close to a decade ago. She'd never even seen it, as it was his deal. Anyway, she brought everyone up here to check it out with her since my wife's family operates River Bend Vineyard and Winery outside of Delphine in Bastrop County."

"Must be nice to be able to treat your friends that way." The sheriff checked his watch. "Okay, come on, let's go see how those statements are going, and you two can give Jesse yours. Then we'll go from there."

While they waited for the sweeper team to arrive, everyone finished their statements. Nico explained the trouble they'd been having of late with Roger Thompsen, one of the other shareholders, and the mess the man had made in the fermentation room on the previous day.

"Sheriff, is it possible that this is just a sick joke, just another attempt at sabotaging the winery?" Miranda asked. "I mean, I can't believe that there's actually a body in that Iron Maiden."

Masters rubbed his chin and glanced at Jackson. "I suppose it's possible, Ms. Rollins."

"But you don't think that's likely, do you?" Elise asked.

"I don't know. I guess I don't see how doing something like this as a prank in a remote room of the castle where only the occasional tour group ever goes would make much of an impact."

"Yes, but, Sheriff, Thompsen knew that we were going to be here touring the castle today," Miranda insisted. "And he's already caused a number of problems over the last month or so."

"That may be true, but I'm not gonna speculate on the what ifs. We need to wait for the team to arrive and do their work. Once that contraption is opened up, we'll know soon enough what's what."

The sheriff's tone, though civil enough, smacked of finality and shut down any further questions or speculation. Fortunately, the investigative team arrived ten minutes later and went to work on the Torture Chamber, documenting as much as possible before they were ready to open the Iron Maiden.

Dr. Fred Wilcox, the Shiloh County Medical Examiner, had come along with the team. The doctor reminded Jackson of Doc Nagle, Bastrop County's coroner—an older country doctor with an inquisitive mind and a keen eye for details. He was standing by, but the look on his face after he'd scrutinized the scene spoke volumes, in Jackson's opinion.

After they'd waited a tense forty-five minutes or so, the lead investigator came out to give the sheriff a rundown.

"We've done all we can in there, Sheriff. It's a pretty confined area. We can start on the Armory as well, but we're ready to open up the Iron Maiden whenever you are."

"Thank you. You and your team just stand by for a minute. We'll be right in." Sheriff Masters turned to Jackson and Jim. "I'd like you two to come with me, please."

"Sheriff, we're not—" Jackson began, but the sheriff put up a hand and interrupted him.

"Look, Jackson, I know this isn't your jurisdiction—far from it— and this may turn out to be nothing. However, if this ends up being something ... more, it seems to me that you two may have some insight that would be beneficial for the investigation I'll have to conduct." Masters gave Jackson a hard stare. "Now, you can say no, and I can't force you, but I'm askin' for your assistance."

Jackson looked at Jim, who shrugged. "I'm good with it," he said.

Turning back to the sheriff, Jackson nodded. "Okay, then. We're right behind you."

"Good deal."

They followed Masters through the Armory and on back to the Torture Chamber with young Deputy Navaro bringing up the rear. Jackson could see that the sweeper team had been thorough with their work and were waiting for the go-ahead to open the Iron Maiden. At Masters' nod, they did just that.

What they found inside was not pretty by any stretch of the imagination.

As Miranda had prophetically said earlier, Roger Thompsen would not be perpetrating sabotage, pranks, or causing trouble of any other kind going forward.

"Ah, geez," the sheriff muttered. "Not exactly what I'd wanted to find, but there it is. Guess I'm not all that surprised though I sure did hope for a different outcome."

"If he's got a wallet on him, Sheriff, we'll find it and see if we can ID him pronto," the sweeper lead said.

"No need, really," Jackson replied quietly. "Though I know you'll want to confirm, but this is Roger Thompsen. Or at least, the man we knew as Roger Thompsen."

"Well, now. That's unfortunate," Masters replied. "That's gonna open a whole new can of worms. As I said before, we haven't dealt with this kind of thing in the county since I've been here, and that's over a decade now. It's mostly just been suicides, accidental deaths, hunting mishaps, that sort of thing. Never had a bizarre situation like this, that's for sure." He paused for a moment and frowned. "Although, we did have an argument that got out of hand a few years back over in Pinedale. That ended with a homicide, but it was fairly cut and dried. This?" The sheriff shook his head. "I don't know what to make of this. Human beings can be so vicious to each other over the least little thing."

Turning, he addressed Dr. Wilcox, who was studying the body in situ. "I know it's way early, but can you tell me anything yet, Doc?"

The doctor grimaced and responded with an unmistakable tone of irritability. "I can tell you that he's dead, that he undoubtedly has a number of puncture wounds from the spikes in this ghastly contraption but not much more than that until I get him on my table. So, don't even ask me about time of death."

"What an awful way to die," Deputy Navaro murmured in a stressed tone, his face taking on an upsetting hue of grayish-green.

"The Iron Maiden was designed to cause a slow, painful death by exsanguination," Jim said. "The spikes weren't long enough to pierce vital organs but long enough for the victim to slowly bleed to death. The cabinet sometimes had spikes to pierce the eyes as well, but I can see that thankfully, this one does not." He tilted his head with a thoughtful look. "Or maybe they were just removed at some point."

Jackson stared at his partner. "Who are you and what have you done with my partner?"

"Hey, you knew that I was a student of history."

"History, yes. Medieval torture devices, no."

"The Iron Maiden, though it's frequently thought of as medieval, was not actually used in the Middle Ages. That's a myth."

With another glance at the work the doctor was doing, Deputy Navaro swallowed hard and excused himself, making a quick retreat from the room.

Sheriff Masters stared after his deputy with a heavy sigh. "Navaro's a good kid but he's only been on the force for a couple of years, and he's still pretty green. No pun intended."

Jackson jabbed a finger in Jim's direction. "Okay stop. Just stop. See what you've done? You're scaring the children."

Jim tried to hide his grin, failing epically. "Yeah, yeah. But I do feel the need to point out that we all saw this guy alive and well last evening. Add to that, there's a bloody swath leading up to the Iron Maiden, which indicates that Thompsen was bleeding prior to being stuffed into it. The cabinet may have helped move things along a bit, and it'll be the doc's call, but I highly doubt that this *ghastly contraption* is the murder weapon."

"Well, I suppose that's logical, but let's shelve that discussion until he can tell us definitively what killed our victim," Masters suggested, then turned to the doctor. "You about ready to get him out of there, Doc?"

"Yes. I think we've got what we need. Again, I won't really be able to give you any solid data until I can examine him properly." The M.E. stepped back and stripped off his gloves as the team brought in a gurney.

"Alright then. Let's get him out of there."

Once the team had removed Thompsen's body from the cabinet and was preparing for transport, the sheriff turned to Jackson. "We'll let the team finish up here. Once they have Thompsen on his way, the techs will transport that contraption to the lab for further examination as well. Right now, let's go back and talk to the group. We're gonna need to set up some formal interviews, get a little more information."

That would be an understatement, Jackson thought, but he just nodded. He had a sneaking suspicion that this was going to get a whole lot worse before it was all said and done.

THE DRIVE back to Riverside Manor was a solemn affair after learning of the grisly discovery found inside the Iron Maiden. The previous evening had been the first time that any of them had ever set eyes on Roger Thompsen, with the exception of Miranda and Nico. Sheriff Masters had sent the wedding party back to the Manor with a request that no one leave the area without speaking to him first. He'd also asked each of the group to come into his office for formal interviews first thing Monday morning. That left the rest of the evening and a full Sunday to stew over the situation.

Elise studied each of her friends in turn on the drive back. There was a mix of feelings hanging over the group. Apprehension, disbelief, and a sense of avoidance filled the air. Murder was an ugly business, as Elise herself had experienced firsthand over the last few years. And though they had no personal involvement, she really couldn't say that she blamed any of them for wanting some distance from it. However, personal involvement or not, she had questions, and Miranda seemed to be the only other one in the van who wanted more information as well.

And in true Miranda style, she got right to it.

"So, what happened back in that room, Jax?" she asked, glancing periodically in the rearview mirror at him. "How did Thompsen die? And are you going to be working with Sheriff Masters? I thought you said that you and Jim were out of your jurisdiction."

Jackson nodded. "We are. Jim and I have no authority here at all. Sheriff Masters did ask us for our assistance, but we don't know exactly what that will entail yet, and we couldn't talk about it even if we did."

"Yes, but—"

"This is now an ongoing homicide investigation, Miranda," he added, cutting off her protests. "Everyone needs to be mindful of that and stay out of Sheriff Masters' way."

Elise didn't look at him, but she could feel his eyes on her during that last comment and knew it was probably pointedly meant for her. It was a blanket reminder that they were no longer in Texas, and she would get no leeway with the sheriff's investigation. It also meant that prying information out of her new hubby would be harder than usual as well. She'd have to ponder that a bit.

They'd all missed out on lunch and, of course, the planned wine tasting out at the vineyard. So, they opted for a couple of pizzas from the only pizza place in the town and then convened in the little cubby bar at the Manor to digest what had occurred and contemplate how it would go from there. Miranda made the excuse of more phone calls and declined to join them, but Nico met them there and slipped onto the overstuffed sofa next to Madison.

"What a heinous way to end a winery tour, huh?" he said, ordering a beer. "I still can't believe it. I just had a run in with the guy yesterday, and then this?" He shook his head. "What a mess."

"Yes, and he was waiting for Miranda here at the Manor when we got back last night," Madison replied. "That had to have been close to ten o'clock, and his wife was with him. Why would he have gone back out to the winery after that?"

"Maybe he was meeting someone," C.C. suggested.

"Could be. But why that late at night?" Nico sighed. "Though considering the havoc the man had already caused, it wouldn't surprise me a bit if he'd been up to something nefarious."

"Nico, I'm assuming that the winery has security cameras, correct?" Jackson asked.

The man nodded. "Of course. We have a fairly new state-of-the-art system that Miranda and the other shareholders had installed in the last year or so."

"Good. I imagine Sheriff Masters will be in touch about checking the feeds. That could help with determining if the victim was alone or meeting with someone."

"Sure. I know the system rewrites itself every forty-eight hours, but I'm not sure where it is on that timeline. Hopefully it hasn't gone through that process yet."

"That's a good point." Jackson stood up and motioned to Jim. "I think we should probably give that information to the sheriff, if he hasn't already snapped to it."

"You bet," Jim agreed. "Sounds like a plan.

Jackson leaned down and gave Elise a quick kiss. "We'll be back later," he murmured, then gave her a keen look. "Stay out of trouble, pal."

She rolled her eyes at him. "You're such a nag. Go, would you? And be careful."

He grinned and then headed for the door with Jim right behind him. Elise watched them go with a slight smile. Her guy may be on his honeymoon and out of his jurisdiction, but he was right in his element. However, she did worry about what, or who, they might find on that security feed.

If they found anything at all.

5

Elise waited to be sure Jackson and Jim had left the building before focusing in on Nico. She had a feeling that the handsome Italian knew more than he'd shared with them the previous day or with the sheriff this afternoon. She hoped she could get him to spill some details or at least get a clearer vision of who Roger Thompsen really was, as she was sure that there was more to the backstory than anyone was saying.

"So, Nico, how long have you been the primary winemaker at Bella Luna?" she asked.

He shot her a grin. "I studied under Dario Santoro. He was the original winemaker for Bella Luna. I became primary winemaker a little over four years ago after his death. Dario was a great man, an incredible winemaker, and he taught me so much."

"So, you knew him for many years?"

Nico nodded and took a drink of his beer, then seemed to grow pensive. "I did, and I still miss him. My dad wasn't around much when I was young, and then one day he just picked up and left the family behind. I'd just turned sixteen. After that, I drifted, you might say, for a handful of years. I'm embarrassed to tell you that I was in and out of trouble quite a bit during that time of my life."

"But you were so young. It's understandable that you would act out after the trauma of losing a parent, no matter how it happened," Madison murmured. "Seems like you found your way, though."

"Yes, but it took a while. I was in my early twenties by the time I met Dario. He was quite strict, but patient and kind, genuine and wise. Everything my old man hadn't been. Dario showed me what a father/son relationship could be ... should be. He filled a void in me that I'd held onto for far too long. He was the father that I'd subconsciously wished for all those years after mine took off the way he did."

"That's so awesome that you found him, and that he made a difference in your life." Madison smiled at him, then frowned. "Was he ill? When he died, I mean. Was it a long illness?"

"Oh no. Dario was a hale and hardy Italian in his late sixties when he passed." Nico shook his head. "No, one day he was just found out in the vineyard laying in between rows. He'd had a heart attack and died alone, surrounded by the grapes that he'd loved. Truth be told, I think he died of a broken heart."

Elise raised her eyebrows. "Why do you say that?"

"Well, he'd had a falling out with the original owners. They'd been old friends of his from Sicily, but they'd been talked into selling the vineyard in shares for huge profits by an opportunistic real estate agent who didn't care what happened to the vineyard or the people who worked there. Dario couldn't afford to buy in, though he did try to raise enough money for at least a small share. Unfortunately, he fell short." Nico shook his head again and his tone sharpened with an angry edge. "Dario begged them to reconsider but they wouldn't, and no amount of arguing with the owners—his *friends*—made a difference, as they'd made up their minds to move back to Sicily. I think the whole affair just broke him. He loved Bella Luna. It was a part of him."

"Oh, how awful," Madison said, putting a hand on his arm. "I mean, business is business, but still, it seems so cruel. Were the current shareholders part of what happened back then?"

"No, no. If you're thinking about Miranda, don't worry." Nico patted her hand. "Few people had any idea of what was happening during that period. With the exception of Gene Rollins, Miranda's husband, that is. He was the first investor. I don't know how, but he and Dario had known each other for quite a long time, and Gene bought a fifty-two percent share of the vineyard when he found out what was happening so that Dario would always have Bella Luna."

C.C. frowned. "He bought it for Dario?"

"Well, no. You have to understand. Dario was a proud man. He wouldn't have accepted a share of the vineyard as a gift, no matter how well-intentioned. Gene obviously knew that, so he did the next best thing. He bought controlling interest so that no one else could make any changes without his consent and made sure that Dario had complete control over the day-to-day operations."

"But it wasn't enough, was it?" Elise asked, watching him closely.

Nico took a deep breath and let it out slowly along with most of his anger. His smile was tinged with sadness as he stared down into his beer glass. "No. It was a grand gesture by Gene, but in the end, no, it didn't make a difference."

"So, Miranda's husband was the first to buy in, but besides Roger Thompsen, how many other shareholders are there?" Elise tilted her head and studied the man. He had been close to Dario and obviously still harbored some anger for what had befallen the man he'd considered a father figure. Could the way the scenario unfolded with the sale have eventually played a part in Thompsen's death somehow?

"Besides Thompsen? There's one other couple that bought in right after Gene ... and right before Thompsen. William and Grace Moran purchased a thirty percent share."

Elise nodded. "Then if my math is correct, that only left eighteen percent for Thompsen."

"That's right, and it caused quite an uproar at the time. The guy was an ass, shouting about conspiracies, how the Morans were working with Gene to keep him from getting a decent share."

"I take it there was no truth to any of it," Elise said. "I mean, I can't imagine. Sounds like something out of a bad novel."

"Hell no! There was nothing at all." Nico pointed a finger. "However, I think his bluster was just projection."

Elise leaned closer. "Really? How so?"

A hard look crossed Nico's face. "Well, like I said, the original owners were talked into selling by an unprincipled real estate agent."

"Okay. And?"

"A real estate agent that I'm pretty sure had some dodgy ties to Thompsen, though I could never find proof of it."

"So, you think that Roger Thompsen may have been involved with this agent who talked the owners into selling, and that was the reason he was angry? That Gene and the Morans got there first and shut him out, so to speak?" Elise asked with a raised eyebrow.

"And sounds like the reason that he ended up with a much smaller piece of the pie," Tina added. "That would probably tend to make someone like Roger Thompsen pretty irrational."

Nico sighed. "Irrational is a mild word for it. The guy went off the rails."

C.C. made a rude sound. "I'm not sure that it would take much, from what we saw of him the other night."

Elise gave Nico a thoughtful look. "Still, that scenario seems a bit convoluted."

"As well as downright shady," C.C. muttered.

"Well, like I said, I could never find concrete proof. It was just a feeling I had, but I wasn't the only one who felt that way."

C.C. shook her head. "But here's the part that I don't get. If Thompsen was working with this devious real estate agent and they had this plan, how would Gene and the Morans have gotten in their purchases before him? I mean, wouldn't he have had the inside track, been able to jump on it before they ever knew about the listing?"

And what part could that have played into the man's gruesome death years later? Elise thought absently.

Nico grinned and shook his finger at C.C. "Great question, C.C. And the owners had a brilliant solution. See, they came to Dario and explained what they had decided to do before they signed the papers with the agent. They at least got that much right. They gave him first crack at buying in and a short window of time to get the funds together before they actually listed, but like I said, he couldn't do it."

"And that's when Gene stepped in? During that short window of opportunity?" Elise asked.

"Yes, and he brought the Morans with him. So, as a favor to Dario, the owners accepted both offers before Thompsen even had a shot." The Italian shrugged. "I guess maybe you could make a case for a conspiracy, but it wasn't a planned deal. The owners really did feel bad for Dario. I think it was just their way of making amends for the damage that had been done to their relationship with him. Gene was just trying to help an old friend. He had no idea about Thompsen until the guy secured the final eighteen percent of the vineyard and started complaining."

"Sour grapes," C.C muttered, then laughed. "No pun intended."

"Sounds like Roger Thompsen was trouble right from the beginning," Elise said.

"Yeah, but it kind of smoothed out after that." Nico took a sip of his beer. "Don't get me wrong, the guy was constantly complaining about something, but it was just more of a nuisance after his original blowup—and mostly just piddly stuff. Gene and the Morans always seemed to be able to keep him in check."

"So, what changed?" Tina looked confused.

"What do you mean?" Nico asked.

"Well, Gene died in that car accident five or six years ago, right?" She turned to Elise with a questioning look.

"I think closer to seven," Elise replied, then thought for a moment. "But Tina brings up a good point. As far as I know, Miranda hadn't had any issues with the man in the years since Gene's death. At least, she's never talked about it, and I'm assuming, as majority shareholder, she would have been the first call. The trouble just started a month or so ago."

"Right," C.C. agreed. "It got so bad that she finally had to get the lawyers involved. So why now?"

Madison shook her head. "We don't know that for sure. I mean, we only know about this recent trouble after overhearing a couple of phone calls, and she put it off as nothing at first. You know how Miranda is. She could have been having issues with Thompsen off and on for years without any of us knowing about it."

"That is true, Maddy," C.C. replied. "Miranda is pretty tightlipped about her personal life."

"Either way, Roger Thompsen didn't seem to be liked by many people," Elise commented.

Tina frowned. "Yeah, even his wife looked beat down when she came with him to confront Miranda last night. She looked like she wanted to be anywhere but here witnessing his tirade."

Nico nodded. "I'm not surprised. I know his kids wanted nothing to do with him, either."

Elise pondered the conversation and then sighed. "Seems like the sheriff is gonna have a difficult time sorting out Thompsen's murder. This is a small town and a rural area, so he'll probably be able to come up with some suspects and put together enough pieces of the puzzle, but I don't think it's going to be a walk in the park."

DEPUTY NAVARO MET Jackson and Jim at the castle door when they got to Bella Luna. Jackson had called the sheriff before they'd left the B and B to tell him about the security feed and let him know they were coming back out.

"I've been watching for you guys. Sheriff Masters had me wait here," Navaro told them when they'd arrived. "The sheriff's in the office on the second floor. That's were the security setup is. They're looking at the feed now ... or at least they were getting ready to when I came downstairs. Come on, I'll show you where the office is."

"The feed hadn't rewritten yet?" Jim asked as they followed the deputy across the castle atrium and started toward the stone stairway to the right.

Navaro shook his head. "I don't know. They were just starting on it, but I don't think so." The deputy stopped and turned to Jackson. "So, I know you told the sheriff that you've had some crazy scenes in your jurisdiction, but have you guys handled many cases like this? I mean, homicides? I've only been on the force for three and a half years, and I've never seen anything like this in all that time. I mean, sure, the occasional dead body, but never a murder."

"We've had several murder investigations over the last few years but, no, nothing like this, so you're not alone there, Deputy," Jackson told him.

"Call me Jesse," Navaro said and then ran a hand through his hair. "But you've investigated murders, and that's more than I can say. Did you solve them all?"

Jim laughed. "We did solve the ones we've had in our immediate area of the county, not that it was easy. It's particularly hard when you're having to investigate friends and acquaintances as suspects. That's a dicey situation, especially in a rural area where everybody knows everybody."

"And the murders you've handled? They were committed by people you knew?"

"Not all of them, but a couple were." Jim shrugged. "That's hard, but you find that under certain circumstances, even those you think you know well can be capable of terrible things."

"Well, this Thompsen guy didn't have many friends in Meadowview, that's for sure. Just the opposite from what my abuela says."

Jackson frowned. "Did you and your grandmother know Roger Thompsen?"

"I didn't know the guy but I'd seen him once or twice. I should have recognized him when we found him in that torture cabinet, but I was just so shocked. Guess that's not a great excuse in this line of work."

"As good as any," Jim said. "That was a pretty gruesome scene."

Navaro made a face. "Anyway, I don't live in Meadowview—I moved to Murphey to be closer to work—but my abuela does. She knows Thompsen's wife. I don't know if she'd ever met him, though."

The deputy turned and started up the stairs. "Come on, the office is up here."

They climbed to the second floor and followed Navaro to the winery office three quarters of the way down the corridor where they found Sheriff Masters and a couple of techs. One of the techs sat working on a desktop computer in front of a double monitor setup while the other went back and forth between the desk and a small electronics room along the back wall.

"Now, try it again," the tech called from the other room.

The woman at the computer began typing and then smiled. "That's it. Okay, let's see what we can find."

Sheriff Masters looked up at Jackson and rolled his eyes. "I hate this electronic crap. Can't do anything these days without it. Can't do anything with it. And God forbid something misconnects, or you lose a password, or some other idiot thing."

"Patience, Sheriff," the woman at the computer crooned without taking her eyes off the screen in front of her. "We're getting there."

Masters scrubbed his hands over his face. "I have no patience for any of this, Molly. Just give me some good news, already."

Jackson stepped around the desk to look at the computer screens. "Jesse said he didn't think the feed had rewritten yet, so what's the problem?"

The tech glanced over her shoulder. "Looks like someone messed with the router and the settings. We're just getting to the feed now." She turned back to the screen. "Ah, here we go. Oh, no. For the love of—"

"Oh, no what?" Masters asked. "Talk to me, Molly."

With a sigh, she turned and shook her head. "The feed is set to rewrite at midnight every forty-eight hours, which, by the log, should have been tomorrow night."

"*Should* have been?" Jackson asked.

The woman looked up at him. "Yeah, but there's nothing here."

"What do you mean there's nothing there? Are you telling me someone reset it manually?" Masters asked. "If that's the case, we should still be able to retrieve at least the last twenty-four hours, right?" At the look on the woman's face, he narrowed his eyes. "Molly?"

With a heavy sigh, she shook her head. "The system wasn't reset, Sheriff. The feed was wiped."

Masters stared at her for a long moment. "*Wiped*?" he finally ground out. "As in, the last forty-eight hours are just *gone*?"

"Unfortunately, I think so, yes."

"Is there any way to recover any of it?" Jackson asked.

Molly rubbed her eyes as if she'd been staring at the screen too long. She gave another sigh. "I can't answer that. This is a bit beyond my wheelhouse. We'll work on it, and I know a guy in Portland that is a genius with these kinds of systems. I'll give him a call and see if I can get him over here as soon as possible. He owes me a favor or two."

Masters gave a short nod. "You do that. Get me something. Anything." He turned to Jackson. "In the meantime, can you two follow me back to the office? I'd like to go over where we are so far. I also just got a text from Doc Wilcox. He's got something for us."

Jackson nodded. "Absolutely. I told Elise I'd be back later. She's used to me being held up with work." He checked his watch. "It's four-twenty now. As long as we get back for dinner, we should be fine."

"Speak for yourself, pal," Jim muttered. "I can guarantee you that Tina will not be as forgiving about it. We are on vacation, you know."

"And I'm technically still on my honeymoon, so quit your whining, buddy."

Masters shook his head and grinned. "I'll do my best to get you both back as soon as possible and keep you out of the doghouse. Let's go."

Twenty minutes later, they were in the sheriff's office and staring at a murder board that Jackson thought was in a style surprisingly similar to his own.

"It's a bit old school," Masters said when he saw the look on Jackson's face. "But it's just how I keep it all straight in my head whenever I have a particularly convoluted investigation. Unfortunately, it's a bit sparse yet."

Jim stepped up beside Jackson and gave him the side eye. "Something you want to tell me, son? Are you two somehow related?"

At Masters' quizzical look, Jackson rolled his eyes. "He thinks he's so funny."

"You could take this board and put it in our office, Sheriff. It would be right at home there with its twin."

The sheriff nodded. "Well, that should save some time, shouldn't it? May not be shorthand, but close to it."

Jackson laughed. "Guess so. At least we'll all be on the same page."

Jim pulled a small spiral notebook out of his pocket and waved it at Jackson. "Not to be outdone, my friend," he said with a laugh.

"Now that everyone's in their comfort zone," Masters began. "Let's get this party started."

6

___

"I beg your pardon?" Elise turned, a tube of lipstick in her hand, and stared at Jackson for a moment. "What do you mean the security feed was wiped?"

"Just what I said," Jackson replied in a dry tone.

It was almost seven o'clock and they were about to go to a late dinner. Jackson had gotten back from the sheriff's office in Murphey much later than planned, and by the time he'd arrived, she'd been near to starving and quite irritable with it. Of course, looking on the bright side, because of her irritability and the fact that he'd been so late, she'd guilted him into disclosing more details of the current investigation than he would have normally offered.

But this tidbit was unexpected, to say the least.

"How is that possible? I mean, that the entire feed is gone?"

Jackson shrugged. "When Molly—the computer tech—finally got the settings back online and pulled up the feed ... well, there wasn't anything to pull up."

"And are you telling me that there's no way to retrieve any of it? Come on, they can do some really amazing things these days. I can't believe that hours of security video are just ... gone."

"I asked that very same question, as I am not as slow as you obviously seem to think I am."

She smirked at him and then rolled her eyes, ignoring his sarcasm. "And?"

"*And* ... the answer was undetermined. She said that it was outside the area of her expertise, but evidently, she knows a guy who may be able to recover something. Molly said that he was the best she knows of with this kind of thing, so she was going to see how soon he could get over here from Portland. However, I'm not holding my breath at this stage of the investigation."

Elise turned back to the mirror to finish applying her lipstick. "So, what else did you boys uncover that made you so late getting back? Couldn't have been just the wiped feed scenario. Like, who had access to the security system? Had to be someone who knew their way around the winery, knew where the system was located, right?"

She watched him in the mirror as he folded his arms and frowned at her.

Then he narrowed his eyes. "You're just gonna milk the fact that I was a little late for all it's worth, aren't you?"

Their eyes met in the mirror. "A *little* late? Try close to three hours, pal, but who's counting?" She turned and gave him a big, bright smile. "So, you know it, Deputy. That'll teach you to stick to a schedule. Besides, we're on our honeymoon," she crooned that last part and coupled it with a very cheesy pout.

He snorted. "Oh, brother. That's just so pathetic, even for you, El."

"J-a-a-a-x," she wheedled. "I'll tell you mine, if you tell me yours."

"Elise Brianna, this is not my case. And you need to keep your pretty little nose out of it." He wagged a finger at her. "Do not get me into trouble with Sheriff Masters. I will let him throw you into the clink for interfering with an investigation. Don't think that I won't."

"Oh, please. I know that you won't, 'cause that would be a bad look all the way around. And besides that, what would you tell Gram when you had to go home without me?"

Jackson burst into laughter. "Miss Abby would probably applaud me, and you know it. She knows what a snoop you are." He winked at her. "Of course, that and she likes me better."

"Boy, you just keep dreamin', my friend. Anyway, I am not interfering. I promise. We were all talking about the winery after you and Jim left, and then Nico just kinda spilled the beans." *With a few well-placed questions, that is,* she thought. "Seriously, Jax, he laid out how the shareholders came to be in the first place, and I'm telling you, it wasn't pretty. It seemed to involve some possible earlier shenanigans by Roger Thompsen in cahoots with a shady real estate agent. Anyway, there is definitely something there that could've played into what's happening now."

When he didn't say anything but continued to stare at her, she crossed her arms, mirroring his stance, and cocked a hip. After a moment or two, she watched another smile tug at the corners of his mouth. Good Lord, she loved him with all of her heart, but he was so easy.

Finally, he caved, as she figured he would eventually. Shaking his head, he chuckled. "You are incorrigible, you know that?"

"One of the many reasons that you love me, right?"

Scrubbing his hands over his face, he relented. "Okay, we did compile a list of people who would have had access to not only the winery but the office and security setup as well."

"Well, sure. That would be the best place to start." She immediately closed her mouth and pressed her lips together at the annoyed look that crossed his face.

"Really?" he asked in a sarcastic tone. "Do you want to hear this or not?"

She quickly put up her hands in surrender. "Sorry, sorry. Please, do go on."

Jackson blew out a breath. "Turns out, the list is fairly short. First, obviously all of the shareholders had access, so Roger Thompsen, William and Grace Moran, and Miranda."

"Please. Miranda may have had access, but I can't see her wiping the security feed. I mean, what for? In addition, she's nearly allergic to most technology with the exception of her cell phone. And she was with us for dinner and the partial tour of the castle afterward. We all came back here together, remember?"

Although, now that she'd said it out loud, she suddenly remembered seeing Miranda heading out the front door of the Manor after their encounter with Roger Thompsen as she and Jackson were climbing the stairs to their room that evening. Unfortunately, she could see that Jackson might be thinking the same thing. Had he seen Miranda leaving then as well? Where had Miranda been going at ten o'clock at night? She did look a bit rough the next morning when she came into the dining room.

She shook her head. "Look, Miranda is in great shape and all, but do you really see Miss Thing finagling Thompsen's body into that Iron Maiden all by her lonesome? Because I sure don't. Add to it, you know how she reeeaaally doesn't like to get her hands dirty."

"I don't dispute any of that. Everything you just said is absolutely true." Jackson nodded then put up a finger. "However, she could have had help. Miranda has never been above paying someone else to do anything she doesn't want to do, and she has plenty of green to back it up. Which is also true, and you know it. Plus, we both overheard her conversation with Thompsen out on the veranda at the Lodge the night of the rehearsal dinner. She was pretty clear about her feelings. As I recall, she said she would, and I quote, 'do anything to take you down.'"

He put up a hand when she opened her mouth to object. "Now, does that mean that I think she killed the man or had a hand in his demise? I really don't see it, but it doesn't mean that I don't think for one hot minute that she's not capable of it."

Elise threw her arms wide. "Jax! We're talking about Miranda here."

"Uh-huh. And as my partner always says, in our profession, you find that under certain circumstances, even those you know well can be capable of terrible things. And until Miranda can be well and truly cleared, she stays on the list of suspects, El. You know how this works."

"Okay, fine," Elise said, huffing out an exasperated breath. "So, who else is on this list?"

"Nico, for one. After all, we ran into the man out at the winery on our after-dinner tour that night. He had access, and there's no telling how long he'd been there before we showed up. He would have had plenty of time to do whatever he wanted."

"True," Elise murmured, thinking about the man's anger toward Thompsen the night in question and the way he'd talked about the sale of the vineyard earlier that afternoon. "You said the list was fairly short. Is that it?"

Jackson shook his head. "There was one other we added, at least, so far. Roger Thompsen's daughter, Cara, has been acting office manager for the winery for the last two years. Sounds like she and her father did not see eye-to-eye on many things, and they didn't have the best relationship."

"I suppose that everyone will have to give statements as to where they were when the coroner finally gives Sheriff Masters the time of death, right?" When he didn't answer, she stepped into his bubble and took hold of his chin. "Right?"

"Sure."

"Sure? Could you *be* any more non-committal?" She could almost see the wheels turning. There was something else, something he was holding back. "Jax, what are you not saying? I can see that there's something."

After a long moment, he reluctantly gave in. "Yeah, well, that's what we'll be doing on Monday morning, getting those statements. Because Dr. Wilcox gave us not only the time of death but the cause of death as well. That's why Jim and I were so late getting back. We were meeting with him."

"*What?*" Elise shoved at his chest. "Way to bury the lead, Landry."

"Look, El, I shouldn't be talking to you about the case at all." He looked thoughtful for a moment. "Although, I'm pretty sure that

Tina is prying every bit of information that she can out of my partner as we speak, so I suppose you would've just gotten it all from her later. When it comes to Tina, Jim literally has no firewall these days."

"Right. So, don't make me beg her for crumbs. That would just be embarrassing." She grabbed his shoulders and gave them a shake. "Come on, give it up. What was the verdict? How did Thompsen die and when?"

Jackson blew out a breath. "Time of death was in the wee hours of the morning. The window is sometime between midnight and two a.m.."

"We found the scene just before noon, so he'd been dead for hours."

"Yes."

"And the cause of death? It wasn't the Iron Maiden, was it?"

"It was not."

Elise threw up her hands in exasperation. "Well? What killed the man?"

To her annoyance, he slipped an arm around her waist and pulled her up close. "You're kinda sexy when you're digging through murder clues, you know that? I never noticed this phenomenon back home. I have to say, I find it both arousing and troubling all at the same time, and I'm not sure if that's a good thing or a bad thing."

"*Jackson!* Tell me," she cried.

He chuckled, and then his smile faded. "The murder weapon was a dagger or knife of similar length with a curved tip. Another thing we'll be looking for at the winery. We're meeting there at eight o'clock tomorrow morning, though that place is huge and finding it could be on par with a needle and haystack scenario. If it was hidden, it could be anywhere." He frowned. "On the other hand, whoever killed him could have taken it with them. In that case, it may never be found, which would make this investigation even harder than it already is."

"If it was me, I'd start with the walls of both the Armory and the Torture Chamber." When he started at her with a blank look, she sighed. "Come on, Jax. Did you not get a load of the array of knives and daggers adorning every square inch of the walls? Whoever did this could've just taken one down, used it on Thompsen, and put it right back where they got it. I'd be looking for something missing or askew on the wall. Or at least something with the right shape and length."

"Okay," he said slowly with a surprised expression. "That's a good point. I'm sure Sheriff Masters has already snapped to that, but if not, I'll make sure to mention it."

"And there's something else."

Jackson gave her a tired look. "Yes?"

"If he was killed with a knife or dagger, then the puncture wounds from the Iron Maiden wouldn't have made any difference, right?"

"Probably not much. I suppose it's possible that they could have sped up exsanguination a bit, but Thompsen would have bled out fairly quickly with or without that medioeval-looking contraption. The autopsy showed that the murder weapon gave his aorta a decent slice. Death would have come within a short period of time."

Elise thought back to the scene as they'd found it, before the Iron Maiden had been opened. "Then whoever did this must have gotten him into the cabinet almost immediately."

"Because?"

"Because there was just that swath of blood leading up to the Iron Maiden and a pool around its base. The would mean that Roger Thompsen was ... run through, for lack of a better phrase, right where he'd stood and maybe dragged to the cabinet." At Jackson's grin, she frowned. "What?"

"Nothin'. It's just that ... well, that's a pretty dang good conclusion, darlin'. And incidentally, spot on with the leading theory so far."

Thoughts continued to swirl in Elise's head. "But here's the thing, if Thompsen died so quickly, he probably would have dropped like a stone the minute he was stabbed. I mean, I can't imagine him essentially getting stabbed in the heart and yet staying on his feet, right?"

"Yeah, not likely."

"And Thompsen was a small man."

"What are you getting at, El?"

"Well, I guess one person could have done this, but isn't it more likely that there was more than one person involved?"

"That is yet to be determined. Dr. Wilcox said that the placement and angle of the wound indicates that someone of similar height delivered the blow, and probably used the weapon left-handed."

Elise shook her head. "Someone of similar height would have

needed to have considerable strength to drag him to the Iron Maiden and get him into it on their own, don't you think?"

"That would probably be a fairly good assumption in that scenario."

"And y'all haven't found anything in the way of forensics with the Iron Maiden yet?"

"We haven't gotten the report back from the sweeper team." Jackson sighed. "And you have got to stop watching all those police procedurals, pal ... or at least join the force. You're starting to scare me." He took her by the arm. "Come on. Enough talk about murder. It's getting late, and you're wrecking my appetite. Let's go eat."

"But I haven't told you about our conversation with Nico yet and all the things that we learned," she sputtered as he barely gave her enough time to grab her purse.

"Later," he barked, as he pulled her out of the room.

THE LATE DINNER with the group at The River Wild—a seafood restaurant just up river from the B and B—started out a bit stilted with no one wanting to bring up the issue of Roger Thompsen's gruesome murder. Elise thought it felt almost like an unspoken pact that no one wanted to break. They'd been seated in a small room off of the restaurant's main dining area, and once they'd given the waiter their orders and he'd returned with their drinks, Miranda was the first to break ranks after he'd walked away.

"Okay, shall we address the elephant in the room, friends and neighbors?" she asked, leaning back in her chair and sipping her cocktail, her gaze sweeping the table. "Or did y'all just want to spend the next hour or so in uncomfortable conversation circling it like vultures?"

"Geez, Miranda." C.C. shook her head. "You know, you always have such a way with a turn of phrase."

"Thanks, C.C. It's a gift."

Elise watched the surly smile spread across Miranda's face. *She's right in her element,* she thought. *I wonder if she even realizes that she may be one of the prime suspects.*

Madison sighed. "Well, I, for one, have just been trying to put it out of my mind."

"And how's that working out for you, darling?" Miranda asked in a silky voice tinged with sarcasm.

"Not well, not well at all, and thanks for asking." Madison made a face. "After the last few homicides we've lived through in the Delphine area, it's scary that someone could have done this sometime between when we were there that night and the next day when we … found him." She looked toward Jackson at the other end of the table. "I don't see how y'all are going to solve this crime and put this crazy person behind bars anytime soon, Jax."

"This happens everywhere, not just in Delphine, Maddy," Tina pointed out. "But the timing here is pretty rotten, I'll give you that."

"Well, I'm not worried about it at all," Miranda announced, also looking at Jackson. "They'll find out who did this when they look at the security feed, right Jax?"

Jackson and Jim exchanged glances.

"Right, Jackson?" Miranda narrowed her eyes and repeated her question using his full name when he didn't answer.

"We'll see," he said quietly. "You know this isn't our case, and we can't talk about an ongoing investigation, Miranda."

Tina frowned. "Oh, come on. You have to tell her, Jackson."

"Tina." Jim sighed and shook his head.

"What? She's going to find out come Monday anyway, right? She doesn't have to be gobsmacked with it, Jim. And I can't see how it's going to compromise your precious investigation if you give her a heads up."

Jim ran a hand over his face. "That's not the point, darlin'."

"Okay, then what is the point, *Deputy*?"

Elise felt a bit sorry for Jim getting the business from Tina that way in front of everyone, but kept a straight face when Jackson turned to her with a frustrated look. She smiled to herself. At least it wasn't her blabbing this time.

"I'm going to find out what come Monday?" Miranda, who'd been watching the exchange with increasing interest, asked in an aggravated tone. "Come on, people, speak!"

"The security feed out at the winery has been wiped," Tina continued, glaring at Jim. "So, they'll be looking first at whoever knew where the security system was located and had access to it. They're taking those statements along with the interviews on Monday."

Elise watched Miranda sit back in her chair with a stunned look and finish the last of her cocktail in two quick gulps. She signaled a passing waiter and ordered another.

Turning back to the group, she nodded at Jackson. "So, that would be Thompsen, his daughter, Cara, Nico, the Morans ... and me," she said, ticking off each of them on her fingers. "The six of us, correct? Did I miss anyone?"

Jackson shook his head. "Nope. Got 'em all in one. Of course, we could find others, but that's the list so far."

"Well, I suppose we can count Roger Thompsen out, considering," she replied, wrinkling her nose. "But I would think you could cross me off the list too as I was with this group that entire evening; with dinner, the tour, and that unfortunate ambush by Thompsen at the Manor when we got back from the winery."

"I do hope so," Jackson murmured. "I guess it'll all get sorted on Monday when everyone has an interview and gives their statements."

Elsie watch as the two stared at each other for several long moments—watched Miranda nervously turn away—before their waiter interrupted the uncomfortable silence with their meals.

And with what felt like a collective sigh, just like that the conversation turned from murder to food.

7

Jackson was up and out early the next morning after a short phone call touching base with the sheriff. He and Jim stopped at the Java Hut—which thankfully was open early on a Sunday morning—on the way out of town so that Jim could get his morning fru-fru coffee that he liked so well. Jackson also got himself a tall latte, which, unlike Jim's consistent morning ritual, was an occasional splurge for him. It had just hit seven-thirty when he pulled the rental car into a parking space at the winery and shut down the engine. They were thirty minutes early and Masters wasn't there yet, so they sat sipping their coffees and discussing the case while they waited for him to arrive.

"Sorry about last night, Jax," Jim muttered.

"What? Oh, you mean Tina's big reveal. No worries, buddy."

Jim shook his head. "It's gotten so hard to keep anything of importance from that woman. I tell ya, she could wheedle a pearl out of an oyster without even breaking a sweat."

Jackson gave his partner a sheepish grin. "I hear you, but I wasn't all that discreet with Elise, either, so don't beat yourself up. It's a slippery slope, my friend, and gravity can be a bitch. In the forty-five minutes before meeting y'all for dinner last night, I gave up just about everything we'd done and learned on the case to date. So, what Tina blabbed wasn't news to Elise. The only difference is that it's usually Elise doing the blabbing. She's the lead Nosy Parker, if you know what I mean."

Jim chuckled. "Oh yeah, I do indeed. It's exhausting sometimes, isn't it? But I'd say that we're both all the better for having them with us. Not sure what I'd do without Tina."

"You got that right. Plus, I will confess that my blabby wife is actually a pretty good sleuth and had some interesting ideas to share before dinner last night."

"Oh, really." Jim perked right up. "Do tell."

"Well, first off, she was spot on with our theory of there being possibly more than one person involved with Thompsen's murder."

"Interesting. Great minds, right?"

Jackson nodded, then took a sip of his hot coffee. "And it wasn't just a fluke, either. She walked me through it step by step. It was very methodical, logical." He went on to describe Elise's reasoning.

Jim whistled when Jackson finished. "Well, well, well. Go, Elise, go. Sounds like a family affair in detecting could be in your future, old son."

Jackson nearly spit out a mouthful of his coffee. "Dear Lord, don't even say that out loud. That's all I need. It's bad enough as it is." He narrowed his eyes at his partner. "You know, I could put a bug in Tina's ear about that idea, see how you like it."

Shaking his head, Jim chuckled and put up a hand. "Enough said, buddy. I don't think either of us want to go down that road, now do we?"

They sat in silence for a few moments, each with their own thoughts, before Jim seemed to remember that they hadn't finished their conversation. "So, what else did Mrs. Landry have to say?"

"For one thing, it was her suggestion that prompted me to call Masters this morning. The very first thing she said when I told her about the murder weapon was that, if it was her, she'd be looking at the walls of the Armory and Torture Chamber."

Jim nodded. "And that is a dang good catch, right there. There are all sorts of swords, spears, axes, and most importantly, blades displayed on those walls."

"Yep. So we look for something missing or 'askew', as she put it. She pointed out that someone could have taken a weapon off the wall, stabbed Thompsen with it, wiped it down, and put it back on the wall."

"Another interesting theory, which makes sense. From the description the doc gave us, I would think that an antique blade or dagger would be just the thing, and right there at hand. I guess we'll see soon enough." Jim looked impressed. "Those are some solid detecting instincts Elise's got goin' on."

Jackson laughed. "Oh, and that's not all she had, my friend. No, she wasn't done by a long shot. That was just the appetizer, what we talked about before dinner. *After* dinner was a whole other info dump."

"Really? About what?"

"Oh, just a quick rundown of the recent history of the vineyard and winery."

"What?" Jim's mouth dropped open. "How on God's green earth would she have found that out ... and when?"

Jackson laughed at the look on his partner's face. "Yeah, I know. Kinda boggles the mind, right? I'll go through it nice and slow because it's a lot. See, after you and I left the rest of the group and came back to the winery yesterday afternoon, it seems that they had a nice long chat in the cubby bar where our new friend, Nico, told an in-depth story of how it all came to pass. And as my lovely wife put it, it wasn't pretty."

Jackson started at the beginning and told his partner the whole convoluted tale about Dario Santoro, the original owners, the sale of the vineyard, and how the shareholders came to be. When he finished, Jim looked a bit stunned.

"You're right. That is a lot to wrap your mind around and connect all the dots. It's like something out of one of those nighttime TV soap operas from the eighties and nineties. Seriously." Jim looked out at the vineyard and frowned. "So, did she give you any names? Like maybe this sketchy real estate agent, for starters? Sounds like most of the key players are either dead or out of the country. Kinda hard to run it all down if there's no one left to interview."

Jackson shook his head. "Nope. Might be a good conversation to have with Miranda, though. Maybe Gene left that kind of information with her. And either way, Mrs. Rollins is gonna have some explaining of her own to do."

"Oh yeah? Why's that? Wait ... does it have anything to do with that uncomfortable silence between you two last night at dinner right before the food arrived?"

"It does." Jackson told Jim about how he and Elise had seen Miranda leaving the B and B that night after the ugly scene with Thompsen when they'd gotten back from the winery.

"Where was she going at quarter to eleven at night?"

"Yes, that's what I would like to know." He turned to watch the sheriff's cruiser pull into a spot next to them. "Monday's interviews are shaping up to be a whole lotta fun. Come on, partner. Let's see if the four of us can find a murder weapon."

They both climbed out of the car, and after greeting Sheriff Masters and Deputy Navaro, followed them into the castle building.

"So, that was a good thought you had about the weapon, Jackson," Masters said as they headed down the hallway toward the Armory. "What's that old adage about great minds thinking alike? I had the same thought last night after we met with Doc Wilcox, but I was too tired to come back and spend the rest of my evening scouring this place. Some things are best left for fresh eyeballs, know what I mean?"

"I do," Jackson agreed. He wasn't about to mention that it hadn't been his idea but Elise's. That would lead to more confessions than he was prepared to make. "I figured you would've snapped to it as well."

They stopped outside the Armory doorway, and Masters turned. "Okay. The doc says we're looking for something with a ten to twelve inch blade that curves slightly at the end. So, let's look closely at the walls first for anything that could fit that description. Of course, any blank spots where something seems missing as well."

"It would be nice if what we find lines up with El—uh, Jackson's theory of someone using a weapon displayed here to kill Thompsen, then wiping it and replacing it," Jim said, then continued quickly to cover his slight blunder. "I mean, that would be the easiest, even if it had been wiped. Forensics could probably pick up any blood traces that were missed."

Masters paused and narrowed his eyes in Jim's direction, before nodding. "Yeah," he said slowly. "If it was only that easy."

For the next ten minutes or so, the four of them studied the walls of the Armory, scrutinizing anything that looked as if it could fit the description that the doctor had given them.

At the fifteen minute mark, Jim cleared his throat from one corner of the room. "Uh, gentlemen, I think we may have a winner."

Jackson stepped up beside his partner to see what he was pointing at. "Geez, that's one scary looking blade, isn't it?"

"It looks similar to a jambiya or a khanjar. With that sheath, it could be either, so I can't be certain. Though neither of those would fit in with this collection of weaponry at all."

"Why do you say that?" Masters asked, stepping up on the other side of Jim.

"Well, they both originated in the Middle East, though in different areas. Then again, this collection is really a mish-mash of different origins, countries, different *styles*, for lack of a better word. But I'd say this dagger looks like it fits the design we're looking for. I'd gauge it to be ten or eleven inches in length. Even with the sheath in place, it curves slightly at the tip. And, it would be within easy reach."

Masters nodded, pulling on a pair of latex gloves. "Well, let's just take a closer look-see, shall we?"

Stepping between a display of shiny armor and a rack of long spears, the sheriff scrutinized the weapon where it hung on the wall. "Hmm, it does seem like it's not quite seated right within its bracket, slightly wonky. Perhaps like it was put back in haste but not checked very well?"

He took a couple of closeup photos of it as they'd found it before gingerly removing it from the brackets and taking it off of the wall. Jackson and Jim stepped closer for a better look.

The sheriff carefully slipped off the sheath. "This could be our murder weapon, and hopefully so, but it looks pretty clean," he murmured. "We'll get it back to the lab and see what the techs can tell us." He replaced the ornate sheath back onto the dagger and dropped the weapon into a bag. "In the meantime, we keep looking. If we find anything else that fits the criteria, we'll take back everything we find." He stood for a moment scanning the walls. "I just don't understand. Why would they keep all this dangerous weaponry right out here in the open. I mean, in this day and age, it seems like it would be an insurance nightmare. Some teenager takes something like this dagger off the wall, starts messing around and ends up hurting themselves or someone else? Idiocy, in my opinion."

Jim nodded. "And there doesn't seem to be any security in either of these rooms that I can see. No cameras, nothing. Then again, most of this stuff is probably only replicas, just copies of the real antiques."

"Still, these are real weapons for the most part," Jackson replied. "The sheriff's right, it's a dangerous collection to have hanging on a wall for anyone to grab, new or old. Most of those blades and spears are razor sharp."

His partner nodded. "Agreed."

"Well, come on, then," Masters said. "Let's get this done."

They spent another hour giving the Armory and then the Torture Chamber a good going over but found only one other knife that was close to the right design. Unfortunately, it didn't have the curved tip they were looking for but they took it with them anyway, just in case.

Back at the office, Jackson gave the sheriff the same run down he'd given Jim earlier with the history of the vineyard sale and the bad blood that seemed to stem from it as it pertained to the victim.

"That's good work, Jackson, and quick," Masters said when he finished. "Who did you hear all this from?"

Jackson hesitated, running his tongue around his teeth. "Actually, Sheriff, my wife told me about it. Evidently, when Jim and I came back here yesterday afternoon, the group was sitting in the cubby bar at the Manor shooting the breeze, and Nico Ricci told them the whole story."

"Well, that could be important. Tell *Elise* good thinking and job well done ... all the way around," the sheriff said glancing at Jim and then grinning at Jackson.

Great, Jackson thought. Obviously Jim's earlier blunder had not gone unnoticed.

Then the sheriff cleared his throat. "Of course, all of that history is just that, and was a long time ago, but there are definitely a few threads we can tug at in that whole saga. Who knows what we'll find."

"And what part it all played in what's happening here today with the murder," Deputy Navaro added. "I mean, if it played a part in it at all."

Masters looked a bit surprised by his young deputy but gave a brisk nod. "That's a good point, Jesse." Then he blew out a breath and turned to his case board. "Okay, so let's see where we are, sort it all out, and give it some order. Then we'll look at next steps and figure out where we go from here."

With that, the four of them sat down at the conference table to compare notes.

ELISE DIDN'T HAVE much trouble getting Miranda out and away from the B and B for a drive and some lunch with Madison, C.C., and Tina in tow. Her friend was all but bursting with questions from the minute they got into the van.

"Okay, El," Miranda said as she maneuvered the van out of the parking lot and onto the highway heading west out of Meadowview. "Give me some good news."

"What do you mean?"

"Please. You're always the one sleuthing, mucking about in Jackson's investigations. I know you've got a bead on things. What have you found out so far?"

"You mean, other than the security video being wiped?" C.C. asked.

Miranda scoffed and glanced at C.C. in the rearview mirror. "Tina may have wrangled that much out of Jim, but I have a feeling that Mrs. Landry here has wrangling skills that the rest of us only dream about." With a quick look at Elise, the woman smiled. "So, give it up, El. What else do you know?"

Buckle up, I'm goin' in, Elise thought. "Well, the first thing that I will say is that you need to get your story straight, my friend."

There was another quick look from Miranda. "What's that supposed to mean? What story?"

Elise turned to her with narrowed eyes. "Really? How about where you went after Thompsen's tirade on Friday night?"

Miranda didn't turn to look at her this time but Elise could sense the wheels turning.

"I-I was at the Manor with y'all. Remember? We all went into the cubby bar after he stormed out with his wife in tow."

There was a murmur of agreement from the girls in the back-seat, but Elise tuned them out, as she had information the three of them did not.

"Miranda, this isn't a game. A man's been murdered, a man you'd had an antagonistic association with over at least the last few weeks, probably longer. And you were seen leaving the Manor at quarter to eleven that night."

"What?" Tina blurted from behind. "Jim never said anything about that."

"Jim doesn't know about it ... yet." Elise continued to watch Miranda's face. "But he will by tomorrow morning."

"Well, that's just ridiculous," Miranda began in an annoyed tone. "Who said they saw me leave?"

Elise sighed, and her heart sank at her friends implied denial. Because she knew better. "Miranda, Jackson and I were the ones who saw you leave as we were going up to our room that night."

"Oh," Miranda murmured after a pause. "I see."

"Yes, and considering that Thompsen was murdered only hours after you left the Manor, you need to be very clear in your interview tomorrow about where you went. Because trust me, it will come up, and if you're not truthful, Jax will know and it won't look good." She turned to her friend. "And in addition to all of that, your end of several contentious phone conversations were overhead, and not just by me and Jax. So, putting those aside, where were you going so late on Friday night?"

Miranda licked her lips, and then shook her head. "I can't tell you that, Elise. There's more on the line here than my guilt or innocence."

"Miranda, this is all just circumstantial evidence for now, and neither of us think you had anything to do with Thompsen's death. However, the guys have to go by the evidence, and although the security video was wiped, they still may be able to recover some or most of it."

The implication hung in the air like a dark omen, and no one said a word.

"You don't need to worry about that, Elise," Miranda finally said quietly. "I won't be on that video even if they can recover the entire thing. You have my word."

"That's good to know, my friend, but I'm gonna give you some tough love here. The guys are going to need more than your word to cross you off of the suspect list, and they can't do that if you don't give them the tools. That starts with the truth. I will also remind you that this is not Jackson's case. You know as well as I do that Jax and Jim are way out of their jurisdiction. Sheriff Masters, while he seems like a competent, by-the-book kind of guy, is the one in charge. And he doesn't know you like we all do."

There was silence in the van for a few moments before Miranda eventually nodded. "Okay. You're right, Elise, but I'll need to think it all through first. Like I said, it's not just about me."

"That's all fine, but you need to think fast, girl. Tomorrow will be here before you know it, and then it will be the sheriff asking the questions." They rode in silence for a few more miles, and Elise thought about everything Nico had told them the day before and wondered what information her friend might have to fill in some of the blank spots.

"Miranda, how much do you know about the sale of the vine-yard back when the shareholders bought in and about the original owners, how it all went down? Did Gene tell you any of it?"

"Yes, he did," Miranda replied slowly. "Not all of it in the beginning, mind you, and I rarely paid much attention back then, anyway." A reminiscent smile crossed her face, and she shook her head. "That man was always buying something or selling something. Most of the time it felt like he was trying to get rid of as much of his accumulated wealth as he could, but it always seemed like everything he touched turned to gold. I truly think it baffled him. Anyway, I suppose that I should be grateful for that, because I'll never spend what he left behind in my lifetime, no matter how hard I try."

"But he did tell you the story?" Elise asked.

"Yes, but why are you asking about the sale?"

"Well, Nico told us the story, at least his version of it, yesterday. I was just wondering how much you knew about how Gene and the Moran's bought their shares, and about Thompsen's role in the whole mess."

Miranda blew out a breath. "Oh, that, yes. The year before Gene died, he sat me down and told me everything. Elise, what's this all about? Do you think it's connected in some way to what's happening now?"

"Yeah, why do you want to know about that?" Madison asked. "Wasn't it years ago?"

Elise nodded. "It was. But I'm beginning to think that, though it may have been years ago, the past always has a way of rearing its ugly head with unresolved issues just when it's least expected. And sometimes those issues can be deadly."

8

"So, Miranda, when exactly did the problems with Roger Thompsen actually start?" Elise asked when they were seated at a corner table for lunch at a lovely little bistro in the small village of Tarrytown, halfway to Pelican Point. "Because I'm gonna venture a guess that it's been going on for a lot longer than the last few weeks. Yes?"

Miranda took a sip from her water glass and, with a smile, shook her head. "You really don't miss a trick, do you, El? Yes, you're correct. Roger Thompsen has been a problem for a very long time, practically from the beginning."

"Since he threw a hissy fit for being deprived of the majority of shares he was hoping to get his hands on?"

"Again, correct. The bastard," Miranda sneered. "Of course, like I said, I knew nothing about it in the beginning. Oh, I knew that one of the buyers was disgruntled over something, threatening to sue, blah-blah-blah, but it was Gene's deal. I had little interest in his business transactions at that point."

"Until Gene sat you down and told you about what was going on with the vineyard."

"Right." Miranda's eyes flashed with her rising temper. "I was furious. Not to speak ill of the dead, but Thompsen was a reptile, a menace with no moral compass, no compassion for others, and certainly, no redeeming qualities whatsoever. All he cared about was money and how much he could make for himself without regard for anyone who happened to get in his way."

"Like his poor wife," Madison commented. "Did you see the way he treated her Friday night at the Manor?"

"Yeah. The way she sat with her head bowed and her shoulders slumped," Tina added. "Her posture alone spoke volumes. I mean, it was obvious that she's been beaten down for years. You don't get that cowed overnight, right?"

"I've never seen Venia looking anything but beaten down," Miranda murmured. "I do feel bad for her, having to live with that man day in and day out, and I often wondered why she stayed with him at all. But then, not everyone has the courage or strength to walk away from the evil they know."

"So, you've actually been here before now, haven't you?" Elise asked. "I mean, you led everyone to believe that you'd never seen Bella Luna until this trip, but what you just said kinda belies that fact, doesn't it?"

Miranda grinned at Elise. "I can see now that I really need to be more careful what I say around you, Mrs. Landry. The Deputy is rubbing off on you." The woman took a breath and let it out slowly. "Yes, El, I've been here many times and knew Thompsen before this trip. I've been dealing with his idiocy off and on since Gene's car accident, which, by the way, happened on one of his trips up here."

Elise put a hand on her friend's arm. "Oh, Miranda, I'm so sorry. I had no idea that Gene's accident happened in this area."

"No worries, El. I found a place for what happened years ago. It's just a minor twinge every so often. Anyway, yes, I've gotten to know all the players in this little soap opera since then."

"So, are there more Thompsen kids in the mix other than this Cara?" C.C. asked. "I sure hope not."

Miranda took another sip of water and then glanced at C.C. over the rim. "Oh, there are more children, alright. In fact, two strapping boys."

"Well, that's unfortunate," Tina muttered. "I suppose they're just as cowed by the man as his wife."

Miranda set her glass down and wiped away the condensation from the side of the glass. "And you would be wrong in the extreme, darling."

"Oh?" Elise asked. "I know that his daughter, Cara, wasn't close to her father, right?"

"How did you— oh, of course, the gossip in that little burg is always flowing. Their relationship, or lack of it, was no secret." Miranda nodded. "It was common knowledge."

"Yes, Jax told me that she and Thompsen didn't see eye-to-eye on much, that they weren't all that close."

"You can say that again. Cara's thirty-two and the oldest of the three kids. She's been the office manager for the winery for a couple of years now. She's sharp, ambitious, and aggressive. And let me tell you, 'not all that close' is an understatement. Cara despised her father."

"Oh, my!" Madison exclaimed.

The conversation paused as their waitress came by and took their orders, but Tina jumped back into it the minute the waitress walked away.

"And the sons? Where are they now? How was their relationship with their dad?"

"The middle child, Brian, lives in the area and also works for the vineyard. Earl Rutherford is the vineyard's foreman, and Brian is his right-hand man. Brian's never really had much good to say about the 'old man', as he likes to put it, but he's a hard worker, and I don't think Earl has any complaints with his job performance." Miranda tilted her head and gave Tina a considering look. "Truth be told, I think the distance between father and son stems from the fact that Brian has never been good enough for his father. Nothing he's ever done seemed to please the man, and Thompsen always let him know just how disappointed he was no matter who was around to hear."

"That's just so lame," C.C. said. "People like that shouldn't have kids."

"So, I guess it's possible that Brian would have access to the winery, as well, right?" Elise asked. "Maybe have access to the office? He's the foreman's right hand man. His sister's the office manager. Not much of a stretch to think he could get into any area at any time."

Miranda stared at her for a moment, and she could see that her friend was considering this new angle. "I suppose you're right. I don't know him that well, so I really couldn't say."

"What about the youngest child?" Elise asked. "Is he in the mix as well?"

"Well, Gabriel is a musician, and while no longer a child, was possibly Thompsen's greatest disappointment. He left this area at eighteen for the bright lights of L.A., and has had some success as I understand it. He comes back off and on. In fact, he's been back in Meadowview for the last few months, but I expect he'll be taking off again soon."

"Does he work for the vineyard, too?" C.C. asked. "Or is he still making music?"

Miranda laughed. "Oh, no. Gabe has never had any interest in the vineyard other than drinking Bella Luna's wine, that is. And before you ask, he's never had much of a relationship with Thompsen, either. Being the baby of the family, he's always been a bit of a momma's boy, and from what I've seen, he's very protective of Venia. I think she's the reason that he's come back from time to time, to make certain that she's okay." She sat back and sighed. "However, now that Thompsen is no longer around to make Venia's life miserable, I wouldn't be surprised if Gabe's gone within the next couple of months. He's made a life for himself in Southern California."

There was another pause as the waitress came back with their drinks. "Your orders should be coming right up, ladies," she said before she walked away.

Elise thought about everything Miranda had just told them and wondered about the main focus of Nico's story, Dario Santoro.

"Miranda, Nico told us about the previous winemaker, and how he was basically shut out of buying any shares of Bella Luna, the vineyard that he loved. I'm assuming you knew him as well."

"Yes, I knew Dario." The woman's eyes took on a distant look, as if remembering the old winemaker. "Such a sweet, sweet man. He was treated so poorly … and deserved so much better."

"Sounded like Gene had known him for a long time before buying into the vineyard," Elise said.

"Yes. They were old friends from another time in both their lives."

"Nico said Dario was a father figure to him at a time when he really needed one. Did Dario not have children of his own? A family here in the area with him?" Elise watched Miranda's face as the walls came down, the shutters snapping into place, and thought, *Ah-ha, there it is. Whatever she's hiding lives right there in that spot.*

But before she could get any further, the waitress was back with their food. So, she gave it a rest until they were just about finished with their lunch.

"So, Miranda, I got the feeling that you don't want to talk about Dario or any possible family members. So, I won't push, but you have to be aware that Sheriff Masters probably will." When her friend just continued to stare at her in stony silence, she went on. "However, I do have one other question."

Miranda sighed, and the look on her face told Elise that she wasn't pleased, but then she nodded. "Okay," she said slowly. "And what would that be?"

"It's about the sale. Do you know the name of the real estate agent who handled it? Nico was not very complimentary and didn't tell us her name. However, he seemed to think that this woman had snookered the original owners into selling, that perhaps she'd been working with Roger Thompsen all along on the sly. It sounds like a few of the key players are deceased or no longer in the area. Do you know her name and if she's still around?"

"That she would have been working with Thompsen does not surprise me in the least. Yes, I know that heinous bit—uh, yes, I know her name. Rochelle Griffin," Miranda spat out the name as if it tasted bad on her tongue. "Unfortunately, she's still hawking real estate in Murphey. Anyway, in my opinion, she's as immoral and unscrupulous as Thompsen was so that tracks. Gene did tell me that she was pretty pissed off when the owners—who were old friends of Dario's—gave Gene and the Moran's first bid as a favor to Dario before they signed for the listing."

"Yes. Nico did tell us that much."

C.C. grinned and pointed at Tina. "So, that *is* how Thompsen ended up with the smallest sliver of the pie."

Miranda nodded. "The scuttlebutt was that Griffin's worthless husband, Todd, was also furious at the time."

"Why? Was he part of the deal, too?" Tina asked.

Elise watched the evil grin spread across Miranda's face. "Oh, no, darling," she drawled. "Our little Todd was fuming because dear Rochelle hadn't included him in any of it. I'd never actually met the man, but the way that I heard it, they were on the outs long before the deal came along, but I think that was finally the end of things between them. She was working the entire deal behind his back."

"Ouch." Tina winced. "I can see why the guy would have been a bit torqued. I mean, his wife is crafting a deal that will garner her a nice chunk of change, and he knows nothing about it?"

C.C. winked. "Yeah. Big 'ole bummer for our man Todd."

"Where's this Mr. Griffin now?" Elise asked. Her mind was spinning with all the new details that Miranda had shared. She couldn't wait to fill Jackson in on all the dirt.

"He's still around. In fact, I do believe that he's living right here in Meadowview. Coincidentally, I think he and Cara Thompsen may have been an item for a while, may still be, but I'm not sure." Miranda pursed her lips and gave Elise a studied look. "Elise, it's obvious that you think the sale of the vineyard may have played into all of this somehow," she finally said. "But I just can't see how it would matter. And if it does, why is it important now?"

Elise shook her head. "I can't quite see it yet, myself, but somehow, I think it is important. And something tells me that there's more here to link up besides the sale and Thompsen's murder. We just need more information and then to connect the dots."

JACKSON STARED at Elise in stunned silence before scrubbing his hands over his face in frustration. She was going to be the death of him yet, or at least give him an ulcer of epic proportions. "Geez, woman, I've only been gone for a few hours. Exactly how and where did you get all this new information? You are starting to freak me out."

He'd gotten back from Murphey later than he'd hoped—again —and she'd started flinging information at him the minute he'd walked through the door.

Elise giggled. "Don't look so surprised. I didn't go beating the bushes or interrogating anyone, if that's what you're thinking. Well, I suppose you could say that I did bully Miranda a bit."

"Ah, so the geyser of info was from Mrs. Rollins?"

She nodded. "We went to lunch earlier today, then ran out to Pelican Point to see David and R.J. at the theater." She put up a hand before he could open his mouth to scold her. "And before you say anything, it wasn't like we left the area. I mean Pelican Point is only an hour or so away, and I promised the boys that when this whole investigation was wrapped up, we'd all come back over for a full visit before heading back to Texas." She sighed. "David did make me swear that we wouldn't bring any of the bad juju with us when we came back. He said the murder at the Opera House before they left Texas was one murder too many for him."

"Uh-huh. I know how he feels." Jackson shook his head. "So, back up and give me the first part of that info geyser again. The part about the real estate agent. We've started looking at the sale, those involved, etc., but have only just scratched the surface."

"Her name is Rochelle Griffin, and her office, Griffin Realty, is right there in Murphey. Miranda said the same thing as Nico, that the woman is bad news and was probably working with Thompsen during the original sale, but the owners basically outsmarted them by taking both Gene's and the Moran's offers upfront, before they'd signed the contract with Griffin's agency."

"Okay, I can see how that would piss off Griffin, and Thompsen as well if he was working with her. Here she's expecting a huge commissions on multiple sales, but then it all goes sideways." He frowned. "But why would that be important now? It was almost a decade ago. That's the part I can't see."

"Me, either, to be honest, but it's good that you're looking into it because I think whatever was going on under the surface back then is somehow connected to Thompsen's murder ... and possibly other events."

"Other events? Like what?" Jackson asked, as he pulled a clean shirt out of the closet where Elise had insisted they be hung. "And why do you think that, El?"

"Miranda wondered the same thing." Elise sat down on the edge of the bed as he changed shirts for dinner. "And I-I'm not really sure. It's just a gut feeling, Jax. Something's missing. I don't think we have all the pieces yet, but the connection is there somewhere. I'm sure of it."

"Did Miranda give you any other names that could possibly be connected? The original owners moved back to Sicily not too long after the sale, the winemaker ... what was his name?"

"Dario Santoro?"

"Yeah, he died over four years ago, right? Gene's gone." Jackson shrugged and tucked his shirt into his jeans, then grabbed his jacket. "Other than Miranda, Nico, and the Morans, there has to be others besides Rochelle Griffin to have a chat with about what happened back then. Because I'm beginning to think that we may have made a wrong turn somewhere and there's a dead end looming up ahead."

"Oh, don't worry about that just yet, love" she said, and brought him up to speed with the rest of the conversation they'd had with Miranda, including her stalling about where she'd gone on Friday night when they'd seen her leaving the building, how Gene had told her the saga of the sale the year before his death, and then about Rochelle Griffin's ex, Todd, and his possible connection to Cara Thompsen.

"Well, well, well," he murmured when she'd finished. "That's an interesting twist, isn't it. The Griffins' marriage falls apart because of the sale, and Rochelle's ex possibly ends up involved with Thompsen's daughter. Gives a bit more heft to the notion that maybe Roger Thompsen and Rochelle Griffin had been working together. Jim was right. This is starting to feel like one of those smarmy soap operas."

"That's not the first time I've heard that comparison over the last couple of days. Anyway, to be fair, Miranda did say that she wasn't sure how much of what she'd heard was real and what was just malicious gossip." She put up a finger then. "But here's something else, and it was a *real* touchy spot for Miranda, so you'll need to tread carefully here when you ask her about it."

"What's that?"

"Well, like I said, Miranda wouldn't give me any details about where she'd gone on Friday night, said she couldn't tell me because she said, and I quote, 'it's not just about me.'"

Jackson nodded. "So, you think she's covering for someone else?"

"Has to be. See, when we got around to Dario Santoro, she got really quiet and reflective, said how he'd been the sweetest man and hadn't deserved how he'd been treated."

"Okay ... and?"

"Well, when I asked if Dario had any children or family with him here in this area, she completely shut down. I'm not kidding, Jax, you could literally see the walls snap into place." Elise shook her head. "I did warn her that whatever she was hiding, whoever she was protecting, Sheriff Masters would dig into it until it all came out. That didn't even make a dent."

"She still wasn't talking?"

"Totally stonewalled me, but did say that she just needed some time to think it all through before the interview."

"Ain't got a lot of time left, since tomorrow is interview day," Jackson said, dropping his keys in his jacket pocket. "So, she better think fast."

"Exactly what I told her." Elise stood up and kissed him on the cheek before slipping into her coat. Then she just stood there for a moment with a faraway look in her eyes.

"What?" he asked her.

She blinked. "What do you mean, 'what?'"

"You've got that look on your face again that gives me heartburn. The look that says there's something else pinballing around in that brain of yours."

She made a face at him, but then nodded. "I was just thinking about the whole story Nico told us yesterday. He also spent a lot of time reminiscing about what a wonderful man Dario was, how he was the father Nico had wished for so long after his deadbeat dad had left the family high and dry."

"Yeah, so?"

"Well, he just about gushes over Dario but never mentions the old winemaker's family? Don't you find that a little odd?"

"Okay ... maybe."

She narrowed her eyes at him. "And then I ask Miranda a simple question about Dario's family, and she turns to stone." She grabbed her purse, turned, and started for the door.

"You think they both may be shielding someone. Perhaps someone from Santoro's family?" Jackson asked as he opened the door for her.

She patted his cheek as she stepped out into the hall. "I don't know, Deputy. But I think it might be a good thread to tug, don't you?"

9

J ackson and Jim met downstairs in the dining room at just after seven o'clock on Monday morning. They grabbed a quick breakfast and a much needed coffee to go before heading over to the Sheriff's Office in Murphey.

Today was interview day for those they could schedule. The rest would be handled over the first part of the week. Although this wasn't their case, per the sheriff's request, Jackson and Jim would be sitting in with each interview on the docket. Masters wanted to meet with them and Deputy Navaro at eight-thirty to go over a few things before they got started. It was sure to be a long and tedious day for all of them. Add to it, there wouldn't be much down time in the schedule today, as in between interviews, there would be more digging.

And thanks to Elise, they had quite a bit of digging to do.

"I am much obliged to you both for stepping up like this," Sheriff Masters told them when they all sat down at the table in the conference room next to his office. "We can use all the eyes and ears we can get on this case as I'm sure you are aware. And just so you know, I've been in touch with Sheriff Halbrook in Bastrop. Wanted to let him know how much I appreciate your time and assistance." He gave a nod in Jackson's direction. "Especially on your honeymoon, Jackson. I will see that you both are compensated appropriately."

"That's very good of you, Sheriff," Jackson acknowledged. "These kinds of cases are never easy, and don't get me wrong, Jim and I are happy to do whatever we can, but I'm just not sure how much more help we can be. I mean, we're not from around here, far from it. So, we don't know the players, the lay of the land, or really even where to begin."

Sheriff Masters laughed and shook his head. "This from the man who's handed me several starting points just in the last couple of days."

"Now, to be fair, most of the information that I've *handed* you actually came from my nosy wife who can't seem to help herself, even where our investigations back home are concerned."

"Amen to that," Jim added with a shake of his head, then muttered, "And lately, Tina's right behind her."

"I tell you, half the time Elise drives me crazy." Jackson scratched his head. "However, she is incredibly tenacious, and sometimes I think she could get information out of a pile of rocks. I have no idea how she's gotten the information here that she has."

"Huh. Well, I can't wait to have a sit down with Mrs. Landry." Masters gave another bark of laughter and winked. "In any case, maybe we should just sign her right up to assist."

Jackson put up both hands and gave the sheriff a horrified look. "Please don't even suggest that especially within her earshot.

Giving my wife any form of validation will just egg her on, and that's all I need. It's hard enough to keep her from nosing around our investigations as it is."

Jim snickered and pointed a finger at Jackson. "What did I say the other day about detection running in the family?"

"Don't push it, partner. I am not above putting that little bug we also talked about in Tina's ear, and I'm not kiddin'."

Now it was Jim's turn to put up his hands, but this time in surrender. "Okay, okay. No need to get nasty about it."

Jackson thought for a moment and then turned to Masters. "Having said that and, with some embarrassment, I do have some fresh and relevant information that I should probably share with you right up front before the interviews get started."

"Oh? Is that right?" Masters gave him a sly look. "And, is this *new info* from the lovely Mrs. Landry as well?"

Scrubbing his hands over his face, Jackson was sure he was never going to hear the end of this from Jim—or Masters, for that matter—but nodded. "Yes, yes it is."

He proceeded to relate everything that Elise had told him the night before. The sheriff made notes while Jackson laid it all out, as did Deputy Navaro. When he'd finished, he sat back and waited.

After a moment and a few last scribbles on his pad, Masters looked up with a straight face. However, Jackson did notice that the man's lips were twitching ever so slightly, as if he was struggling not to laugh.

The sheriff took a deep breath and let it out slowly. "I do believe

I may have a sit down with Mrs. Landry after her interview today to discuss a possible employment opportunity."

Jackson sighed. *Yep, gonna have to live with this for a while*, he thought. "You're very funny, Sheriff. However, I would be careful going down that particular road, if I were you. You might get more than you bargained for, and then you'd be in the same predicament as we are ninety percent of the time back home."

The smile bloomed again on the sheriff's face, and he cleared his throat. "Seriously, this is some good work. I have questions about some of these very things on my checklist, but we haven't had the time or manpower to get to them yet, so this may be just the thing to get this case moving forward, maybe connect some of the dots." His smile grew. "I'd ask you to give your wife my thanks, but I know that probably wouldn't set well. So, I'll just say that I would appreciate it if you'd give her a bit more leeway, so to speak, over the next week or two."

"I'll take it under advisement, Sheriff," Jackson replied.

Amusement flickered in Masters' eyes before he shook his head and refocused on the task at hand. "Now, I am expecting to hear from the sweeper team sometime today or tomorrow regarding any forensics they collected from the scene at the winery, including anything they may have found with the Iron Maiden. We can only hope to catch a break there, though I'm not holding my breath." He shuffled through some of his notes, then looked up. "However, let's set that whole mess aside for later, as well as all but the most pertinent of this new info, and get back to these interviews, shall we?" Masters opened another folder and began laying out the forms for each interview scheduled for the day, six in all.

And then they got down to business.

First up on the docket this morning had been Miranda, but she'd rescheduled her interview for the end of the day, so Nico Ricci was coming in at nine-thirty. After what Elise had told Jackson about how Nico and Miranda had both avoided talking about Dario Santoro's family, he was eager to dig into that subject with the man. What they learned from Ricci today, if anything, would be helpful when Miranda finally came in for a chat in the late afternoon. Jackson decided to go out and wait for Ricci in the lobby and greet him when he came through the door.

Jim followed him out to the lobby a few minutes later and sat down next to him. "So, do you think we're gonna get anything of worth out of Ricci this morning? I mean about Santoro's family?" Jim asked, mirroring Jackson's thoughts.

He shrugged as he kept an eye on the parking lot through the long window next to the door. "I guess we'll find out. I think getting him to reveal any secrets will be a helluva lot easier than pulling anything out of Miranda without some sort of incentive."

"Ha! Too right, my friend. To tell ya the truth, that woman has always scared me just a little bit."

"There's a good reason for that, buddy." Jackson turned with a grin. "That's your subconscious telling you to beware, that she could probably take you down and eat you alive if she was of a mind. It wouldn't be pretty, that's a certainty."

"I know you're mostly kidding, but unfortunately, I think there is some truth to that."

"Anyway, if she and Ricci are both stonewalling over Santoro's family, there's got to be a reason, something there. I think Elise may be right. They may be covering for or protecting the same person, possibly a family member. I'm hoping that if we can get to the heart of it with Ricci, maybe Miranda will give it up as well."

"Knowing that woman, it seems like a pretty big maybe," Jim said skeptically.

"Could be. However, we are fixin' to find out." Jackson gestured toward the window where Nico Ricci could be seen getting out of his little sports car in the parking lot.

At nine-thirty on the dot, Nico walked into the lobby.

"Hey, Nico," Jackson stood up and greeted him. "Thanks for coming in and for arriving so promptly. Sheriff Masters will be right out and then we can sit down and talk, maybe get you in and out as quickly as possible. I'm sure you have plenty of work to do out at the winery."

Nico nodded. "You can say that again. The sheriff okayed me for the fermentation room so that's good. Work at the castle is never quite done, if you know what I mean."

"I do indeed."

Before they could get much beyond meaningless pleasantries, Sheriff Masters came out of his office up the hallway and strode toward them. "Mr. Ricci. Thanks for coming in so early this morning. Come on back and we'll get this over with."

Nico followed the sheriff back to Interview A with Jackson and Jim bringing up the rear.

Once in the room, Masters gestured to the table as Deputy Navaro closed the door behind them. "Have a seat. Can we get you anything before we start? A cup of coffee? Soda? I will tell you that the coffee here in the office is not the swill that you would normally expect in a police station. I take my coffee very seriously and, not to toot my own horn, but it's quite good."

"I will attest to that," Jim added. "Almost better than I make at home." He glanced over at the sheriff with a smirk. "Almost."

Nico chuckled but shook his head. "I'm good. I think I've already had my caffeine quota for the day, but thanks."

"Alright then. We'll get started." Masters shuffled through one of the folders on the table and then looked up. "Oh, and this interview is being recorded just so you know."

"I figured it would be," the man acknowledged. "Murder investigation and all."

With a nod, Masters, with elbows on the table, leaned in. "Okay. Why don't we start with the sale of the vineyard."

This obviously took the Italian by surprise, as evidenced by the stunned expression that crossed the man's face. He covered fairly quickly, but looked back and forth between the sheriff and Jackson. "I-I'm sorry? The sale? That was almost a decade ago. I thought these interviews were just to update our original statements regarding Roger Thompsen's death."

"Well, now, you are correct," Masters acknowledged with another nod and stared hard at the man. "However, a few things have come to light which seem to connect the two. As I understand it, several of the main players are now either out of the country or deceased. And you were around back then, so I was hoping that you could fill in some of the blanks for me, if you can."

Jackson watched the man process this, the wheels turning at a rapid pace. After a moment, Nico blew out a breath. "Uh, okay. I don't know what all I can tell you but I'll do my best. What do you want to know?"

Masters looked down at his notes, making a show of scanning along with his pen. Then he looked up with narrowed eyes. "Tell me about Dario Santoro."

"Dario?" Nico sputtered, now clearly rattled. "Why do you want to know about him?"

"He was the winemaker back then, correct?"

"Well, sure, but what does that have to do with anything?"

Masters perused his notes again, giving Nico the impression that they knew something that he did not. Jackson had to hand it to the sheriff. For overseeing a very rural county, he had himself some mean interview skills. Jackson couldn't imagine playing poker with the man.

"See, the way I've heard it, Mr. Ricci, is that Dario Santoro kinda got screwed over when the original owners sold the vineyard in shares, and that Roger Thompsen was smack-dab in the middle of said screwing and perhaps instigated the whole thing."

Masters glanced at Jackson, and he read the intent loud and clear. It said, *sending you in, pal. Go get him.*

Jackson wasted no time in doing just that and sat forward. "Nico, we're aware that you were close to Dario. We heard about the conversation you had with Elise, Madison, Tina, and C.C. on Saturday in the cubby bar, about how much Dario loved the vineyard and how poorly he'd been treated. Miranda said much the same thing. You told them that you couldn't prove it but that you thought Roger Thompsen was working with ... a Rochelle Griffin? Evidently, she was the real estate agent for the sale?"

"She was, however, I would use that title loosely." Nico replied after a moment, gauging his words carefully. "And yes, I know that she and Thompsen were working together, maybe on behalf of someone else, but I could never find a concrete connection. So, no, I couldn't prove it."

"It sounds to me like there were some real hard feelings over the way it all shook out. Roger Thompsen in particular was pretty angry about being blocked from getting a hold on the majority of shares he was looking to acquire, wasn't he? I can't imagine this Rochelle Griffin was too happy about it, either." Jackson shook his head. "I mean, she would have stood to make a tidy profit off the sale had Gene Rollins and the Morans not snapped up the bulk of the shares before the owners signed with her, right? The fact that there was only a paltry eighteen percent left by that time seems like it would have been quite a blow to her as well."

Nico gave a slow nod, and again, his answer was cautious. "I would say that's an accurate assumption. They both expressed their displeasure about it at the time, but it blew over after a while."

Jackson tilted his head and raised his eyebrows. "Blew over? Or smoldered under the surface?"

"What do you mean?"

By the look on the man's face, Jackson could see that Ricci knew exactly what he was getting at, but spelled it all out for him anyway. "I'm talking about all the trouble that Thompsen caused out at the winery. You told the girls that it was just piddly stuff, right? Now you're telling us that it all kind of 'blew over', but that's not quite true, is it? You want to tell us when it actually started and what that looked like? Because Miranda says

Thompsen was a problem right out of the gate and the disruption he caused continued to escalate."

"Okay, yes, the trouble did start with the sale." Running a hand over his face, Nico relented. "Look, Miranda didn't know about any of it in the beginning. I know Gene told her about it before he died, but she didn't see it like Gene did on his trips up here, like the rest of us did. Thompsen was livid with the outcome of the sale, made noises about conspiracies, possibly suing, though he didn't have a leg to stand on there."

"And then?"

Nico stared down at his clasped hands on the table in front of him. "It is true that things did sort of die down for a month or so, but then the real trouble started. It was just little things to begin with, vandalism off and on around the vineyard, minor theft, stuff like that. No one connected the dots at first."

"But then it got worse?" Jim asked. "And those dots started to link up?"

"Yeah, you could say that. It escalated to break-ins, expensive gear going missing then turning up somewhere else on the property a week later, irrigation equipment being damaged," Nico replied. His voice was steady, but as he looked up, Jackson could see the man's anger in his eyes. "But there was nothing that could ever be traced back to Thompsen. It was so frustrating because we knew it was him or someone he'd probably paid to do it. That's why Gene had the security cameras installed on the property."

The sheriff frowned. "But that only covers the castle and the immediate winery area, correct?"

"True, but it did put an end to the issues that were occurring around the castle itself, which is another reason we were sure Thompsen was behind all the problems."

"And who is 'we?'" Jackson asked.

Nico blinked. "I beg your pardon?"

"You keep saying 'we.' Who else thought it was Thompsen? You told the girls that you weren't the only one who was thinking that Thompsen was the guilty party. I'm assuming Gene was of the same mind."

"Well, I was just an apprentice winemaker back then, but I over-heard conversations with the others. Yes, Gene, but Dario and William Moran as well. They all thought the same thing."

"It had to be hardest on the winemaker, though, right?" Jackson asked, softly. "I mean, to be shut out of buying into the vineyard, loving it the way he did, and then to watch it being attacked in that way."

Nico swallowed hard. "It wasn't just hard on Dario. It took several years but I think it destroyed him. Gene tried to help by acquiring the majority share of the vineyard when Dario couldn't, but it wasn't enough. If you want to know the truth, I think the whole nasty business played a factor in Dario's death in the end, so that's something else that I will place firmly at Thompsen's feet."

"I suppose that's understandable." Jackson nodded. "After all, you told Elise that Dario was a father figure to you after your own father left the family. Sounds like he felt the same way about you."

"Yes. That's true." The man tapped a finger on the table. "But I'll tell you another thing that I've not told anyone else. Though I have no proof of this either, I've always felt that the car crash that took Gene's life was also suspect."

The sheriff looked up at that and frowned. "Really. Why do you say that?"

"Go back and look at the reports. I'm telling you, it was a fishy deal. But then, again, I was an apprentice back then and no one would have taken me seriously. That's just my opinion."

Masters made a note on his pad. "Alright. I will do that."

Jackson thought for a moment. If the accident that had taken Gene Rollins' life was found to be part of this, it would open up —as the sheriff had put it earlier—a whole other can of worms, and the investigation would take on a much larger scope. However, as stunning as that thought was, he still hadn't gotten to the question that he'd been waiting to ask throughout the entire interview, the question he'd been about to ask when Nico brought up the subject of Gene Rollins' car crash. He got to it now before they got farther afield. "Nico, did Dario Santoro have children of his own?"

Taken by surprise again, Nico blinked several times and paled. "I, uh, what does that have to do with this investigation?"

Jackson sighed. "Surely, being so close to Dario, you would know if the man had children. Is there a reason you don't want to say? I mean, we can do a bit of research but it would be easier for you just to tell us."

Storm clouds brewed again in the Italian's eyes and his voice took on an edge. "It's just that I don't want innocent people traumatized any more than they already have been."

"So, Dario Santoro had other children in the area, is that correct?"

"Yes," Nico hissed. "Dario's daughter lives in the area."

"Mr. Ricci, can you tell us where you were on Friday night into Saturday morning?" Masters asked him suddenly. "We have the earlier statements about the wedding party running into you out at the winery during their impromptu tour between eight and nine o'clock Friday night, but we need to know where you went after that, where you were between midnight and two a.m. Saturday morning. It's just to dot the i's and cross the t's, so to speak."

Watching the man closely as he hesitated, Jackson smiled to himself and thought, *He's thinking, how much do I say? And how much can I leave out?*

"When I left the winery, I went to a friend's house. I got there a little after nine."

"And how long were you there?"

"If you must know, I spent the night. Then ran home at about eight-thirty the next morning to shower before heading out to the winery for the full tour Miranda had scheduled."

"Uh-huh." Masters made a show of scribbling notes on his pad. "And this friend's name and contact information?" he asked before looking up at the man expectantly. "We will need to confirm the timeline. Again, i's and t's."

The storm in Nico's eyes erupted into a full-fledged fire.

"Her name is Adrianna Santoro," he spat. "She's Dario's only child ... and my fiancé."

10

Since Miranda had been MIA, Elise, C.C., Madison, and Tina caught a lift to the sheriff's office in Murphey from a local service and had shown up en masse for their interviews at one o'clock. Though there were four of them, it hadn't taken long for each to update their original statements, as there wasn't much to update in the first place. With the exception of Miranda, they'd all been together at Riverside Manor Friday night and knew nothing of the murder until—as a group —finding evidence of a crime scene on Saturday at just before noon.

Elise had been the last to give her statement update sitting across from Sheriff Masters and Deputy Navaro, with both Jackson and Jim taking seats against the back wall of Interview A. The questions asked of her had been mostly routine—which she figured had been the same for the other women—until near the end of the interview when it became clear that Jackson had relayed the information she'd given him. And though the sheriff was careful at first with these last questions, it was also quite obvious that he knew exactly where the information had been garnered.

"So, Mrs. Landry—"

"Elise, please, Sheriff," she cut in. Looking over his shoulder at Jackson, she grinned. "The Mrs. Landry thing is still pretty new."

Masters cleared his throat. "Alright, then. Elise. Just a couple more questions, a few things that I'd like to clear up. It's come to our attention that Mrs. Rollins was with the group on Friday night but left the Manor at just shy of eleven o'clock. Is that correct?"

This time, she avoided looking in Jackson's direction but nodded. "That's right. We—Jax and I—were the last to head up to our room after leaving the cubby bar, and we saw her going out the front door as we made our way up the stairs. Although, to be clear, she could have just been going out to the van to retrieve something she'd forgotten, but then came back in after we'd gone to our room."

Masters nodded. "But you don't know that for sure, do you? You only saw her leave, correct?"

"Yes."

"And later? Did you ask her about where she went? If she'd just gone out to the van for something she'd forgotten?"

Elise sighed. "I did. Us girls took a drive on Sunday to see some of our friends in the area, and I did ask her that."

"And what did she tell you?"

"As I'm sure you already know, she wouldn't tell me where she went or who she'd been with."

"So it was clear that she hadn't, in fact, just gone out to the van for something but had indeed left the Manor."

"Correct."

The sheriff made a few notes on his pad. "Did she give you a reason why she wouldn't tell you where she went or who she was with?"

Elise nodded. "She said that there was more on the line than her guilt or innocence, that it wasn't just about her."

"Her guilt or innocence?"

"Well, yes, we'd talked about the security video at the winery being wiped, and I was concerned about her refusing to confirm where she'd gone, but she told me that even if the video could be restored, she wouldn't be on it, which indicated to me that she hadn't gone to the winery."

"But there again, you can't be sure, as you only have her word— or indication, as you say—for that."

"True."

"And the other part? What did you take that to mean?"

"I-I don't—"

"When she said that it 'wasn't just about her'?" Masters repeated and leaned forward. "How did that strike you, Elise?"

"Well, I suppose, that she was protecting someone, or maybe covering for someone? But that's just an opinion, a feeling, Sheriff. I could be wrong."

"Uh-huh." Masters tapped his pen on the pad in front of him and then looked up at her, his gaze direct. "Elise, I'm certain you're aware that we're looking into the original sale of the vineyard because it was you who put that particular bug in Jackson's ear."

Elise glanced briefly at her husband, knowing she'd probably hear about this later. "Sheriff, I really didn't mean—"

Masters put up a hand. "No, there's no need to explain or to worry about Jackson. Although, *he'll* probably not be all that happy about it, ongoing investigation and all, I actually appreciated the suggestion. After looking into it so far, I'm of a mind that you may be correct, that there's something not quite right in that whole mess. I think we're going to find that the sale is where everything started, but we're just not there yet." The sheriff looked down at his notepad again, as if thinking through something in his mind. After a moment, he continued. "Elise, you asked Mrs. Rollins about the sale, didn't you?"

"I did."

"And you asked her about the original winemaker? Dario Santoro?"

"Yes. Miranda liked the man very much, and while she didn't know him well when her husband Gene bought into the vineyard, I suspect that she came to know him quite well after Gene's death, because she spoke very fondly of him."

"And when you asked her about any family Mr. Santoro may have had?"

Elise frowned. "She ... uh, well, she pretty much shut down."

"Meaning?"

"Meaning that it was clear she wasn't going to talk about that ... at all. I got the feeling that was a very touchy subject for her."

"Do you have an idea of why? Do you think maybe a family member of Mr. Santoro's was perhaps who she was protecting?"

Elise shook her head. "I really couldn't tell you that, Sheriff. I would just be speculating, but as I said, she basically shut down at the mention of Dario having family in the area. However, I will say that, at the time, I did think that perhaps it was why she was stonewalling, that there was someone she was shielding, and that, yes, they might be related to Dario."

"Thank you for your insight, Elise. We're going to speak to Mrs. Rollins later this afternoon, so we'll be asking her about all of this when she comes in."

Elise looked him in the eye. "Sheriff, full disclosure? I did tell her that at the end of our conversation, that I wouldn't push but that you most certainly would. She said she just needed some time to think it through, but I told her that she needed to make it snappy, that she didn't have much time left."

"You are quite the pip, Elise." Masters chuckled.

"Thanks … I think."

He put up a finger. "There is one other point that I'd like to discuss before we're finished here."

Elise was hesitant but tilted her head, considering. "And that is?"

"We're going to also be chatting with Cara Thompsen tomorrow to see what she can tell us about her father's involvement with a possible scheme pertaining to the vineyard sale." He leaned down on his elbows. "Todd Griffin and his ex-wife, Rochelle, who, as you know, was the real estate agent for the sale are also on the schedule for the next day or two. I'd like you to repeat what Mrs. Rollins told you about the rift during that time between Mr. Griffin and his ex-wife."

Now Elise frowned. "But Sheriff, obviously Jax has already passed that information on to you. And, besides, it's really all just hearsay. I mean, even Miranda called it scuttlebutt, just rumors that were going around back then."

"That's true, but I'd like to hear it from you, what she actually told you."

"Alright." She blew out a breath and thought for a moment, trying to remember Miranda's words as clearly as possible, before nodding. Then, she went back over their conversation as closely as she could remember it.

When she finished, the sheriff made a few notes and paused. "When Mr. Ricci was here this morning, he said that he was sure that Rochelle Griffin and Roger Thompsen were working together during the original sale, and that they may have been working on behalf of someone else. Did you and Mrs. Rollins talk about that possibility?"

"Yes, Nico did tell us that on Saturday, but he didn't say anything about them working for someone else." Elise shook her head. "And, no. Miranda never said anything about that. She didn't seem to know any of the finer details about the sale, and definitely not about the possibility of Rochelle Griffin and Roger Thompsen working together on it. I don't think it was something Gene ever touched on with her, but I can tell you that she wasn't surprised by that supposition. In fact, she thought it made perfect sense, that they were two of a kind. Both immoral and unscrupulous."

"But she never mentioned any other possible players, someone they might be working for behind the scenes?"

"No. I would say ..." She paused and caught Jackson's eye, then thought better of making any suggestions.

"Yes?" The sheriff prompted, not letting her off the hook. "Go ahead, finish your thought."

"Well, I wouldn't presume to give you advice on your investigation in any way, but from what I've gathered, that would be a good subject to discuss with both Cara Thompsen and Todd Griffin."

Masters chuckled again. "Oh, trust me, it is on my 'to do' list." He slid his notepad into the folder beneath it, and folded his arms over the top. "In the meantime, is there anything else you'd like to tell me, any other thoughts you've had or information you've ... *acquired* about the sale and its possible connection?"

Elise glanced at Jackson again, who just shook his head. Looking back at the sheriff, she smiled. "No. Not that I can think of at the moment, Sheriff."

Masters returned her smile with a knowing grin of his own and gave her a pointed look. "Well, if you think of anything else that may be pertinent, please feel free to ... uh ... pass it along."

Elise couldn't quite believe hear ears. Was the sheriff really implying that she—as Jackson would say—continue to poke around in an ongoing investigation?

Oh, I bet Jax is just loving that, she thought, but only nodded and said, "I'll keep that in mind, Sheriff."

SHERIFF MASTERS SAT at the conference table with papers spread out in front of him and a frown on his face. Jackson could see that the man was working through something in his head and wasn't quite ready to share.

He could definitely relate.

Jackson was working through his own dilemma at the moment and was not looking forward to talking to Elise about the sheriff's earlier insinuations. Her nosing around in his investigations at home was one thing, and though she usually knew the people she was poking at with her questions, doing so was not without its own hazards. Even folks you knew could be capable of horrific acts when cornered or desperate. However, they weren't at home now, and the people they would encounter here were strangers, which made them unpredictable as well.

"Okay, I want to walk through what we know so far," Masters said suddenly, as if he'd finally come to some conclusions. He held up a report he'd taken from one of his folders. "But before we get started on that, I just received this report from the sweeper team on the Thompsen scene."

"Did they find anything that'll help us?" Jim asked.

"Not nearly enough," the sheriff replied. "At least, nothing conclusive. Now, we did get confirmation that the ornate dagger we collected is definitely the murder weapon, as there were minute traces of the victims blood recovered from around the base of the hilt."

Jim smirked. "Just so darn hard to scrub all the little nooks and crannies when you're hastily wiping down your murder weapons."

"Very true, though not much of a surprise there," Masters replied. "The team did, however, recover a partial print—in Thompsen's blood—on the inside of the Iron Maiden's door where somebody probably took hold of it to pull it open. As there were zero other prints found on that side of the room, and

I mean zero, it seems like in cleaning up after themselves it was the only place the perp, or perps, missed."

"But it's a plus, right?" Jackson asked. "Clear prints?"

"Unfortunately. No." Masters ran a hand over his face. "The prints were obviously made by fingers but they were smears with no print definition."

Jim frowned. "Gloves?"

"Gloves." The sheriff grimaced. "There was one other partial found on the door frame between the Armory and the Torture Chamber, but there again, it wasn't enough to even run through the system."

"What about the Iron Maiden itself?" Jackson asked. "Anything else found there?"

Masters shook his head. "Not much. The outside of the door had been wiped down, but there was a bit of trace blood in the—as Jim put it—nooks and crannies on the outside of the door as well. Probably from when they closed it up with Thompsen in it. On the inside, other than the weird partial print, it was mostly just Thompsen's blood and fibers from his clothes."

"That's disappointing." Jackson narrowed his eyes. "So, to leave almost zero trace evidence behind, whoever did this had to have taken quite a bit of time to clean up after themselves."

"Yep." Masters nodded. "And without the security video to worry about, they probably had all the time they needed. But then again, I wasn't holding my breath for any stunning revelations here."

"Well, we have made some headway, Sheriff," Jesse said.

"We've made a bit of progress, yes, but not nearly enough." He made a couple of neat piles out of the scatter of paperwork he'd been going over, then looked up at Jackson and Jim. "Now, let's bring you two up to speed with what Jesse and I did yesterday evening after you went back to the Manor. Though I was not looking forward to it, we went out to talk to Venia Thompsen and her two boys."

Jackson nodded. "Crossing the family off the list ... if possible. Always a good place to start."

"Exactly. It seems that none of the Thompsen children were very fond of their father, so it was of paramount importance to get their whereabouts at the time of his death." He rolled his eyes. "You never know. Anyway, I also wanted to talk to Mrs. Thompsen about the events of Friday night, namely the incident at the Manor and their movements after they left the site."

"And what did she tell you?" Jim asked.

Masters perused his notes. "She said that Thompsen was 'very angry after the confrontation', and that she was terrified on the drive home, as he was 'driving like a mad man.'" He looked up. "Her exact words."

"Well, that's not hard to imagine," Jackson said. "When we all got back to the Manor, Thompsen was already wound pretty tight. And it was much worse by the time he left."

Jim nodded. "Yeah, he was just about foaming at the mouth when he headed out the door. And his poor wife, well, he basically snapped his fingers in her direction as he flew past her. I remember thinking that the drive home was probably gonna be just a might harrowing, by the looks of him."

Masters' face was grim. "Mrs. Thompsen said that when they got to the house, her husband didn't even get out of the car. He just told her to go into the house and stay put, that he'd be back after he took care of some business."

"Now, what kind of business would he be taking care of at that time of night?" Jim wondered. "I mean, it had to have been ten o'clock or just after when they left the B and B."

"She didn't know, but her younger son, Gabriel, corroborated her story. Evidently, he was there when she came in, and he told her he'd stay with her until Thompsen came home so she wouldn't be alone. However, I got the feeling that the reason he stayed was to make sure his momma was okay *after* his daddy got home. It has been noted that Mr. Thompsen had a reputation of taking things out on Mrs. Thompsen from time to time, and that Gabriel had been her protector on several occasions. Anyway, the boy ended up staying the night because his daddy never did come home."

"So, sounds like those two can be crossed off the list," Jackson surmised. "How about the other son, Brian?"

The sheriff scratched his head. "Now, the jury's still out there. He said he was with some friends who own a vineyard over in Dundee. Stayed with them overnight. He gave us their contact information but we haven't had time to chase down the alibi yet. Jesse's gonna do that later this afternoon."

"You bet, Sheriff," the deputy said. "I'll get it nailed down as soon as we're done here."

Masters nodded. "Good deal. So, that will take care of the immediate family with the exception of Cara Thompsen, but she's scheduled to be in here tomorrow at eleven. We'll get her statement and whereabouts then."

Deputy Navaro looked at his notepad. "I spoke to Adrianna Santoro about an hour ago. She confirmed that Nico Ricci, her fiancé, was with her Friday night and stayed until a little after eight a.m. Saturday morning. So, we can probably cross him off the list of suspects, right?"

"For now," Masters qualified, then ran his pen down the list on his notepad in front of him. "The other shareholders, William and Grace Moran, live in the Eugene area, which is a good three to four hour drive from here on a good day. Plus, they were at a fund raiser in downtown Eugene on Friday night until well after one o'clock Saturday morning, which has also been corroborated, so that puts them in the clear as well. Although, we may want to talk with them about the sale, so I told Mr. Moran that I'd be in touch at a later date."

"Our possible suspect list seems to be dwindling at a pretty significant rate," Jim pointed out. "And I'll be danged if I know where we go from here."

Masters shook his head. "Oh, I have no such concerns about the path forward, Jim. I'm of a mind that we start by looking real hard at the sale of the vineyard and those involved. Short of an unexpected confession within the next twenty-four hours or so, that's the first place we go from here." The sheriff turned to Jackson. "I find myself with the same itch about that sale that your wife seems to have, Jackson. Like I told Elise, I think the sale's where everything started."

Jackson nodded. It was a logical path forward—to go back to the beginning. The more he'd thought about it, the more he, like the sheriff, had started to believe that something from the past was behind Thompsen's death. Something had taken place that had set the whole thing in motion, but what specifically that was, he had no idea. However, he agreed with Masters, it was starting to point to the sale of the vineyard. Unfortunately, it was going to take a lot more digging to uncover what that could be, for sure.

Masters gave Jackson a narrow-eyed look and pointed at him with his pen. "Here's another thing that I've been pondering on. I want to do some research on Gene Rollins' accident, see if it was as fishy as Mr. Ricci seems to think it was, and if so, if there's some connection to the sale there, too."

The sheriff got up to make another pot of coffee. "But in the meantime, we've got one more interview in about an hour and a half." With his back to them, he continued. "And I would very much like both of you to assist with it, maybe run a tag-team scenario."

"Miranda." Jim rolled his eyes at Jackson. "And *I* would very much like to defer to you on this one, buddy," he muttered beneath his breath.

"Thanks so much," Jackson replied quietly, but nodded at Masters when the sheriff turned back to them. "I can do that, Sheriff. I will say that I would definitely love to hear her answers to some of the questions on my list."

Masters came back and sat down while the coffee brewed. "Excellent. Then let's go over both your list and mine, see about any overlaps, and then get our game plan set." The sheriff gave Jackson a wily look. "Speaking of scuttlebutt, I have heard that Mrs. Rollins can be a bit prickly and is no pushover."

Jackson burst out laughing. "Oh, man. You have no idea. That may be the biggest understatement of the year."

"You can say that again," Jim agreed.

Masters nodded. "Okay then. Let's get to it."

A little over an hour later, the trio had sketched out their game plan, ran it through a few times, and had given it a final tweak. In the thirty minutes or so before Miranda was due, Jackson went over the questions on his list, questions that he would be posing to her himself.

Part of him wanted to know where she'd been Friday night, mere hours before Thompsen was murdered, and who she was obviously covering for. Another part of him hoped that they could clear her from any involvement. He'd told the sheriff everything Elise had shared with him, which she had verified in her interview, so really, it was up to Miranda to clear herself by being forthcoming and truthful. Jackson knew that Miranda was aware he'd also seen her leaving the Manor late on Friday night, so she couldn't really deny it, but would she stonewall them here in the interview when they asked her about it? He'd just have to wait and see.

He didn't have to wait long.

At four-thirty on the dot, Mrs. Miranda Rollins sauntered into the lobby of the Sheriff's office with a smug smile on her face and accompanied by her attorney.

———

11

"Good afternoon, Mrs. Rollins." Sheriff Masters stepped forward and greeted Miranda warmly, as if they were old friends about to have a chat to catch up rather than sitting down for an interview during a homicide investigation. "Thanks so much for coming in this afternoon. We really appreciate it."

Jackson had to struggle to keep a straight face as Miranda responded in kind.

"You're very welcome, Sheriff. I do apologize for having to reschedule at the last minute this morning," she drawled, then gave him a small pout. "I hope I didn't put a crimp in your day."

Masters waved away her comment with a hearty laugh. "Good Lord, no. Don't you worry about that at all. We've got quite a few interviews set up over the next couple of days, so we had no trouble filling the time this morning."

"Well, that's a relief, isn't it?" Miranda turned to Jackson with a twinkle in her eye that said the fun was just beginning. "Jackson," she nodded in acknowledgement.

"Miranda," he replied with an amused look.

She tilted her head. "Where's Jim? I thought he'd be here as well."

"Oh, he is," Jackson replied, nodding toward the hallway. "He's waiting for us in Interview A. I see you brought a friend along with you."

"Oh, geez, where are my manners?" She turned to the sheriff and gestured to the tall, stoic man standing next to her. "This is Warren Davis ... my attorney. I hope that's not a problem, Sheriff."

"Problem? Why, no. Not at all. Although, you do understand that this is just an interview, but if it makes you feel better, that's fine." Masters reached out and shook Davis' hand, then continued in a friendly tone that edged right up to 'country bumpkin' status. "Come on back. We'll get this over just as quick as we can and get you both on your way."

Jackson smiled to himself. He had to give it to Miranda. She was smart as a whip, sometimes too smart for her own good, but showing up with her attorney was a pretty sharp move. Although he was certain it was a move designed to throw Masters off his stride, Jackson doubted it would make a dent in the sheriff's armor. Dillon Masters may preside over a small rural county, and was doing a pretty good impression of a friendly country sheriff at the moment, but Jackson knew that he'd had been around the block more than a few times. In addition, he was damned sure that Miranda had given her suit a full rundown of her concerns long before they'd shown up this afternoon.

Miranda and Davis followed the sheriff down the hall with Jackson and Deputy Navaro bringing up the rear. As they entered Interview A, he watched her give a coy wave to Jim—who was already sitting at one end of the table looking uncomfortable—before he closed the door and sat down at the other end with Masters sitting between them. Deputy Navaro took a seat against the back wall.

On the other side of the table, Miranda's attorney pulled out a chair for her before seating himself next to her and opening the leather folder he'd removed from his briefcase.

This ought to be an amusing little side show, Jackson thought, knowing Miranda's fondness for drama and bravado. According to Elise, their pal Miranda was hiding something ... or someone. They'd see just what questioning she'd try to avoid. That would be instructive, and he figured it was the reason for bringing the attorney with her in the first place; intimidation and, of course, to see what she could get away with.

The sheriff opened his own folder on the table in front of him and took out his notepad. "Now, though this is just an interview, it is being recorded. You understand," he looked back and forth between Miranda and Davis expectantly, but when neither voiced an objection, he continued. "So, will you both please state your names for the record?"

Miranda hesitated with a quick glance to Davis, then complied. "Miranda Louise Rollins."

Davis followed suit. "Warren Davis III, Mrs. Rollins' attorney."

"Okay, then, moving on." Masters cleared his throat, a congenial smile still firmly in place, and put up a finger. "However, before we get to updating your original statement, there is another subject that I'd like to discuss first."

Miranda hesitated again, clearly cautious. "Alright," she finally replied.

Jackson could almost see the wheels turning in her head.

"I'd like for you to tell me …" Masters paused, his pen hovering over his notepad. "… what you may know about the original sale of the vineyard in as much detail as you can remember."

Like Nico Ricci, this line of inquiry right out of the gate obviously took her by surprise, though she recovered much more quickly than the winemaker had. However, a frown did settle over her features. Jackson suspected that she'd been expecting to start off with the questions she was hoping to delay or avoid altogether, which was the reason Davis was here with her.

She glanced at Jackson. "Why are y'all so interested in the sale, Jax? Elise hammered me on that yesterday … as well as other things." When he didn't respond but continued to stare at her with an amused look, she shook her head and turned back to the sheriff. "Look, I have a feeling that you've already heard this story, Sheriff. This seems like a huge waste of time. Both mine and yours."

Masters laid his pen down and leaned back in his chair. "Yes, we have heard various bits and pieces of the story from several other sources, but I'd like to hear the full version from you. See, I don't look at getting all of the correct information as a waste of time, do you?"

Jackson kept his face passive but had to struggle not to laugh at the irritated look Miranda gave the sheriff.

He's very good at this, he thought.

Finally, with an exasperated huff, she relented. "Fine. I'll play along … for a bit. What do you want to know?"

"Well, as I understand it, you weren't part of the original sale, that it was your husband's purchase, correct?"

"That's right. It was Gene's deal. He was always buying something." She glanced at Jackson again. "As I told Elise, I was never interested in his financial wheeling and dealing back then. I didn't find out about any of it until the year before he died. That's when he told me about the whole sordid mess."

Masters nodded. "Then, why don't you start right there, when he laid it all out for you."

Miranda heaved another heavy sigh, and it was obvious that she wasn't pleased, but she did as he asked. The story that she wove was more detailed than the bits and pieces she'd told Elise, or at least, it was more detailed than what Elise had told Jackson. She walked them through the problems Gene and the Morans had endured with Roger Thompsen from the beginning, and then elaborated on all the struggles they'd had with the man in the years after her husband's death. It was a tale filled with betrayals, deceit, vandalism, suspected sabotage, and quite a bit more.

"And that's about all I can tell you, Sheriff," she said when she'd finished her story.

"That sounds like you've had a long haul of struggles, Mrs. Rollins," Masters murmured. "I am sorry to put you through this, but I think that it's important. I believe we need to understand the past to know how we got to homicide here in the present."

Miranda put up a hand. "Trust me, Sheriff. I'm all for that, if you think it will help. I want to know how this all happened—and why—just as much as you do. Maybe more. I'm tired of the ugliness that's been hanging over the vineyard for far too long. It needs to be cleared up. And soon."

And soon? Jackson thought. *That was an interesting turn of phrase.*

"Glad we're on the same page here," the sheriff said. "To be clear, your husband never mentioned anything about the possibility of Thompsen working with the real estate agent during the sale, did he?"

"He did not, though looking back, I'm sure that he had his suspicions. He just never said anything about it to me."

"And nothing about any other possible outside entities working from the shadows?"

"From the *shadows*?" Miranda raised her eyebrows and laughed, then waved away her amusement. "Sorry, that just sounds so clandestine, so diabolical." She shook her head. "But, no, if he suspected some kind of scheme, he never mentioned it."

The sheriff picked up his pen and made a few notes, then turned to Jackson, which was his cue to dig into his own questions with the woman.

And he was more than ready.

Leaning forward, Jackson thought, *my turn* ... "So, Miranda, can you take us through your movements from Friday's after-dinner tour of the winery through Saturday late afternoon?" he asked.

He could see that this was the part of the interview she'd been waiting for, the reason she'd brought her attorney with her, but Jackson had a couple of aces up his sleeve that he didn't think she would see coming. He watched as the hard look came into her eyes, but there was a brittle smile on her face.

"Of course," she replied, though her tone was slightly strained. "I'd be happy to walk you through it."

She took them smoothly through the ride back to the Manor from the winery, the surprise of finding Thompsen waiting for her, and the ugliness of what followed. It was all neat and tidy, he thought, and felt very well-rehearsed.

"Then we all went into the cubby bar for a much needed drink," she added at the end, and the look she gave him felt like a dare. It was like she was silently goading him, *'Go ahead, ask me more. I'm ready for you.'*

But he didn't think she was. So, he called her bluff.

"And then?"

She stared at him and the rest of her stiff smile faded, her tone becoming just a wee bit snappish. "And *then* ... I went to make some phone calls, one of which was to Warren, here."

"I can corroborate that," Davis said quietly. "Mrs. Rollins called me about ten-fifteen, not long after Mr. Thompsen left Riverside Manor, to give me a rundown on what had just occurred."

Jackson made some notes of his own and then looked up, ignoring the attorney and pinning her with a direct look. "And then?" he repeated.

Frustrated, a touch of anger fired up in her eyes. "Jax, I'm not going to sit here and hav—"

He shook his head, cutting off the beginning of what he knew would be a diversionary rant. "Come on, Miranda. We both know that Elise and I saw you leaving the Manor at just about quarter to eleven Friday night. It seems like a pretty simple question. Where'd you go?"

When she continued to glare at him in stoney silence, he put up a hand. "Let's do this. How about I help you out a bit. So, one of the calls you made was to Mr. Davis here, but I'm betting at least one other call was to someone you really don't want to talk about. I'm also betting that's where you went when you left the Manor ... to see Adrianna Santoro, Nico's fiancé." He smiled at the shock that crossed her face. "How am I doing so far, pal?"

"How did you—" She stopped herself abruptly, then closed her eyes for a moment, her anger fading to be replaced by something else. Apprehension? "Look, Jax ... I-I can't."

"It's all gonna come out anyway, Miranda. Might as well tell us everything now." When she still didn't say anything, he continued. "Don't you want to get it out there in your own words? I mean, look, my gut says that you didn't have anything to do with Thompsen's death, but my gut doesn't mean squat here. And it also doesn't mean that I don't think you're more than capable of it."

"Gee, thanks, Jax."

Davis leaned forward. "There's no need to be antagonistic, Deputy. This is only an interview, correct? What you think is not—"

"It's okay, Warren," Miranda murmured, putting a hand on the attorney's arm. "Actually, Deputy Landry is quite right. I think we're *all* capable of terrible things." She met Jackson's gaze head-on. "But I didn't have anything to do with that man's death."

"Then give me the rest of your story. Help me cross you off the list," Jackson replied. "And tell me about Adrianna Santoro."

For a moment, Jackson thought she was going to refuse to answer, but then she finally gave a slight nod.

"Adrianna has lived here in Meadowview since Dario became winemaker for Bella Luna, and long before the sale. When the original owners—who were Dario's friends from Sicily—sold the vineyard and went back to Italy, Dario's wife left him and went back with them. However, Adrianna stayed here with her father." Miranda's eyes took on a faraway look, and a half smile played across her face. "She'd always been daddy's little girl. Adrianna worshiped Dario, and she loved the vineyard because he loved it. She was completely devastated when he died. See, she'd watched her father slowly give up on life, on his dream of owning a vineyard.

"Gene bought the majority of shares knowing that Dario wouldn't accept the gift of ownership but to give him the control over the vineyard and winery, to try to give the man a piece of that dream, or as close to it as he could. He'd also tried to protect both Adrianna and Dario from the shit-storm swirling around the vineyard during that time, but then he died. Though Dario did his best to continue shielding his daughter, Adrianna saw her father struggle with all the malice and spite that Thompsen had spread and, along with the sale, it all simply broke him. And then he died as well."

She looked up at Jackson with a world of sadness in her eyes and cleared her throat. "Can I get some water, Jax? Then I'll tell you the rest."

"You bet."

"I'll get it," Deputy Navaro said, and left the room.

They sat in silence for several minutes until the deputy came back with Miranda's water. She cracked the bottle open, took a few sips, and then nodded.

"So, here's the rest of the story. I've felt immensely protective of Adrianna since Dario's passing. She was always a really good kid, and she was adamant about staying here and not going back to Italy where her mother lives." Miranda looked over at Jackson, an impish grin spreading across her face as she rolled her eyes. "Did I say kid? She's in her early thirties now. Anyway, she and Nico had been dancing around each other for years, but then they finally got together and then a year later, engaged. At that point, a delicious notion came to me. I decided to gift them my majority share in the vineyard as a wedding present."

Jim whistled and his eyes went wide. "That's ... really generous, Miranda."

She shook her head and her eyes filled, spilled over. "No, Jim. It has nothing to do with generosity. It has to do with what's right. Gene would have done it in a heartbeat. And Dario ... well, Dario would have loved the idea of his only child living out his dream."

For as many years as Jackson had known Miranda Rollins, this was a side of her that she'd kept well hidden.

She may be a bad-ass with a hard outer shell most of the time, but inside? She has a big, gooey center, he thought. *Who would've known?*

Deputy Navaro handed Miranda a small box of tissue, and she smiled up at him. "Thank you," she murmured, and took a tissue to dab at her eyes.

"Do they know about your plan?" Jackson asked. "Nico and Adrianna?"

Miranda rolled her eyes again, and her tone was pure sarcasm. "No, Jackson. Like I said, it's going to be a wedding gift. Duh."

Jackson smiled. "Okay, point taken. So, that's where you went when you left the Manor that night?"

"Yes. One of the other calls I made was to Nico. He was actually the one I wanted to talk to. He was at Adrianna's, so I went there. I needed to make sure he knew about what happened with Thompsen at the Manor, wanted to warn him to stay clear of the man." Miranda gave Jackson a wry look. "I went in person because ... well, Nico is a lovely man, but he does have a bit of a hair trigger."

"Yeah, I had a hunch about that," Jackson replied. "So, when did you get there and how long did you stay?"

Miranda twirled the tissue she held around and around between her fingers as she chewed on her bottom lip. "I got there a little after eleven and stayed until just after one. I got back to the B and B about twenty minutes later."

"Can anybody verify that? Anybody see you come in?" he asked, knowing the probable answer. At one in the morning, more than likely, there wouldn't be anyone awake to see her return.

She slowly shook her head. "Regrettably, no. There was no one around at that time of the morning. I went up to my room, took some pain killers for a growing headache, and went to bed. I woke up with my alarm at seven-thirty, got ready for the day, and came down for a coffee to go just before we left for the winery." She gave him a sour look. "So, no, I don't have an alibi, if that's what you're getting at."

Jackson glanced to Masters, silently handing the tag-team baton back to the man. He'd gotten answers to his questions. Maybe not all the answers he'd hoped for, but answers to the ones that were nagging at him. Unfortunately, without an alibi for the time of Thompsen's death, Miranda would have to stay on the suspect list, but at least they could bump her down a few pegs for now.

"Okay, then. I think that's all for now. We'll let you know if there's anything else," the sheriff said. He closed his folder and smiled. "Thank you for coming in. I know this wasn't easy for you."

"I'll walk you out," Jackson said.

In the lobby, she turned to him before leaving and laid a hand on his arm. "Thanks, Jax."

"For what?"

"For making this easier than I thought it was going to be. You're really quite good at this, you know."

"Well, now. That's quite a compliment, coming from you."

"Stop." She slapped at him playfully. "Seriously. I probably made it harder on myself than it needed to be. I should have trusted you from the start. I'm just protective of Adrianna and don't want to see it all dredged up for her again."

"That's understandable," he replied, then smiled. "Look at you. Miranda Rollins. A woman with a heart of gold. Who knew?"

She leaned in at that and grinned. "You better just keep that to yourself, my friend. Slander's a thing these days. Remember, I have my attorney with me."

"Yeah, yeah. Get outta here and stay outta trouble."

She laughed, and he watched her and Davis cross the parking lot and drive away, feeling like a weight had been lifted from his shoulders. At least, for now.

He went back to Interview A and gathered his things. Masters had planned to do some research on Gene Rollins' accident and had gotten the reports sent up from records that afternoon. Jackson, Jim, and Deputy Navaro would be digging into the backgrounds on Rochelle and Todd Griffin first thing in the morning before the next round of interviews, so Jackson and Jim headed back to the Manor for an early dinner.

Elise jumped him the minute he walked into their room.

"Well, you're back earlier than I thought you'd be," she said, clearly apprehensive.

"Yep. Miranda's interview didn't take as long as I expected it to."

"Did you find out where she went on Friday night and who she'd been protecting?"

"We did. Finally. She made it harder than it needed to be, but then, that's Miranda."

"Well? What did she tell you?"

He narrowed his eyes at her and shook his head.

"Come on, Jax. I'm the one who gave you the information in the first place."

With a sigh, he told her everything Miranda had told them in her interview. When he'd finished, she sat down on the edge of the bed with a surprised look. "Wow. She's going to give them the controlling shares of the vineyard and winery as a wedding present? That's ... well, that's amazing."

"I know. It was quite the revelation. However, she still doesn't have a solid alibi for the time of Roger Thompsen's death."

"Oh, come on, Jax. Do you really think she went from Adrianna's place after one in the morning and met with Thompsen at the winery, then killed him? All by herself?"

Jackson shook his head again. "No, I do not, but that doesn't matter. She doesn't have an alibi that can be corroborated. So, as we've previously discussed, she stays on the list for now. However, she does get kicked down the list a few levels."

Elise frowned, but nodded. "I suppose that's better than nothing." She paused for a moment, then looked up at him uncertainly. "Jax, I'm sorry about today."

He sat down next to her. "About today?"

She frowned. "Well, yeah. About ... you know ... what Sheriff Masters said. I really never meant to get you into hot water with him or cause any ... weirdness. You know?"

He shook his head. "You didn't do either. I had a feeling he was going to ask you some pointed questions because he'd figured it out. He'd basically guessed where the info I was giving him came from." He took her hand. "Now, I'm not necessarily jazzed about the whole thing, but if he's okay with it, well, it's not my case, is it? However, as long as you don't get too crazy about it and this doesn't carry over to Bastrop County and my jurisdiction, I'll look the other way. For now."

She grinned at that. "That's good. Because I think I found something that could be important."

Jackson ran a hand over his face. "Woman, could you not even wait a day or two before diving into the deep end?"

"This isn't about the murder, Jax. Well, it may be indirectly, but anyway, it's more about the sale."

To his amazement and disbelief, she jumped up and retrieved a little notebook from the table. "Listen to this," she said as she sat down next to him and flipped through a few pages. "There's another player. I mean, I think that there is. His name is Miller

Hensen, and he's a land developer. It seems his company, Hensen Enterprises, had been looking into large parcels of land in the area around the vineyard for quite some time."

"So? What does that prove? I suppose there've been a lot of developers looking at land all over the county. Just because this Hensen may have been looking at land around the vineyard at one point isn't a concrete connection. He's probably not the only one."

"You're right, but hang on a minute. It took some digging, but I found a whole article on him and some of his previous acquisitions in the county, and there was a brief mention of the Bella Luna sale."

"Okay, but he didn't actually acquire any shares of Bella Luna, El. And even if he did, as just a shareholder, he couldn't really do any developing without the other shareholders agreeing to it."

"Yes, but the article called it 'the *sale* that got away'. Evidently, Hensen doesn't usually lose out on something he really wants. And it sounds like he'd anticipated buying Bella Luna outright, that he was looking to scoop up *all* the shares not realizing that the original owners had already accepted offers from Gene and the Morans."

Jackson squinted at her. "Where in God's name did you find this information?"

She stopped and stared at him for a moment as if he was terribly slow. "Geez, Jax. On the internet, where else? Try and keep up." She waived a hand in the air. "Anyway, here's the best part. This guy, Hensen, is quite mysterious. He keeps a pretty low profile from what I could gather, but I found a couple photos with the article, and one of those photos was of a grinning Hensen cozied up to none other than Rochelle Griffin."

12

Early Tuesday morning, Jackson, Jim, and Jesse met up with Sheriff Masters at the office to get started on their planned research into Rochelle Griffin and her ex-husband, Todd, before Cara Thompsen arrived after lunch for her interview. Jackson came armed with the new information Elise had given him the night before regarding Miller Hensen and his possible connection to Rochelle Griffin, who'd been the real estate agent of record for the vineyard sale, such as it was. Sitting around the conference table with the team, he spent about twenty minutes bringing everybody up to speed.

"Well, isn't that an interesting turn of events? A possible connection between the real estate agent and a land developer." Masters got up and went to his case board when Jackson had finished, adding Hensen's name directly below Rochelle Griffin's with a question mark out to the side. "This may just end up giving some heft to the theory that someone was working the deal from the background."

Crossing back to the conference table, the sheriff opened his folder and spent a few minutes perusing his notes. Then he frowned and looked up. "Okay, so here are some things we need to figure out pronto. First, were Thompsen and Griffin really working together from the start like Nico Ricci suggested? If so, were they working the deal on their own or were they working on behalf of someone else? And finally, was that someone else this Miller Hensen?"

"And also, was the plan to buy the entire vineyard?" Jesse added. "Seems like if this guy was involved, and he's a developer interested in the land, wouldn't he need to buy the whole thing outright?"

"Exactly." Jackson nodded. "That's what I've been thinking."

"Yeah," Jim agreed. "Wouldn't want any pesky co-owners or shareholders holding up his plans, right?"

"Of course, this is just some new information. It doesn't really confirm or deny if Hensen was actually part of some kind of scheme or not," Jackson replied. "Like Jesse said, he could've just thought to buy the whole vineyard and then found out that the majority of the shares had already been sold after the fact. The article that Elise found was pretty vague about Bella Luna. It indicated that Hensen had lost out on the sale, but it was only a brief mention. It was more focused on Hensen's background and business history."

Masters walked back and studied the case board again, as Jackson was prone to do during his own investigations at home when something was nagging at him.

"Here's another possibility that's been rolling around in my head." The sheriff glanced back at Jackson. "You said that there was a photo of Hensen and Griffin all cozied up, right?"

"Yeah," Jackson confirmed. "I've got a copy of it on my phone. I can send it to you."

"Good. Do that." Masters glanced at the board. "So, what if Hensen was the guy pulling the strings in the first place, maybe even funding Thompsen?"

Jackson raised his eyebrows. "Oooh, that's an interesting thought."

"Do we know what Thompsen's financial situation was? Did he even have the funds to buy in, and if not, where did he get the green to snap up that last eighteen percent of the shares? It was a much smaller portion, but it had to have been pricey just the same."

Jim scribbled some notes into his little notebook. "I can surely get on that and find out, Sheriff."

Masters continued to stare at his board. "What if Griffin was feeding the developer the information on the vineyard sale as it progressed, and he was in on the scheme from the start on the back end. Thompsen could've just been the face out front."

"Or maybe the three of them came up with the scheme together," Jesse added.

Masters turned from the board and jabbed a finger in the deputy's direction. "Bingo. Ricci was sure that Griffin was the one who talked the owners into selling in shares as opposed to selling the vineyard as a whole. Hensen has the funding but he wants to keep a low profile, so they get Thompsen to make the offer."

"Thompsen could've already been involved with Griffin and it was a three way partnership," Jackson speculated.

"Yeah, but either way, why all the cloak and dagger stuff?" Jim asked, shaking his head. "I mean, it doesn't make a whole lotta sense to me. Why have Thompsen as a front man? And why talk the owners into selling in shares, for that matter? If this guy, Hensen, prides himself on always getting what he wants, why not just make a top end offer for the whole damn thing?"

Jackson frowned. "Good point." He walked over to the board and stood next to the sheriff for a moment, and then he rapped a knuckle on the board under Hensen's name. "From the way it sounded in the article that Elise found, Hensen is known to be a pretty ruthless business man and sharp as they come. He prides himself on his business acumen. Maybe the share deal was some kind of smoke screen."

"A smoke screen?" the sheriff asked. "What do you mean?"

"Well, when Elise told me about the Bella Luna sale being mentioned in the article, I said, 'so what?' Why would it matter if Hensen had been looking for land to buy in the area? That doesn't necessarily mean anything. I mean, there were probably a lot of other development companies looking to do the same thing, right?"

"Ah, I think I see where you're going with this," Jim said, nodding. "If you've got other development companies sniffing around the area, then you do your best to control the sale and stay in the background. It would be pretty unethical, but talking the owners into selling in shares and then funding an unknown face to gobble up as many of those shares as possible—preferably all of them—would be a damn fine smoke screen. After all, you don't want to get into a bidding war with other companies, do you? Especially on a lucrative property of this size."

"No." Masters stepped back and sat down at the table, shaking his head. "No you do not. Part of that business savvy would be getting the best deal for your money and not over paying if you can help it. You get into a bidding war and all bets are off. If you really want the deal, you're gonna have to outbid everyone else, and you'll end up paying through the nose for it in the end."

"This way, getting the owners to sell the vineyard in shares, theoretically, you'd end up with the whole enchilada for a lot less before anyone else is the wiser. That is, if things go as planned." Jim gave his partner a considering look. "It would be convoluted for sure and dicey at best, but if it worked? That, my friend, would be a pretty diabolical strategy."

"Precisely." Jackson grinned. "Plus, Hensen's company has a boatload of capital. Elise and I did some research on him last night." He looked back at the board. "There again, this is all just guesswork. Anyway, the owners threw a wrench into that kind of thing working when they sold the bulk of the shares to Gene Rollins and the Morans as a favor to Dario Santoro."

"True enough. But remember, the real estate agent didn't know the owners had made that side deal until they finally signed with her," the sheriff pointed out.

"Yeah, and we have several sources confirming how ticked off both Rochelle Griffin and Roger Thompsen were about that," Jim added. "Although, I still can't see what this whole mess has to do with Thompsen's murder. I mean, it wasn't his fault the sale went south on them, so what would be the motive for killing the guy over a failed land deal that he had no control over?"

"Well, maybe we'll get lucky with Cara Thompsen, and she'll know some particulars about what her daddy was up to and with whom." Masters stood up and looked around the room. "In the meantime, Jackson, you and Jim split up the digging on the internet and get us some hard data on the Griffins, as well as Thompsen's financial situation, if you can. Preferably something that will confirm some of these crazy theories and give us a solid path to follow." He turned to his deputy. "Jesse, I need you to man the front desk and make those calls we talked about last night to my contacts over in Terence, see what they know about this Hensen character. Hopefully, something more will break there."

"What are you going to do, Sheriff?" Jesse asked.

"The accident reports from the car crash that killed Gene Rollins came through yesterday afternoon, but I didn't get to them. I'm gonna sift through those and see if there's anything to be found. Ricci seemed to think that the accident was fishy, that it was maybe not such an accident at all. So, I'll try to either confirm the theory or at least put that one to bed."

As the sheriff left the room with Jesse close behind, Jackson and Jim got busy, and three hours later, Jackson's eyeballs were burning from staring at the screen of the laptop he'd been using. He felt like they were no farther along than they had been. He'd been looking into anything he could find on Rochelle and Todd Griffin, but had only found the basics. Todd had filed for a divorce not long after the Bella Luna sale went sideways, which coincided with Miranda's 'scuttlebutt' about the Griffin's relationship being on the rocks and the sale fiasco finally putting an end to it. However, it really didn't move the case along or give them anything they hadn't already known.

"Okay, I came up with some interesting info on our victim," Jim said, coming in from the other room carrying the small laptop that he'd been using. He placed it on the conference table and then sat down across from Jackson, flipping through his little notebook. "Thompsen definitely did not have the capital to buy the vineyard outright, let alone the eighteen percent share that he ended up with."

"Really?" Jackson sat back and rubbed his tired eyes. "Do tell."

Jim shook his head. "Couldn't get into details of his finances, of course. The sheriff is going to have to put a request in there, but from what I could find on my own, the guy was underwater big time. No way did he have the funds to buy into the vineyard like he did. So, someone had to have helped him along. From the looks of it, even his house here in Meadowview has a second mortgage."

"Huh. Interesting, Well then, maybe the theory of outside funding isn't that far off the mark."

"Yeah. More like spot on. You find any possible connection with the Griffins?"

Jackson frowned. "Nope. Todd filed for a divorce not long after the sale business, but that just matches up with the rumors and hearsay floating around. Miranda told the girls that their relationship was about done when Todd found out that Rochelle had the vineyard sale cooking and hadn't clued him in. Him filing for a divorce so soon after finding that out confirms the gossip, I guess."

Jim nodded. "I'm kind of interested to see how Cara Thompsen's interview goes this afternoon. I mean, it seems like all the Thompsen kids had very little use for him. If she and her daddy had such a bad relationship, I'm thinking she's got some dirt to tell there. Plus, if Miranda was right, and Cara had been with Todd Griffin for a time, and is maybe still with him, she could have some telling insight there as well."

"Agreed." Jackson stared at the case board for a moment, and then turned back to Jim. "Hey, on another front, Molly was just here a bit ago looking for Masters. She's the computer tech that worked on the security feed when we found that it had been wiped."

"Yeah, I remember. What did she want? Any good news there?"

"No, not yet, but she was looking to update him on the recovery process. Masters had gone down to the archives for some report he was missing, and she couldn't wait, so she asked me to have him give her a call." Jackson wiggled his eyebrows. "Her specialty computer guy finally got over here from the big city, and she seemed pretty hopeful."

"That's great. Maybe he'll be able to recover some of the video, and we can get this wrapped up and go home."

"Buddy, from your mouth to God's ears."

They spent another forty-five minutes running more in-depth queries, but neither were having much success by the time the sheriff came back from the records department followed by Deputy Navaro.

"You two have any luck with your research?" he asked when he and Jesse sat down at the conference table with them. "Jesse here sketched a bit more in on Hensen from what he got from the guys over in Terence."

"I didn't get much more about the Griffins other than what we'd already heard gossip-wise." Jackson hooked a thumb toward his partner. "But Jim found some interesting stuff on Thompsen."

"Yeah," Jim said. "I can't see how he could've bought into the vineyard the way he did without someone else funding him." He went through everything he'd found with his research into the man's finances. "That's about all I could get without hacking into his actual finances or bank records, which I don't have authority to do, but I'm fairly certain that what's there won't be pretty."

The sheriff nodded and then turned to his deputy. "Jesse, put in a request. We'll take a look-see at how bad it really was and where he might have gotten the funds he needed to snag his eighteen percent. We also need to check on who else may be listed on the deed for those shares."

"You find anything on Gene's accident?" Jim asked.

"Maybe." Masters sat back and narrowed his eyes. "Ricci may have been correct about the whole thing being hinky. I still have some questions that I need to follow up on with the team that went over the rig when it was retrieved from the scene, but it's not looking like a cut and dried accident to me. Ricci may have been right, but we'll see. If so, that'll be just one more puzzle to unpack." He sighed and looked at his watch. "It's almost noon. Why don't we grab some lunch and meet back here in forty-five minutes or so? We'll make sure we've got all the bases covered before Ms. Thompsen arrives for her interview at one."

CARA THOMPSEN WAS ten minutes late and full of apologies when she finally walked through the door and Jesse ushered her into Interview A. Jackson and Jim sat along the side wall with Masters and Jesse sitting across from the woman at the table.

"I'm so sorry, Sheriff. I know that I'm a bit late. I got hung up at my mom's. My brothers and I are working through the funeral arrangements with her, and it's not going well."

"I understand," Masters murmured. "These kinds of things are never easy. I'm sorry for your family's loss."

Cara smiled. "Thank you, Sheriff, but as you probably know, I didn't have a great relationship with my father and neither did my siblings. We're just trying to support our mother and get her through this ordeal." She sighed. "Although, she'd never admit it, but my father's death is probably a huge weight lifted from her shoulders."

Masters frowned. "Why do you say that, Ms. Thompsen?"

The woman's gaze skittered back and forth between the Sheriff and Deputy Navaro. Jackson could tell from his vantage point that she'd realized how her comment had come across and was now gauging how to say what they'd all heard—that Roger Thompsen had been an abusive, overbearing husband and father. After a moment, she licked her lips and made her decision.

"Come on, Sheriff. I'm sure that you've heard the rumors. Let me just confirm that they're all true. Roger Thompsen was a horrible man who treated his family like dirt, especially my mother. Of course, that's only because us kids wouldn't take his crap once we got old enough to rebel. She, on the other hand, would never fight back. She'd just let him beat her down."

"He was physically abusive?"

Cara smiled. "Gabe, my little brother, was always worried about that. He's the baby of the family and momma's little angel. But I don't think so. Dad's abuse was usually verbal and mean-spirited, but not physical that I'd ever seen. Sometimes he'd withhold things from her as punishment, mostly money. She was supposed to pay the bills but sometimes she didn't have the funds to do it. Any late notices and she got the riot act, so sometimes Brian or I would help her out when Dad was in one of his moods."

"And did that happen often?"

She shrugged. "Didn't use to."

"But that changed?"

"Yes. It did."

"When? How long ago?"

The woman considered. "I guess that it's been more frequent over the last couple years. Everything would be fine for a while, Dad would be flush, and bills would be paid. Then, out of the blue checks would start to bounce, bills would go unpaid, he'd be edgy and turn ugly to everyone around him. Gabe lives in L.A. most of the time, and Brian and I don't get around to the house as much as we should, so, like I said, Mom got the brunt of his abuse." She stopped and gave the sheriff a cautious look. "Why are you asking about all of this? You can't be seriously looking at the family for Dad's murder?"

"It's usually the first place we start with this kind of investigation, Ms. Thompsen. Standard procedure, eliminate those closest to the victim. We've already talked to your mother and both of your brothers."

"So, this interview is to eliminate me?"

Masters nodded. "If we can, yes, but before we get to that, I've got some other questions that I'd like to go over with you."

Jackson watched the frown settle over the woman's face, and her gaze darted back and forth again. *There's that cautious look again,* he thought. *What's got her so jittery?*

She finally nodded. "Okay," she said slowly. "What questions?"

The Sheriff flipped through his notepad, as he'd done with the other interviews. "Well," he began as he glanced up and pinned her with a look. "Let's start with the sale of the vineyard. You were around for that, right?"

"The *sale*?" She gaped at Masters, clearly shocked. "What does that have to do with anything? It was what? A decade ago?"

Masters nodded. "It was, but some information has recently come to light regarding the sale that may have directly impacted what's happened with the vineyard over the last few months leading up to your father's death."

Jackson watched Cara's face. She was clearly more than rattled now. *Oh yeah. There's definitely something there that she's uncomfortable with,* he thought.

"What information," she demanded.

"How much do you know about the sale of the vineyard, Ms. Thompsen? About your father's role in it?"

The woman's mouth opened and closed a couple of times before she actually spoke. "I'm not sure what you mean."

Jackson was certain that wasn't true. He could see it on her face as plain as day from where he sat. Masters obviously thought the same, and called her on it. Then he bluffed his way past her denial and into their theories at the speed of light. Jackson had to work to keep the grin off of his face.

The sheriff leaned forward. "Now, Ms. Thompsen ... Cara ... that's not exactly true, is it?"

"I-I don't—"

"See, there have been a few allegations that your father and Rochelle Griffin, the real estate agent for the sale, were working together on behalf of another party to gain control of the vineyard. We understand that the plan was to break up the vineyard and develop the land. Did you know about that plan?"

Jackson watched the woman's shoulders suddenly slump, a look of resignation crossing her face. And just like that, she blew out a breath and folded like a house of cards. He had to admit, it made him skeptical.

Hmm, that was a whole lot easier than I thought it would be ... or should be.

"Okay, yes, I found out about their stupid scheme. Way after the fact, of course. I was just in my twenties and starting an internship at the winery when the sale went down. He and I fought about it on several occasions after I found out." She sat back and gave Masters a look of disgust, but blurted out the rest. "He was such an idiot. He thought he was this big deal, but he was just Rochelle Griffin's lap dog. He wouldn't have even been part of the scheme if Hensen hadn't put up the money."

"Miller Hensen?" the sheriff asked quietly, stringing her along. "He was the developer looking to buy the land, correct?"

She nodded. "Dad was supposed to buy controlling interest, but the Falcones, they were the original owners, had made an agreement with Dario Santoro for Gene Rollins and William Moran to purchase shares before they signed with Rochelle." Cara gave a laugh that Jackson thought was just short of hysterical. "It's funny because Rochelle was the one to talk them into selling in shares. She and Hensen had this plan, but that went to hell in a handbasket when the Falcones accepted Gene's offer and then the Moran's. She and Hensen were left out in the cold."

Masters looked over his notes again, made a few new ones. "But that wasn't really the end of it all, was it?" he asked when he finally looked up at her.

The jittery look was back in her eyes, but Cara slowly shook her head. "Both Dad and Rochelle were furious about being shut out, and I imagine Hensen was pretty livid as well. From what I understand, Rochelle had assured Hensen that the scheme would work out for all of them. They weren't about to let it go. That's what Dad and I argued about. I guess there had been problems from time to time going back to the date of the sale."

"Sabotage, vandalism, damaged equipment. Problems like that?"

"Yes," she replied quietly. "Over the last few years, I had my suspicions that my dad may have been behind the problems we were having recently but I could never confirm it."

The sheriff nodded. "We've heard the same thing from others about the earlier problems as well."

"Yeah, well, I finally caught him in the act one night. We argued about it again. See, when the sale went badly for them, he and Rochelle planned to make it so difficult that the other shareholders would give up and sell."

"But that didn't happen."

"No, Gene Rollins was a good man. He wouldn't be bullied, so the whole thing kind of died down for a while." She sighed, and a look of sadness filled her eyes. "But then Gene died. And it started all over again. My dad thought he could intimidate Miranda, after all, she was just a woman. He has ... had no respect for women."

"And Miranda Rollins wouldn't be intimidated?"

Cara gave another hysterical laugh. "Not even a little bit."

With that final answer, Masters nodded again. "Okay. I think that answers most of my questions. Just one more thing before we finish up here. I'm going to need to know where you were between midnight and two a.m. last Saturday morning."

The woman's mouth dropped open, and she shook her head. "You can't think that I actually killed my own father. I mean, sure we weren't close ... okay, he disgusted me ... but come on."

The sheriff laid his pen across his notepad and leaned on the table. "Look, Cara. You've told me that he was abusive to the entire family. You've admitted that you and your father argued—and recently—about the problems he was causing at the vineyard, that you actually caught him in the act of sabotage. I need to be able to cross you off the list. Now, where were you?"

The woman swallowed hard and blinked several times before finally nodding. "Okay. I was with a friend. We had dinner at about seven-thirty Friday night, and then went back to his place to watch a movie."

Masters picked up his pen and made some notes. "And what time did you leave?"

"I-I didn't. I spent the night." She fidgeted in her seat. "I went home at about ten o'clock the next morning."

He looked up at her. "And this friend's name and contact information?"

At first, Jackson thought she wasn't going to respond, but then came the answer that he'd been waiting for.

"I was with Todd Griffin. I'm pretty sure you have his contact information."

"To be clear, you were with Rochelle Griffin's husband Saturday morning during that time."

"Her *ex*-husband, and yes, that's correct."

"Okay. Thank you, Cara. You've been very helpful. We'll be in touch if we need more.

13

"So, what Miranda told us on Sunday was true," Elise mused. "Cara Thompsen and Todd Griffin were definitely an item. Still are, it seems. Interesting."

Jackson snorted. "I'm not sure how interesting it is, but yes, Cara blurted that out at the end of the interview."

They were having dinner in the Riverside Manor dining room while the rest of the group opted for pizza a few blocks away. With Roger Thompsen's murder and the resulting investigation, they'd all been spending so much time together that Elise was happy to have a quiet dinner alone with Jackson. It was a nice break, though murder was again tonight's topic.

She watched him frown as he cut into his steak. "What?" she asked.

He looked up and gave her a questioning look.

"I can see something rolling around in your noggin. So, what is it?"

Jackson laid his knife down next to his plate and gestured with his fork. "You have x-ray vision now, darlin'?"

Elise grinned at him. "Don't need it, love. It's as plain as day. Your face says it all. So, what gives?"

He plopped a juicy piece of steak into his mouth and considered her as he chewed.

"Jax, come on. Tell me what you're thinking."

He swallowed and then took a sip of his beer. "Okay, what I found more interesting about Cara Thompsen's interview was what she didn't say." He waved his fork dismissively. "Oh, don't get me wrong. The confirmation that she and Griffin have been —and still are—an item was good information to have. Also, the fact that Masters bluffed her so easily into confirming that her dad, Rochelle Griffin, and Miller Hensen were in league for the sale scheme from the get-go did connect some crucial dots for us, but it was actually something else that popped for me."

"Really? What was that?"

Jackson picked up his knife and cut himself another piece of steak. "I guess it was mostly her demeanor."

"Her demeanor? What do you mean?"

"Well, for one thing, she came in all flustered with a 'I'm so sorry I'm late, Sheriff. I was helping my poor mother with the funeral details' apology. You know, like, nothin' to see here, just doing my part. But the minute the sheriff started asking about the sale and her dad's part in it, she got all nervous and jittery. Then she tried to play dumb." He smirked at Elise. "She's a terrible liar, by the way. Anyhow, it didn't take much to get the whole scheme out of her. Then she goes into what a terrible person her dad had been. I mean, you could hear the suppressed anger in her voice. He may have been her dad, but she really did not like Roger Thompsen."

Elise nodded as she picked at her Cobb salad. "Yeah, Miranda told us that Cara was sharp and ambitious ... and that she despised her father."

"Yep. That's pretty much what came through in her rant." Jackson stared across the dining room for a moment. "And at the end of the interview, she *really* didn't want to tell Masters where she'd been when her dad was killed. For a minute, I thought she wasn't going to tell him."

"Huh. Maybe she just didn't want to have to explain about her relationship with Todd Griffin."

Jackson shook his head. "I think it was more than that. Again, it was her manner rather than the information we got from her that had my radar up. No, it was obvious that there was something else there, something she definitely didn't want to talk about."

"Another tantalizing puzzle to unravel?"

"More like another one to add to the growing list of puzzles to unravel. At this rate, we may not be going home anytime soon. Or, at least, you may be going home without me."

"Huh-uh. No way am I going anywhere without you, love." Elise said, forking up a last bite of her salad. She dabbed her lips with her napkin. "You know, I'm interested to hear what Todd Griffin has to say when he comes in for his interview. He's up next, right?"

"Yeah. He's coming in at eleven tomorrow morning. I'm gonna be watching that sideshow with a close eye, believe me. I'm pretty sure he and Cara will have hooked up by then to sync their stories, so I'm not sure how much we'll get out of him of any worth. I would've preferred to talk to him this afternoon after her interview and not given them that chance, but he was conveniently unavailable."

Elise picked up her iced tea and stared down into the glass, then took a small sip. "I have a feeling that the sheriff will get quite a bit out of him."

"Why do you say that?"

"Well, Miranda said that Todd was furious when he found out about the vineyard sale, that Rochelle had this scheme going and he'd been left out of the loop."

"Sure. You find out that your wife has a deal on the back burner that's gonna bring her a huge payday and she doesn't make a peep? I can imagine that would've pissed him off but good."

"Yes, and all indications are that the Griffin's marriage was in big trouble long before that. It sounds like he filed for divorce right after finding out about the scheme."

Elise smiled and nodded at a couple who came into the dining room, watching them sit down at a nearby table next to the fireplace. Leaning in, she kept her voice low. "Jax, I've heard some pretty ugly things about Todd Griffin, and he doesn't sound like the type to let bygones be bygones, if you know what I mean. Word is that he got a real sweet deal with the divorce."

Jackson stared at her for a moment and then shook his head again. "What 'word?' Where are you hearing all this stuff. We've been here for less than a week."

Elise giggled. "You are so cute when you're baffled." When he just continued to stare at her, she sighed. "Come on, Jax. It's amazing what you can glean by just listening. It's like you said with Cara's interview. If you listen closely enough, sometimes you can pick up more than if you just pound folks with questions."

"I guess."

"Plus, I'm not from around here. That makes me almost invisible to people when I'm out and about. People don't think about being careful around folks who don't know the individuals or situations that they're gossiping about." She pushed her salad bowl to the side and continued to sip on her tea. "Anyway, I'm figuring that Todd used the sale scheme as leverage to get that sweet divorce deal out of his wife."

"A little bit of blackmail between ex-lovers?" Jackson wiggled his eyebrows.

"Exactly. I bet he'll be quite forthcoming with all of the juicy gossip if the sheriff pushes the right buttons, and I think you'll be surprised about how easy that will be. Of course, I've never met the man, I'm just going by what I've heard."

Jackson rolled his eyes. "Okay, Columbo. I'll take it all under advisement," he said, and signaled for the check.

TODD GRIFFIN SHOWED up at the sheriff's office for his eleven o'clock interview on Tuesday morning with ten minutes to spare. As opposed to Cara Thompsen who'd been ten minutes late for her appointment.

Jackson watched Griffin climb out of a pricey Porsche Boxster, and though the day was overcast, he adjusted the aviator sunglasses he wore before striding toward the building. The man was casually dressed in jeans and a snowy-white, button down shirt under a dark brown leather bomber jacket. As he neared the door, he ran a hand through his dark hair, and Jackson caught the flash of what looked like a Rolex peeking out of the jacket cuff at his wrist.

The guy obviously has expensive taste. The spoils of a successful divorce settlement?

Griffin was a buff guy and tall—Jackson gauged him to be just over six feet—with a muscular frame which probably saw the gym at least a couple times a week.

"Good afternoon, Mr. Griffin," Masters greeted the man as he entered the lobby. "Thanks for coming in."

Griffin smiled and shook the sheriff's hand. "Not a problem, Sheriff. I'm not really sure why I'm here or what I can tell you, but I'm glad to help, if I can."

The sheriff nodded. "Well, it's appreciated. Come on back, and we'll get started so that we don't monopolize too much of your time."

They headed back to Interview A, Masters leading the way to where Jesse was waiting by the door, with Jim and Jackson following. As Jackson got to the room, the deputy leaned in and spoke quietly. "I've got some calls to make for the sheriff, so I'll be at the front desk if you need anything."

"Okay. Thanks, Jesse," Jackson said as the deputy closed the door behind him. He rounded the table and took his place on the sheriff's right-hand side.

"Okay," Masters said as he opened the folder in front of him and looked up at Griffin. "This is being recorded, so would you please state your name for the record?"

The man nodded. "Sure. Todd Griffin."

"Thank you."

The sheriff made several notes on his pad and shuffled through some papers in the folder, letting the silence thicken almost to an uncomfortable level as Jackson watched Griffin squirm a bit in his seat. The tactic did the trick, he thought, as Griffin leaned forward and spoke.

"Like I said, Sheriff. I am happy to help in any way that I can with your investigation, but I'm not sure exactly how I can do that. I mean, I didn't know Roger Thompsen and don't have any information about his death."

Masters finally looked up at the man. "But I'm assuming that you'd met the man, correct? I mean, since you and his daughter, Cara Thompsen are ... close."

Griffin shifted in his seat again. "Okay, sure. I'd met him once or twice but that was it. Like I said, I don't know how I can help with your investigation into his death."

"Well, now we will get to that, but I do have some other things I'd like to talk about first."

Todd frowned. "Okay," he said slowly. "About what?"

Masters smiled. "See, we're looking into the original sale of Bella Luna, so we've got some questions regarding that."

The man blinked a couple of times, the only outward indication that he was unsettled by the statement, but Jackson felt that he'd obviously been expecting this.

"Bella Luna? I see."

The sheriff flipped through his notepad. "Now, your wife was the real estate agent for the sale, correct?"

A hard look came into the man's eyes. "My *ex*-wife, yes."

Masters looked up at that. "But you were still married at the time, weren't you?"

Todd sighed. "We were, but I'm not sure what that has to do with anything," he said with mild irritation.

"Well, it's come to our attention that your wife was involved in a kind of convoluted scheme with Roger Thompsen and Miller Hensen, a land developer, to purchase—if not the entire vineyard—at least the majority of shares with a plan to break it up and develop the land."

Griffin shrugged. "So what? That's not illegal, is it?"

"No, not illegal, I suppose, but not exactly kosher, either, is it? Did you have a part in their scheme?"

"I did not." Griffin frowned.

"You didn't know what your wife was planning?"

Jackson watched the man's face color as his anger rose.

"No, I didn't know what my *ex*-wife was planning, nor with whom she was planning the scheme," he snapped.

"At the time." Jackson added.

"What?"

"You didn't know *at the time*, but you did find out later, didn't you?"

Griffin crossed his arms and leaned back in his chair. "Okay, yes, I found out about what Rochelle was doing later."

"How much later?"

Jackson watched the man carefully. Griffin was definitely calculating how to proceed and how much to say. Like Elise had said the night before, they just needed to push the right button to get him talking.

"Did you find out before or after the Falcones signed the contract with your wife's agency?" the sheriff asked when Griffin had yet to answer.

"I found out a few weeks before."

"How? I mean, how did you figure it out?" Jackson asked with a frown. "If the sale scheme was on the down low, how did you find out about it?"

"I'd had a feeling for a while that something was up. Rochelle had been secretive, well, more secretive than normal, and I'd asked her about it a couple of times, but she just kept saying that she didn't know what I was talking about." Griffin sighed and lean forward. "One morning before she left for work, she told me she had an out of town meeting in the afternoon, so she'd be late getting home." He shrugged. "I had a key to the office and the password for the office computer, so I went down there and did some digging while she was gone. She had everything right there spelled out in black and white."

"So, you found all this out when the scheme was still in play, when a big payout for everyone involved was still the prize?" the sheriff asked.

"Yes."

"And she never said anything to you?" The sheriff whistled through his teeth. "That must have been quite a blow. First to find out that she had a deal cooking behind your back, and then to have that deal go sideways when the owners sold the majority of shares before they even signed with her agency. And here she was, the one that had talked them into selling in shares in the first place."

When Griffin held his tongue, Masters continued. "Must have made you really angry. I know I would've been."

"I was. You bet I was, but then my daddy always said that when people do you wrong, don't get mad, get even."

The sheriff nodded. "And is that what you did? With the divorce? You filed not too long after the sale went bad. Did you get even?"

A wicked grin spread across Griffin's face. "I did, indeed. Rochelle and I were just about through before I found out about the hinky sale deal, anyway. And yes, that she'd kept it a secret made me furious. So, I got my pound of flesh by using that information."

"Using it? How so?"

The sheriff asked the question casually, but Jackson knew exactly where he was going with it, as they'd discussed this at length before Griffin had arrived. Just pushing those buttons to see what would pop.

"I told her that I would put the whole scheme out there for everyone to see. That I'd ruin her reputation and Hensen's to boot." He nodded at the sheriff. "You were right, Sheriff. The scheme, though it wasn't technically illegal, was seriously unethical. And this Hensen guy? From what I could tell, he has a rep for being a shrewd business man. There was no way my dear ex-wife was going to make an enemy of him by having this hinky scheme plastered everywhere."

"So, you blackmailed her into giving you a sweet deal in the divorce," Jackson said, using Elise's phrasing from the night before.

Todd laughed out loud and spread his arms wide. "Come on, blackmail? That's a little harsh. She had a choice. I prefer to think of it as creative thinking. After all, information is power, right?"

Masters shook his head, made some notes, and then moved on. "Okay, can you tell us a bit about the vineyard sabotage? As I'm sure you're aware, Ms. Thompsen was here yesterday and told us that her dad was behind those issues from the beginning."

Griffin nodded. "Yeah, like my ex-wife, he was a piece of work."

"I thought you didn't know him that well. You said that you'd only met him a couple of times, right?" Jackson asked, making a show of checking his notes. He looked up, pinning Griffin with a hard look. "Those were your words."

The man's grin faded. "Look, I didn't know him well. He was Cara's dad, so yeah, I'd met him a few times. I say that he was a piece of work because I heard it all from her. I know they'd argued about the problems he continued to cause. From what I understand, the man still hoped to get the other shareholders to give up and sell. I think he and Rochelle were still working with Hensen to get their hands on the vineyard. Evidently, Hensen had big plans for development in the area and the vineyard was his main priority. He was incredibly pissed off that the sale hadn't gone the way Rochelle had assured him it would." He shook his head. "Anyway, Thompsen was definitely behind all the vandalism and damage that was happening out at the vineyard. And what he didn't do himself, he hired out. Though Cara could never get proof."

"Until she caught him in the act?" Jackson asked.

Griffin gave another sigh and nodded. "Until she caught him in the act."

"Okay, I think that's about all for now, Mr. Griffin," Masters said. "Just one more thing. Where were you between midnight and two a.m. last Saturday morning?"

Griffin rolled his eyes. "Cara Thompsen and I had dinner Friday night and then went back to my place and watched a movie," he said without missing a beat. "Cara spent the night and left the next morning around ten o'clock."

Oh, yeah, they definitely sync'd their stories, Jackson thought.

"Alright. Thanks for your time today, Mr. Griffin." The sheriff smiled. "If we need anything else, we'll be in touch."

As though perfectly timed, Jesse opened the door to the interview room.

The sheriff gestured to his deputy. "Deputy Navaro here will see you out."

Once the man left the room, they gathered their things and followed him out. Jackson watched Griffin pull out of the parking lot in his expensive ride and then turned to the others.

"Well, surprisingly, that kind of went to plan."

"It surely did," the sheriff said. "Not sure how much more this gives us though. Let's convene in the conference room and compare notes."

As they headed for the room, the main phone line rang, and Jesse went to answer it. Jim, Jackson, and Masters sat down at the conference table and began to sort through their notes.

"I think the first order of business will be to get in touch with Rochelle Griffin," Masters said. "We're armed with enough to pry some info out of her, though most of it is hearsay."

"Yeah, but it would be good to get confirmation on some of this from her," Jim said. "It seems to be a convoluted mess."

The sheriff shook his head. "You got that right."

Jim ran a hand over his face. "I know we're looking at the original sale to see what started it all, but I am gonna say it again, I still don't see a connection to Thompsen's murder."

"You're not alone, buddy," Jackson said. "I'm having a hard time with that as well."

"Well, we'll see what Rochelle Grif—" the sheriff began but Jesse rushed into the room, cutting him off.

"Sheriff, we've got a problem."

"What's up, Jesse?"

"That phone call was from Chief Whitehall over at city. There's been a suspicious death and he needs us to come right now. Says it may be of interest to us."

Masters frowned. "A suspicious death? Where?"

The deputy's eyes were wide as he looked around at each of them in turn before coming back to Masters. "That's just it, Sheriff. It's at Griffin Realty. The deceased is Rochelle Griffin."

14

S ince Griffin Realty was in an older neighborhood a mere sixteen blocks from the Sheriff's Department, it took them less than fifteen minutes to grab their gear, so to speak, and arrive on the scene. The office was quaint, consisting of a small craftsman-style house that had been turned into a business with a detached garage at the back. As the sheriff pulled the cruiser to the curb across the street, Jackson climbed out of the passenger's side and studied the place.

Griffin obviously took decent care of the building and the landscape was both attractive and meticulously groomed. The house was situated among other homes of similar size and style just off the main drag, which he figured gave it a homier feel and would probably have made it a good choice for a realty business.

There was an ambulance in the driveway behind a small sedan and a dark brown SUV at the curb in front of the house. A magnetic sign on the SUV's driver's side panel held the M.E.'s logo. Masters had parked his cruiser on the other side of the street directly behind another city vehicle.

"Hey, Dillon, thanks for coming so soon," Chief Norman White-hall said, the older officer greeting the sheriff with a handshake when they'd crossed the street to where he stood on the sidewalk.

"Norm," the sheriff replied. "Sounds like you've got some trouble here."

"Well, now this is not how I'd hoped my afternoon would go, I can tell you that."

"Suppose not, but then some afternoons just never go as planned, am I right?"

"That you are," the chief replied with a grin.

"Unfortunately, my afternoons of late have decidedly gone to crap." Masters gave the chief a sour look before introducing Jackson and Jim. "These are the two out-of-state deputies that I told you about who are generously giving us a hand with our homicide investigation which has been a great help to me. Figured they can give us another set of eyes here as well."

"Good to finally meet you two. The sheriff here has had nothing but good things to say about you both," the chief said. "And, another set of eyeballs are always welcome in these situations. The more the better."

Masters nodded toward the office. "Ms. Griffin inside?"

"Yep." Whitehall gestured toward the porch where an officer was sitting on a bench speaking quietly with a younger woman. "That's Darlene Wilks with Officer Metzker on the porch there. Darlene has been working off and on with Ms. Griffin for a few years doing some freelancing, updating the website, changing up the company's site graphics, that sort of thing. Darlene found the deceased about an hour ago. Evidently, she and Ms. Griffin had some kind of production meeting with clients scheduled for two o'clock, so Darlene arrived early to get set up beforehand."

Whitehall looked at his watch, then glanced up and down the street. "Almost the two o'clock hour now. Darlene doesn't have the client contact info to cancel the appointment, so I've been keeping an eye out. Anyway, when Darlene got here and didn't see the Griffin woman's car—which, by the way, is uncharacteristically parked in the garage—she tried the front door. It was unlocked, so she went in ... and found her."

"That little blue sedan in the driveway in front of the ambulance isn't Griffin's car, then?" Jim asked.

"No. That's Darlene's rig."

The sheriff frowned. "Jesse called it a suspicious death when he came in with the news, so what's the deal?"

Whitehall raised his eyebrows and blew out a breath. "Now, that's where things get a little hinky for me, Dillon. At first blush, it *looks* like a suicide. We even recovered a note in the printer tray that she supposedly typed out and printed before she died."

"Supposedly?" Masters asked slowly. "Sounds like you're questioning that now."

Whitehall gave a slight nod. "That's why I said hinky. A closer look told maybe a different story for me. Something just doesn't feel right but danged if I can put my finger on exactly why. Also, there's the fact that Darlene says no way on the suicide. Of course, you can never really know what someone else is gonna do—even those you think you know well—but you take a look and see what you think. I called Doc Wilcox right after I got on scene. He came right over. He's still in there with her now."

The sheriff sighed. "Well, let's go in and take a look, see what's what. Then we'll hear what the doc has to say. I'd also like to see this supposed suicide note."

"I'm gonna let you three check it out on your own. I want to wait out here in case the two o'clock clients show up. Gonna be a helluva shock for them. I left the suicide note in the printer tray right where I found it. Figured you'd need to check it out."

"Good deal. But I'd like to have a quick chat with Darlene before gloving up to go inside," Masters said.

They followed Whitehall up the sidewalk and climbed the pristinely painted front steps to the equally pristine porch. The sheriff crossed to the couple on the bench and addressed the woman.

"Ms. Wilks, I'm Sheriff Masters. I'm gonna go in now and speak with Dr. Wilcox. Once I do that, I'd like to speak with you as well. Okay for you to wait out here for maybe ten minutes or so?"

Darlene's red-rimmed eyes filled again as she looked up at him, but the woman's voice was steady when she spoke. "That's fine, Sheriff. I'm not going anywhere for a bit."

"Can we get you something while you wait? We've got water in the cooler in the back of the cruiser."

She swiped at the tears leaking down her cheeks. "No, Sheriff. Chief Whitehall already asked. I'm good. I'd just like to be done here as soon as possible, if you don't mind."

The sheriff nodded. "Understood. Then we'll try to make this quick with the doc and then be back out in a jiffy."

With that, Masters walked back to the door and took the booties and latex gloves that Whitehall offered. He, Jackson, and Jim all donned the protective gear and then entered the house.

The main room was set up much like a living room would have been with a small sofa facing the fireplace and flanked by matching arm chairs. The coffee table, which rounded out the scenario, offered an array of magazines and real estate flyers. A beverage station stood along the wall to one side with a coffee maker and all the accoutrements to go with it. Through the archway to the right—which would probably have been a dining room in its time—was a show room of sorts containing a desk and two chairs, a bookshelf, and a small credenza. Jackson figured this was where potential buyers or sellers could peruse real estate listings, walk through choices, sign contracts, and the like.

The short hallway running toward the back of the house held a doorway to the kitchen on the right, a small bathroom on the left, and at the very back past the staircase to the second floor, Rochelle Griffin's personal office. There they found Dr. Wilcox and two of his assistants.

As well as the deceased.

Rochelle Griffin was sitting in her chair and slumped over the desk, a pill bottle in her outstretched left hand. Several pills were scattered over the desktop next to her with a few more dotting the carpet below.

"Doc, we have got to stop meeting like this," Masters said with a shake of his head.

The doctor grunted and stood up. "We agree on that much, Sheriff," he muttered.

"Norm says this looks like suicide on the surface but he's not convinced. What say you?"

"We've taken all the photos we're gonna take, so go ahead. Take a closer look for yourself and tell me what you see."

As Masters walked around the desk for a closer look, Jackson followed, and the first thing that he noticed was the position of the woman's body. Sure, she was basically sitting in the office chair, her upper body laying across the desktop, but Jackson could see—or rather sense—what the chief meant about the scene feeling somehow off. Looking down, he frowned. One of the woman's feet was buckled under, as if the chair had been pushed up to the desk with her in it and her foot dragging along behind, while the other foot was stretched out underneath the desk. That just didn't look right to him.

Evidently, Masters was of the same mind.

"Okay, for one thing, I'm not liking the body position," the sheriff said, as if repeating Jackson's thoughts. "I mean, look at her feet."

Wilcox's smile was grim. "That is one odd thing."

Masters narrowed his eyes at the doctor. "One odd thing? What else?"

"Well, it's not my area, but the chief found the 'suicide note' over there in the printer tray." He pointed to the side cabinet against the wall behind the desk that held the printer. "Seemed a bit odd to me considering that she's here at the desk, but then, again, not my area of expertise."

Masters crossed to the printer and carefully lifted the single piece of printed paper from the tray. He read through it, then handed it to Jackson. "That does seem a bit off. Of course, she could have just hit print and then laid her head down and passed out."

Jackson read the note twice through and looked up at Masters in surprise as he handed the note to Jim. "Wow!"

"Exactly," the sheriff muttered and pointed to the note that Jim now was reading. "If what's there is true, our Ms. Griffin here has been a very busy gal."

"I'll say," Jim replied, handing the note back to the sheriff.

Masters laid the note back in the printer tray for the sweeper team and then took in the room as a whole for a moment. Jackson could almost see the man's thoughts whirling before he finally spoke. "Doc, I know you probably can't give me COD, but how about a timeframe?"

The M.E. frowned. "No, I can't tell you how she died just yet, and I won't speculate, but what I can say is that she's been dead for at least twelve to fourteen hours."

"Figured." Masters looked at his watch. "That would make TOD sometime between midnight and two a.m. Anything else you can tell me right now that may have a bearing?"

At this question, the old doctor almost smiled. Almost. "I thought you'd never ask." He leaned over the body and pointed at the back of Rochelle's head. "You can't see it because she's got quite a thick head of hair, but there's a medium-sized hematoma right here in the occipital area."

"Hematoma? Like a lump?" Masters raised his eyebrows. "Like maybe she'd been hit from behind?"

"Again, I won't speculate on that just yet, either, but it's a possibility. Once I get her on my table, I'll be able to tell you more.

The prescription on the bottle in her hand indicates Phenobarbital, which was prescribed to her for treatment of seizures. I've taken samples of the scattered pills and will make certain that's what these actually are."

Jackson stepped forward. "So, Doc, Phenobarbital can kill pretty easily, can't it?"

"Oh, sure. It's a barbiturate. Slows down the brain, can drop the blood pressure. Pheno, Nembutal, Seconal, there's a whole list, as well as four different classifications. Plus, if you add alcohol to the mix you can have yourself a faster ride to the promised land." The doctor nodded. "Many a celebrity has died by overdosing on barbiturates. Of course, back in the fifties it was probably more common than it is today. Back then, they handed them out like candy. Today they've got all these new-fangled designer drugs to choose from with a whole 'nother set of problems."

"Well, let me know once you have more info and a clear cause of death," the sheriff said. "In the meantime, are you done with her here? She ready for transport?"

The M.E. nodded. "Yes, I've done all I need to do for now. We'll go ahead with the prep and get her transported to the morgue if you're okay with that."

"I am. I'm gonna call in the sweeper team right now and then coordinate with Norm on what he may need as well." Masters turned to Jim and Jackson. "Let's give this room another quick eyeball while the doc here gets her ready to go, and then we'll go out and have a chat with Darlene. Once the sweepers get here, we'll regroup."

"Sounds good," Jackson acknowledged.

After another quick scan of the room, Jackson and Jim followed the sheriff back out the way they'd come in as Masters called for the sweeper team. They headed out to the porch where Chief Whitehall waited with Darlene Wilks. The chief stood as they approached.

"I called for a team, Norm," the sheriff said quietly. "If there's anything else you need, you let me know. Did the clients show?"

The chief nodded. "Darlene and I handled that. That whole thing is on hold until they hear back."

"Alright then." Masters looked at Darlene. "You feel up to going through this now?"

The woman blew out an unsteady breath but looked as if she'd settled a bit. "Yes. Let's get it over with so I can go home."

Masters took the seat next to her on the bench that Whitehall had vacated and gave Jackson a considering look. Then he glanced at the driveway before turning back to Darlene. "You know, I really need to stay here and wait for my team. And since the ambulance is blocking you in, it's gonna be a while longer before the doc can transport Ms. Griffin. How would you feel about going back to the office with these two fine deputies here to give your statement? They can bring you back once you're done, and by that time, the ambulance will be gone and you can go home."

This was something that Jackson hadn't seen coming. Of course, he and Jim were assisting the sheriff and had helped with interviews at the station a few times, but that was with the sheriff present. This was new.

Darlene looked back and forth between them, and then finally nodded. "That might be best. I really don't want to be here any longer, Sheriff, and I could probably have my husband pick me up from the station. He can come back and get my car tomorrow, if that's okay with you."

The sheriff smiled. "I'd say that's a mighty fine plan." He pulled the keys to the cruiser out of his pocket and tossed them to Jackson. "I'm gonna stay and go over the room with the team. I can have the chief drop me at the station, if that doesn't take too long. I'll text you if that's the plan. If I'm not back by the time Ms. Wilks has been picked up, and you haven't heard from me, come on back here and get me."

"Will do," Jackson said. "Ms. Wilks, do you want to get whatever you need out of your vehicle and then lock it up before we leave?"

Like someone coming out of a daze, the woman's eyes went wide, and she stood. "Oh ... yes ... that's probably a good idea. But my things are on the sofa in the house, along with my purse and keys."

She looked toward the house, and Jackson could read the anxiety in her eyes.

Jim came to her rescue. "I'll grab 'em," he said. Turning, he went back inside. A moment later he came back out with her things. "Anything I missed?" he asked as he handed over her belongings.

"No, this is all I had with me."

"Okay, let's go lock your car, and then we'll head to the cruiser and wait for Deputy Landry to join us."

Jackson watch them go and then turned to the sheriff with a frown.

"What?" the sheriff asked with a slight smile.

"Are you sure about this?"

Masters chuckled. "Son, I have seen your work. You and Jim know how this goes, and you, my friend, are a heck of an interviewer, so I have no problem with you two handling this. Besides, Jesse doesn't have the experience yet, and he's doing some research for me right now, which is what he's really good at. This will save us some time."

Jackson nodded. "So ... that suicide note ... you know, it seems like ..."

"Seems like what?"

"Well, it *feels* like—"

"Like maybe this isn't a suicide at all? Like maybe somebody was looking for someone to dump every last thing on top of and did a sloppy, pathetic job of making it look like suicide?"

Jackson slowly nodded again. "That's exactly what it feels like. I mean, if the note that was found is real, she confessed to not only killing Roger Thompsen, but also orchestrating the sabotage at the winery and vineyard over the years, *plus* Gene Rollins' death to boot. That just seems like overkill, don't you think?"

The sheriff nodded. "I do. Especially since the fact that we're looking into the early days of the vineyard sale and the *possibility* of Rollins' death not being the accident it was purported to be is not common knowledge."

"True. In addition, from everything I've heard—or should I say, that my wife has heard—Rochelle Griffin may not have been the most scrupulous business woman, but this note just doesn't jibe with her reputation as a demanding pain in the butt with no conscience."

"My thoughts exactly."

"And the chief said that Darlene was adamant that Griffin would never have committed suicide. Of course, like he said, you never really know about folks, right?"

Masters' smile was grim. "No. No you do not. However, I have a sneaking suspicion that what we're gonna find here is that we have yet another murder, this one set up to look like suicide. And done pretty poorly, I might add. Anyway, we'll wait to see what the doc has to say. That'll tell the tale. For now, go get Darlene's interview taken care of ... and no joy riding in my cruiser."

Jackson laughed and shook his head. "I'll try to remember that." He headed down the steps and crossed the street to the rig where Jim and Darlene were already waiting. Sliding behind the wheel, Jackson pulled away from the curb for the short trip to the office.

Masters had obviously called Jesse at the station, because the deputy had the interview room ready for them when they arrived. Once they got situated, Jackson eased into the interview with a bit of background.

"So, how long have you been working with Griffin Realty, Darlene?"

The woman sighed. "I've been doing free-lance work off and on with Rochelle for the better part of three years. This is just such a shock."

"I can only imagine. I guess you knew her pretty well after working with her for so long."

Darlene nodded. "As well as you can really know anyone, I suppose."

"Okay, can you go ahead and take us through this afternoon from when you arrived?"

"Well, we had this meeting with clients set up for two o'clock, so I got to the office at about quarter to one. Rochelle and I were going to get everything ready to go. Her car wasn't in the driveway, so when I pulled in I called her cell from my car, but it went straight to her voicemail. Anyway, I thought I'd just go check, you know, maybe her phone was on the charger or something."

"Uh-huh. Logical."

"So, I tried the door. It was unlocked so I knew she had to be here."

"Why is that?" Jim asked.

"Well, Rochelle was a real stickler about locking up. She would never leave without locking the door, deadbolt and all. She was always saying how she didn't trust her ex."

"Todd Griffin?"

Darlene nodded. "Evidently, she thought that he'd helped to tank a deal she'd put together with some land developer on a sale for one of the vineyards in the area. Sounded like the whole deal had imploded, and she'd blamed him for part of it. That fight had basically put an end to their marriage in a really vicious way. She'd changed the locks after their nasty divorce, but she was still vigilant. Like I said, she just didn't trust him." She waved a hand in the air. "Anyway, since her car wasn't there, I expected the door to be locked. When it wasn't, I figured maybe she was having the car worked on or something, so I went in and put my stuff down in the front room and then went looking for her." She frowned and looked up at Jackson. "It was weird, you know, like really quiet, and I called out to her a couple of times as I walked toward her office. And that's when I saw her."

The woman's bottom lip began to tremble, and blinking back fresh tears, she took a tissue from the box on the table. "I probably shouldn't have gone to her the way I did but I was just so shocked. I could see almost immediately that she was ... gone. I mean, it was pretty obvious, but I couldn't believe it. Part of my brain just wouldn't acknowledge it." One lone tear slipped down her cheek and she dabbed at it with the tissue, shaking her head. "I still can't. It all seems so surreal. I've never found a dead person before."

"Your actions are totally understandable. You did nothing wrong," he said, and slid a bottle of water across the table for her.

"Thanks." Opening the bottle, she took a sip. "Anyway, I stumbled backward and then ran for my purse and my cell phone, called 911. After that, I just sat on the porch bench and waited for the police to get there."

Jackson made some notes and then took a breath. This part was never easy. "Darlene, how had Ms. Griffin seemed to you lately? Was she worried about anything or anyone? Like Todd Griffin especially? Or maybe someone else? Was she depressed or unhappy?"

"No. Nothing like that. She was fine. If I would have seen any change in her behavior, I would tell you, but there was nothing different. And Rochelle wasn't the type to hide things. If something was bothering her, trust me, you knew about it. And I mean, right now."

"Okay, the reason I ask is that I know Chief Whitehall told you about the suicide note that was found in Rochelle's office—"

"Huh-uh," Darlene blurted, shaking her head fiercely. "There is no way that I'll ever believe that Rochelle Griffin committed suicide. No matter what it *looked* like in that office. Just no."

Jackson nodded and spoke gently. "I understand that it's hard to grasp this kind of thing, that someone you know so well could actually do something like this, but the reasons the note listed were disturbing."

She leaned in and her eyes took on the heat of anger. "Look, I will be the first to admit that Rochelle was not the most stellar human being. We worked together and were friendly, but we weren't friends. We had our battles from time to time. She could be mean and ugly, dismissive and condescending. And yes, she was unscrupulous and sometimes had her toes right up to and over the line into dishonesty. I won't dispute any of that. I'm also well aware that she'd done some really despicable things in her life, and while she may have regretted a few of those things, she would never, ever apologize to anyone for them. Nor would she have let anything or anyone drive her to suicide. Never." Darlene took a deep breath and blew it out slowly, then looked Jackson in the eye. "I don't care what was in that note that you found. I can tell you right now that from the sound of it, Rochelle Griffin didn't write it."

ell, I sure didn't see that coming," Elise said with raised eyebrows. "I mean, Rochelle Griffin? Dead by suicide?"

She and Jackson were getting ready to meet the crew for dinner, and he'd just spilled the details of his afternoon, which she was having a real hard time believing, and by the look on his face, he was as well.

"Yeah, wasn't on our radar, either," Jackson grumbled as he checked his phone for messages. "And just when we were starting to make some progress on the Roger Thompsen investigation." He shook his head. "We interviewed Todd Griffin earlier today and hoped to get with Rochelle before the end of the week. And now this."

"But come on, Jax. Suicide? Really? What a coincidence, huh?" she said, tongue in cheek.

He glanced up at her with a bland look. "Yeah, and you know how I feel about coincidences."

She smiled. "I do indeed. And please. A printed note left with her confessing a host of sins, including Roger Thompsen's murder *and* Gene Rollins' death by car accident? That seems a little convenient, don't you think?"

"Why, yes, darlin'. I do think it seems quite convenient. Again, not my first rodeo with murder investigations, remember?"

"I know, I know," she said, putting up a hand. "But you don't believe it any more than I do, right?"

Jackson sighed. "To be honest, I'm not sure what to believe at this point. Just when I think we're getting a handle on things, someone throws a wrench into the mix." He ran a hand through his hair. "Take for instance, in his interview, Todd Griffin told us that he hadn't known about the vineyard scheme that Rochelle was working on until just before the Falcones signed with her."

"So, before the whole deal went south."

"Uh-huh. He said he had a key to the office back then and the password to her computer. He went snooping one day when she was out of town, and that's how he found out about the scheme in the first place." A disgusted look crossed his face. "Man, the guy was just so smug and really proud of the fact that he'd basically blackmailed her into giving him a great divorce settlement by threatening to expose the entire deal and ruin her reputation and that of Miller Hensen's, too."

She raised an eyebrow. "He had a key to her office?"

"Well, yeah, but that was before the divorce."

"Okay, sure, but who's to say that good ole Todd didn't keep a copy of the keys to the office for himself?"

Jackson shook his head. "Darlene Wilks told us today that Rochelle had changed the locks at the office because, after their nasty divorce, she didn't trust her ex. Evidently, she was always vigilant about locking up whenever she left the office. Darlene also said that Rochelle was always complaining about Todd and blamed him for tanking the deal out of pure spite. Which, if true, is even more despicable after blackmailing her with it for a major divorce settlement."

"So, what are you thinking? That Todd could be involved in Rochelle's death? Maybe he decided to slip in somehow and stage a suicide?"

"That's a theory, I guess."

Elise frowned. "But for what purpose? After all this time, I can't imagine it would have to do with the original sale and divorce settlement. So, why kill her now? What would he gain?"

"Hard to say, but it's still too early to make assumptions or any snap judgements." Jackson shook his head. "Again, time of death was between midnight and two in the morning. We don't know if she'd been working late or had gone home and come back. I will say that there were things about the scene that didn't make sense to me or to Masters, things that just felt ... somehow off, but that doesn't necessarily mean anything."

"Off how?"

"The way the body was positioned, for one thing. Also, the doc said that she had a lump on the back of her head that was hidden by her hair. Plus, the 'suicide' note chocked full of confessions? Just seems ... off."

"Sounds like, but I get that you can't really make any judgements without more concrete information to go on."

"No, we have to follow the evidence, of which we have very little at the moment. However, Darlene Wilks was adamant that Rochelle Griffin would've never committed suicide, no matter what the scene looked like or what the note left behind said."

Elise frowned. "Well, you would expect her to say that, right? I mean, especially after finding her friend dead like that, but you never know what kind of turmoil people are dealing with under the surface. Some folks are just really good at hiding their pain."

"But that's just it. Darlene said that they weren't friends."

"What do you mean?"

"The way she tells it, they worked together and were *friendly*, but they were not actually friends. She even said that they'd had their own battles over the last few years. She was very clear-eyed about the kind of person Rochelle Griffin was. She said that Griffin could be mean, ugly, and condescending, that she was unscrupulous, and at times, dishonest."

"Ouch."

"However, she was firm on one thing, for sure. And that was the fact that Griffin would never have apologized to anyone for any of the terrible things she'd done in the past which, by the sounds of it, were plentiful."

"So, no known depression or guilt issues and no regrets that could drive her to take her own life?"

Jackson shook his head. "According to Darlene Wilks, that would be a hard no."

"Interesting."

"Anyway, we don't have anything concrete right now to debunk suicide, just our own eyes and a sloppy scene. So, we'll just have to wait and see what the autopsy turns up, as well as anything the sweeper team finds at the scene. But I can tell you that Masters and I are on the same page. Neither of us believes that this was a suicide."

Elise frowned. "Here's something else that I don't understand. How does this tie into Roger Thompsen's murder?" She put up a hand before he could answer. "Oh, don't get me wrong, I know that the supposed suicide note makes that link perfectly clear by confessing to the murder, but if Rochelle Griffin didn't write that note, then I would assume that Thompsen's killer did."

"That would be a logical assumption. What's your point?"

"Well, what about the rest of it? I mean, beyond a handful of folks that you've interviewed in connection with Thompsen's murder, it's not public knowledge that y'all are looking into the original vineyard sale or the problems associated with it."

"True, but we've only told four people that we're looking into the sale. Nico Ricci, Cara Thompsen, Todd Griffin, and Miranda. Of course, any one of them could have told any number of people that little tidbit after their interviews. There's no way to know."

"But they all have alibis for the time of Thompsen's death."

"As far as we know. Cara Thompsen and Todd Griffin alibied each other, which is always convenient, and for me, always a little suspect. Then you have Adrianna Santoro confirming that Nico Ricci, her fiancé, was with her all night. Miranda, however, is the only one out of the four that doesn't have a concrete alibi. She was with Nico and Adrianna after she left the Manor Friday night, but said she came back to the Manor at around one in the morning, and there is no one to confirm that."

"Well, that's ridiculous, so I won't even speak to that." Elise waved his comment away. "However, the other part of the suicide note that's disturbing is that no one knows Sheriff Masters is looking at Gene's accident, right?"

"During a heated moment in his interview, Nico Ricci is the one who told us about his suspicions over Gene's death. That's what spurred the sheriff into taking a closer look at the accident, but we haven't mentioned that piece of the side investigation to anyone, even those we've interviewed. Masters found that part of the suicide note curious as well. I mean, if Rochelle Griffin didn't write the note, then who else had those suspicions? Or even the knowledge, for that matter."

"Yeah, it kinda gives credence to Nico's theory that Gene's car crash wasn't actually an accident, right? Geez, Jax, that would just be so heartbreaking for Miranda." Elise shook her head. "Anyway, are y'all going to speak to everyone again, find out their whereabouts for the time of Rochelle's death?"

Jackson put up a hand. "Let's not get ahead of the facts, darlin'. We still have to wait for the official autopsy report before we can move forward with anything. And while we do have an approximate time of death, we still don't know exactly *what* killed her. So, as Sheriff Masters is fond of saying, 'that's going to tell the tale.'"

"Do you know how long the autopsy is going to take, how soon you may get the results back from the M.E.?"

"No clue. We didn't have to wait long for Dr. Wilcox to give us the results for Roger Thompsen's autopsy, but I don't know what all he's got on his plate, schedule-wise."

"Speaking of timelines," Elise said as she pulled her coat out of the closet and slipped it on. "Have y'all heard anything more about the security feed? I know the expert you were waiting for finally got over here. Any good news there?"

"Haven't heard. Molly, the County tech, said that she was hopeful but I don't know what she told Masters or if he's had time to call her."

She grabbed her purse and started for the door. "Well, it would be great if this so-called expert could restore the video so y'all could wrap up these confusing investigations and we can all go home. This honeymoon has taken a disturbing turn."

Jackson opened the door for her and chuckled as she preceded him into the hallway. "Jim and I have had that very conversation, pal. So, as I told him, from your mouth to God's ears."

ON THURSDAY, Jackson, Jim, and Jesse spent the morning on various research avenues of the investigation. They'd gotten the green light for Thompsen's financials, and Jim was digging into that. Jesse continued on with the mysterious research Masters had him doing, which Jackson thought was probably associated with Gene Rollins' death, though the sheriff hadn't shared that information yet. Since no one had been able to catch up with Miller Hensen up to this point, Jackson finally made contact with the land developer over the phone.

Hensen had been surprisingly forthcoming and helpful. And though Jackson hadn't gotten a lot in the way of new informa-tion, Hensen had confirmed much of what the team already suspected. The land developer had known about most of what Rochelle Griffin and Roger Thompsen had been up to on his behalf. However, he'd stopped short of admitting any knowledge of the sabotage that had been perpetrated at the vineyard or any potential illegal activity that may have taken place. In that way, he'd been very wily.

Though they'd had their suspicions, the one new thing Jackson had established was that Hensen had been the one to supply the funds for the vineyard shares Thompsen had acquired. After their conversation, Jackson was also able to confirm the man's whereabouts for the time of Roger Thompsen's death, finding his alibi to be rock solid.

Just before the noon hour, Jim stood and stretched. "I need to take a break, work out some of the kinks from sitting all morning."

"Find anything interesting with Thompsen's finances?" Jackson asked without looking up.

"Not really. Only more of what I'd already found on my own. The guy was just about drowning in debt. There would be cash deposits at certain junctures, usually right at the point of over-drawn accounts, but hard to tell where those cash deposits came from since Thompsen was unemployed as far as I could tell." Jim scrubbed his hands over his face. "There's a second on his home mortgage, which he took out a little over a year ago. However, curiously, I did find a separate account that has only his name on it and is holding about twenty large. Still have to dig a little further into that, but need to get some lunch first. You finally talk to Hensen?"

"Yeah. He's very personable ... and very crafty. He did confirm knowledge of some of the steps Griffin and Thompsen had taken on his behalf but not the sabotage or any illegal stuff."

"Shocking," Jim said with a grin.

"Yeah. One thing that I was able to pin down? He admitted that he was the money man behind Thompsen's eighteen percent share of the vineyard, though during that point in the conversation his *personable* slipped just a bit. It was obvious that even now he's still really pissed off about the way the deal went south in the end."

"Okay, that would track with some of what I found."

"And yes, Hensen's development company is the lien holder for those shares, though they're really not much good to him at only eighteen percent. Sounds like Griffin for a time, kept his hopes alive for acquiring full control of the land, but he's pretty much come to terms with the fact that it's a write-off now."

"Wow. Gotta be a hard pill to swallow for a guy like that. You think he'll hold onto the shares and try to wait it out? Or maybe just sell?"

Jackson shrugged. "Hard to know. My gut says he'll cut his losses. His company has a boatload of cash, but those Bella Luna shares don't interest him. That's not what he does, and that chunk of change will probably be better spent elsewhere. But then, what do I know?"

"I'm with ya on that," Jim said with a nod.

"Anyway, other than that, Hensen hadn't heard about Griffin's death but his offices are over in the valley, and it just happened. So, that's not surprising. He did say that he hadn't spoken with her in a couple of months. His alibis for TOD for both Thompsen and Griffin are solid."

Jim nodded. "Okay then. Guess that crosses him off the list. Doesn't mean that he couldn't have paid someone to do them both, but doesn't sound like that's plausible."

"Probably not."

"So, you want to head out for some lunch?"

"I do." Jackson shut down the laptop and grabbed his coat. "How about we try that Chinese place a couple of blocks over. Maybe Masters will be back by the time we've had a bite."

The little Chinese restaurant turned out to be a very good choice, and by the time they'd returned to the office, Sheriff Masters was just pulling into the parking lot as well. They all walked into the office together.

"Jesse, did you get some lunch?" Masters asked his deputy as they crossed the lobby.

The deputy nodded. "I brought my lunch with me today, boss. Ate it while I monitored the phones."

"Good man. Then let's all grab our notes and convene in the conference room. I've got some news and want to hear what you all may have for me."

Once they'd settled at the conference table, Jackson went first. He covered his phone conversation with Miller Hensen and everything that he'd learned from the man.

"Sounds like this Hensen is an oily type but smart enough not to get any of the stink on him from what Griffin and Thompsen were cooking up. He may be slippery but at least we can bump him down the list as a murder suspect."

Jim went next with the financials, disappointing as they were. When he was done, the sheriff snorted.

"A separate account, huh? And with a $20,000 balance, to boot." Masters scratched his chin. "Interesting. Dig into it as far as you can and let me know what you find. In the meantime, I've got a few things here that we need to talk about." He shuffled through some papers in his folder. "Okay, first and foremost, we may have some progress with the security feed."

"Wow. That's good to hear," Jim said with a thumbs up.

"Yes, it is. The security expert that Molly brought over from the valley says he's pretty confident that he can restore what was lost. The bad news is that it's a time consuming process, and there's forty-eight hours to restore and go through to find the section that we need. This guy seems to think it may only take another day or two. So, stay tuned."

"Excellent." Jim grinned at Masters. "No offense, Sheriff. This has been a real good time, but I'm ready to go home. This vacation has been more work than I'd wanted."

Masters laughed. "No offense taken, Jim. I expect you're all chomping at the bit to get home after all of this nonsense." He turned to Jackson. "Especially you and your lovely wife, Jackson. I mean, what a way to spend the end of your honeymoon, huh?"

"To tell you the truth, Sheriff, Elise has been pretty much right in her element with this murder investigation. She doesn't get such a free hand at home, as her husband has no patience for her meddling." Jackson smiled and put up a hand. "Now, having said that, it's been kind of nice to have her to bounce things off of, as well as her feeding us pertinent information. However, I don't know how this is all gonna shape up once we're home. Kinda hard to put it back into the box after it's exploded out onto the scene, know what I mean?"

Jim jabbed a finger at him. "Yeah, and Tina's stepped right into it as well. I'm not looking forward to trying to keep her out of our investigations, either."

Masters shook his head with a grin. "Maybe you two just shouldn't try, Jim. I say, go with it and let them get you the information you need but can't get on your own. They'll be able to go places you can't. Better still, sign them both up and put 'em on the payroll as civilian consultants."

"Oh, Lordie," Jim said, pressing his fingers to his eyes. "What a thought."

"Anyway, back to the case, or should I say, *cases*, now." Masters flipped through his notes. "I talked with Doc Wilcox earlier. He was just starting on the Griffin autopsy, so he may have a concrete cause of death for us by tomorrow sometime. However, the lab results may take a day or two. We'll just have to wait and see if this was actually a suicide or something else."

"That was quick," Jesse said. "Guess the doc had a clear schedule, huh?"

"He did, and we were lucky." The sheriff looks back and forth between Jackson and Jim. "The third thing that I want to update you two on is what Jesse here has found for me and where the Gene Rollins accident issue stands."

"I've been wondering about that," Jackson said. "So, do we have an accident ... or like the Griffin deal ... something else?"

The sheriff took a deep breath and let it out slowly, then he looked Jackson in the eye. "It's looking very much like something else. For now, what I'm going to tell you both stays right here in this room. And that means, not a peep to your lovely ladies. Are we clear about that, gentlemen?"

Jackson looked at his partner and nodded. Jim nodded back. Turning to Masters, he leaned in. "We're clear, Sheriff."

"Good. I don't want a whiff of this getting back to Mrs. Rollins until we've dotted all the i's and crossed all the t's." He paused for a moment, running his finger over his notes, then he looked up. "Since this happened so long ago, the vehicle itself—or what was left of it—is long gone. However, as you know, I've had my guys down at the motor pool going over the reports, photos, and everything else Jesse could get his hands on pertaining to Mr. Rollins' so-called accident over the last week. The result of that study is a bit disturbing."

"So, not an accident?" Jim asked.

Masters shook his head. "Not looking that way. There are some anomalies that we've run across, but without the actual wreckage, the guys are hard put to say conclusively what happened. But add what was in the suicide note to what we've found in the reports, and it becomes a little weightier."

"What else is there, Sheriff?" Jackson asked. "I can see that there's something you haven't told us. Maybe something to make the *weightier* more conclusive?"

"That there is, Jackson," the sheriff replied, his look grim. "Jesse also found one of the motor pool old-timers that was around back then, and he had an interesting story to tell. Seems that he had questions that nobody back then wanted answered."

16

A fter hearing what the sheriff had uncovered about Gene Rollins' death, Jackson had spent a very dicey evening dodging specific questions from Elise. It was like she could sense that there was something he was holding back, and she systematically continued to poke and prod. It was frustrating in the extreme, but he and Jim had both been cautioned by the sheriff not to say anything to anyone. He told her what he could but kept to the talking points that he and Jim had decided on before leaving the station. However, he was well aware that she hadn't been satisfied by the financial information or what he'd learned from Miller Hensen. Although, the possibility of the recovered security video seemed to do the trick for the time-being.

Jackson had to admit that what the sheriff had found out about Gene's car crash was compelling, as it looked as if Gene's rental car may have been sabotaged. When the sheriff had spoken with the retired mechanic who'd been in the department during that time, the man had been adamant that the brakes on the rental car had been tampered with. The lines had been severed and there'd been little fluid left in the system. However, the lead investigator on the case felt the evidence was inconclusive simply because it was hard to tell if the lines had been severed before, or caused by, the accident. Plus, there was an indication of brake fluid at the scene.

In addition, the temperatures had plummeted during the week of the crash, and the roads had been icy and slick. Therefore, the mechanic had been overridden, his suggestion of sabotage relegated to a footnote in the original report and basically disregarded. The previous sheriff had been unwilling to add more trauma to Gene's family without irrefutable proof, of which they had none. Still, though the old mechanic had no tangible evidence, he'd been unyielding in his conclusions and continued to insist that the crash that killed Gene Rollins had not been an accident. Which, if true, meant that Gene's death could well have been murder.

Unfortunately, with all the time that had passed, they had no way to substantiate most of what they'd learned, and Masters was still working on how he would break the news to Miranda, or if he should even try. Jackson was on the fence about that. On one hand, didn't Miranda have a right to know if Gene had been targeted by someone? On the other hand, without concrete evidence, it was all just conjecture, and why open up old wounds if you have no proof? It was quite the dilemma.

By Friday morning, Jackson had no better handle on it all than when he'd started. He and Jim commiserated over what they'd learned on the way to the station.

"I'm right there with you buddy," Jim said, sipping on his hot, fru-fru coffee that they'd picked up on the way out of town.

"Tina was relentless last night, and she wasn't really impressed with my financial hacking and digging skills, either. And, you and I are on the same page with Gene's crash. I have to put a lot of stock into what that mechanic said because he was there. He saw it all with his own eyes. But the fact that there's really no smoking gun, so to speak?" Jim shook his head. "I mean, even in what little photo evidence there is in the file, it's impossible to prove either way if the lines were intentionally cut or whether they were just severed during the crash."

"Exactly. So, what do you do? Especially after all this time has passed," Jackson agreed. "I mean, Masters has a helluva decision to make."

"Too right. Unfortunately, he's also got bigger issues on his plate, especially now with Rochelle Griffin's death on top of Thompsen's murder."

"True, but here's the thing that's really bugging me about Gene's accident. I mean, maybe I can get on board with how it was handled back then because they just didn't have the conclusive evidence, but to have it pop up in Rochelle Griffin's supposed suicide note how many years later? That's just—"

"A bit too coincidental for you, buddy?" Jim finished for him. "I mean, I know how you love coincidences."

Jackson laughed. "Yeah, not so much. Anyway, the best we can do for now is to continue to work the cases and gather evidence. Hopefully, we can get to the bottom of both deaths soon. As for Gene's accident, that will be the sheriff's call if and when he makes it. In the meantime, it's radio silence on that front." Jackson pulled the rental car into the parking lot at the Sheriff's Department and killed the engine. "For now, we keep at it."

"Yep. What do you always say? Something's bound to break."

Jackson nodded. "That's always the hope, my friend. Always the hope."

So, they did just that. They kept at it all morning, making calls, digging into records, and waiting for something to break in either case.

And it didn't take long.

Just after lunch, Jesse came into the conference room with news for the sheriff. "Hey, boss, just got a call from Doc Wilcox. He's got something for you. Wanted to know if you can go on down to the morgue right now."

Masters looked around at Jackson and Jim. "Well, it looks like we've got time to take a breather, don't ya think?"

"You bet," Jim replied. "I'm just about done digging into these financials, anyway."

"I could use a break," Jackson agreed. "Especially, if the doc has something good for us."

With that, they grabbed their coats and headed for the door. Jesse stopped at the front desk to brief Deputy Burrows, who was manning the phones, and then the four of them walked out to the sheriff's cruiser for a ride down to the morgue, which took all of about five or six minutes.

When they arrived, Doc Wilcox was working on his computer and put up a finger. "Give me a second. I'm just wrapping up the preliminary report," he said. Within minutes, he finished and stood. Not one for small talk, he started for the door. "Come on, then. I'll show you what I've found." He stopped abruptly in the hallway and turned to Deputy Navaro. "Jesse, you can wait out here in the hall, if you want."

Jesse's face pinkened, but he shook his head. "I appreciate that, Doc, especially after that last time." Jesse looked at Jackson and Jim. "Suicide we found up in the woods. It was ... not pretty, and I didn't handle it well."

"Happens to all of us, Jesse," Jim replied. "Death is never pretty and always difficult to take. Just some are worse than others."

The deputy turned back to the M.E. "Anyway, I have to get used to it sometime, so I'll come along, Doc."

"Suit yourself." Dr. Wilcox grunted and headed down the hall toward the morgue.

This was the part of an investigation involving a death that Jackson and Jim rarely got to see as Doc Nagle in Bastrop County was a coroner rather than an M.E. He made determinations at the scene and wrote preliminary reports, but any bodies were transported to Austin and the Travis County Medical Examiner for autopsy when needed. The few times that Jackson had been to the morgue in Austin or witnessed an autopsy there had always felt like stepping into a television crime drama.

Surprisingly, this was no exception.

Rochelle Griffin's body was still on the table covered to the neck with a pristine white sheet. Even with the of the lack of coloring in her skin and the slight bluing around her lips, she looked as if she could have just been sleeping peacefully.

"Okay. Gather 'round, gentlemen," the doctor said, gesturing them around the table. "I'll give you the down and dirty of what you'll read in my report." They did as requested, and the doctor continued. "I got the tox report back from the lab this morning."

"That was quick, Doc," Masters said with a frown. "Seems we usually have to wait a week or better for that."

The doctor grunted again. "Business has been slow lately, which is a good thing in my book. The lab was clear, so they got it done PDQ." He waved away the sheriff's comments. "As to the results, our Ms. Griffin here did not die of a Phenobarbital overdose as the scene appeared to suggest. While she did have the drug in her system, the levels were consistent with use for seizure control as prescribed. Also, there were no pills in her stomach contents at all."

"As there probably would have been with an overdose," Jackson said.

"Correct."

"Okay," Masters said slowly. "No surprise there, I guess. I think we were all on that same page, anyway. So, what was the actual COD?"

The doctor frowned. "It *was* an overdose, and the Pheno may have had a hand in it, but it was a massive overdose of fentanyl-laced heroin that actually did the deed."

"*What?*" Sheriff Masters blurted. "Heroin? But how—"

Dr. Wilcox put up a hand, cutting him off. "Hold your water and let me finish, Dillon. I'm gettin' to that."

The sheriff took a deep breath and then nodded. "Okay, okay, go ahead."

"As I told you at the scene, she has a medium-sized hematoma at the back of her head. That was definitely antemortem."

"Is that something that she could have gotten with a fall? Say, earlier in the day before she died?" Jim asked.

"It's hard to say how she got it, but the impact didn't break the skin of the scalp, so there was no bleeding or raw wound. And we found nothing to indicate a fall at the scene."

"So, as we discussed at the time, she could have been hit from behind," Masters said.

"That would be consistent with the hematoma."

"What kind of weapon would give that kind of lump but wouldn't break the skin?" Jesse asked.

The doctor shook his head. "Again, hard to say conclusively. My best guess? You'd be looking for something like a sap or blackjack."

"Wow. That's a blast from the past," Jim muttered. "They were used in the nineteenth century by police, sailors, soldiers, but by the twentieth, they were pulled from police use. They were found to be too dangerous because, even though they were used to knock someone out, you could kill someone just as easily with one blow."

Jackson stared at his partner with a questioning look.

Jim raised his eyebrows. "What?" he asked, arms spread wide. "Again, student of history here."

Shaking his head, Jackson turned to the doctor. "Sorry, Doc. Please continue."

To Jackson's surprise, Dr. Wilcox actually grinned at that. It was the first time Jackson had seen the M.E. even smile since they'd been working with the sheriff.

"Thank you, Deputy. I shall." Turning back to the table, the doctor lifted the sheet exposing Griffin's left arm. "This is the *how* of the overdose, Dillon. I found this injection site during autopsy." He indicated a small, slightly bruised needle mark in the crook of her left arm. "As you know, there was no heroin or drug paraphernalia located at the scene, and with the exception of the prescribed Phenobarbital, the condition of her body gave no indication of habitual drug use."

"So, the obvious conclusion would be that someone gave her the injection, typed up a phony suicide note, and then staged the scene as we found it." The sheriff shook his head. "What kind of idiot thinks that we wouldn't see through a sloppy, pathetic set up like this?" he asked in a disgusted tone to no one in particular.

"Maybe it didn't make any difference to them," Jackson murmured, almost to himself.

Masters turned to him. "What do you mean, Jackson?"

"The sweeper team didn't find any prints at the scene, right? I mean, other than hers, and those were in very specific places, and yet not in places that you'd expect them to be."

"I'm with you so far. Go on."

"So, maybe the staging was just about deflection and buying time, causing confusion."

"And placing blame," Jim added. "Dumping it all on Griffin."

Jackson nodded. "The cherry on top. Whoever did this had to know we wouldn't buy any of it, but they were smart enough to not leave a trace behind."

Masters smiled. "True. Keep going. You're on a roll."

"Well, if we're theorizing here, then I'd say that they would also have to be someone that she knew and was comfortable with.

They get her to meet at the office late on some pretense, then when she turns her back, they knock her out. They type and print the note, then position the body and stage the scene, making sure that her prints were everywhere they needed them to be. And finally, they give her the deadly injection and wipe everything down just in case." Jackson rubbed the back of his neck. "They didn't need us to buy it all. They just needed it to be compelling enough for a diversion, have us waste time with a possible suicide."

"Wouldn't they have to wait around to make sure that she was dead?" Jesse asked. "Like, what if the injection didn't kill her? She'd be able to identify her would-be killer, right?"

The doctor shook his head. "Doubtful she would have lived through the ordeal with the level of the drugs in her system."

"But even so, they could wait and make sure," Jackson said. "It was the middle of the night. They would have had all the time in the world."

After a moment, the sheriff nodded. "That scenario checks all my boxes. Now, how do we unravel it, prove it, and bring whoever did it to justice?"

Jackson shrugged. "By putting one foot in front of the other, working the case, following the evidence. And there's one more thing, Sheriff."

"What's that?"

"I would bet that whoever did this thinks they're the smartest person in the room wherever they go. That means it's only a matter of time before they find out that they're wrong."

≈

AFTER A LEISURELY LATE-MORNING BREAKFAST, and with the Manor's parlor all to themselves, Elise, Tina, and C.C. spent a couple of hours huddled together going over what Elise and Tina had learned from Jackson and Jim by comparing notes. Neither Elise nor Tina were satisfied with the boring financial information Tina had wheedled out of Jim the previous evening, or what Elise said Jackson had learned from Miller Hensen.

"I'm telling you, Jim was definitely holding something back," Tina said, jabbing a finger in Elise's direction. "That man has more tells than a rookie poker player, but no matter what I said or how I sweet-talked, he held firm. And that tells me it may be something big."

"Yeah, Jax has been more forthcoming with info here than he's ever been at home, which obviously has to do with Sheriff Masters being okay with him sharing bits of the case with me. Though Jax is not all that pleased about it, I have shared some things with him that have been helpful to the investigation, so it hasn't taken much prodding to get some details in return as the case has progressed. Unfortunately, my darling husband has very few tells and a pretty impressive poker face, but I could sense he was holding onto something as well."

"So, what do you think it is?" C.C. asked.

Elise shrugged. "Well, I'm waiting for the autopsy report on Rochelle Griffin's death. For a minute, I thought that's what Jax was holding onto, but I don't think that's something he would feel the need to keep from me. I mean, though he was fairly reluctant, he did tell me about Roger Thompsen's autopsy without too much push-back."

Elise looked up and smiled at the couple who'd just come into the parlor and sat down across the room on the sofa in front of the fireplace. She turned back to her friends and leaned in, keeping her voice low. "I mean, we'd already discussed the Griffin scene, and we were both on the same page about it being a homicide as opposed to a suicide, no matter what it looked like. So, I don't really know what the guys are holding back, but I agree with you, Tina. If they're not sharing, it has to be something significant. Maybe something the sheriff specifically told them not to share?"

Tina frowned. "I wonder what that could be."

"I don't know."

"So, what's the plan now?" C.C. asked.

"What do you mean?"

"Well, what do we do next?"

Elise laughed out loud. "I have no clue."

"Oh, come on, El. You always have a plan." Tina complained.

"Not right now, I don't. We'll just have to wait and see what's what later when the guys get back from the office. Maybe we'll find out then what they're hiding. Or maybe they'll have the autopsy results by then, which depending on what's found there, could open up a whole new area in the investigation."

Before they could get any further with their speculations, Madison and Miranda came into the room. The two had gone over to Murphey to pick up some things from Murphey Printing and Stationary for Madison, and Miranda had needed to stop by the Sheriff's Office.

"How was the trip to Murphey? Was it everything that you'd hoped it would be?" Elise asked with a cheesy grin.

"Ha-ha. You're so funny, El," Madison quipped. "The stationary shop was very well stocked, if you must know. They had some really great specialty cards and just what I was looking for in ledgers."

Elise rolled her eyes. "Geez, Maddy. Cards and ledgers? You lead such an exciting life."

"Bite me, El."

Elise giggled, then turned to Miranda. "And you? How did your visit go with the sheriff?"

Miranda plopped down in the wing chair across from C.C. and next to the settee Elise and Tina were occupying. A satisfied smirk eased across her face. "It was short and sweet. I need to go to the office at the winery, but I wanted to make sure it was okay. Masters gave me the go-ahead."

"Really?' Tina asked. "I figured the office, like the Torture Chamber, would be off limits as well, with the security video issue and all."

"Nope." Miranda shook her head. "Evidently, they've taken the security hardware or hard drive or whatever it is down to their lab. The specialist is working on it there, so the sheriff said I could go to the office but the Torture Chamber is still a no-go. To be honest, I don't think I'll go down to that room ever again." She gave an exaggerated shudder. "That scene is something I'll never get out of my head."

"I don't blame you," C.C. said.

"But here's some fun info," Miranda added. "The sheriff said that, come Monday morning, you four can go home."

"What?" Tina blurted. "Seriously? We finally get to go home?"

"Yep." Maddy replied with a grin. "And let me tell you, I am so ready. I almost wanted to give that man a big ole kiss. Plus, I've got so much work piling up at Lodge Merlot."

C.C. nodded. "I'm ready, too."

But Elise frowned. "What about you, Miranda?"

Miranda made a face. "Oh, no. Not me, and not our two fine Bastrop deputies. Evidently, we have to stay until the friggin' bitter end. And I don't know what's gonna happen if they don't solve Thompsen's murder."

"Wait, Jax and Jim have to stay, too?"

"Sad but true, darling."

"Oh, no." Elise shook her head. "Then I'm not going home, either. I've already told Jax that I'm not going anywhere without him. So, I guess I'll be staying as well."

"Good deal. At least I won't be alone." Miranda grinned. "And speaking of alone, you guys want to make a quick trip out to the winery with me? I really need to get some statistical documentation on last month's production from the office to put together a partial shareholder update, but with everything that's still up in the air—namely an unknown murderer still on the loose—I'd rather not go out there alone. Even in the daylight hours."

"Sorry, Miranda," Madison said. "I can't. I have some Lodge business to get done that requires a boatload of phone calls and some rescheduling. That's gonna take me a while."

"I'll go with you," Elise said. "I'd like to check some things that have been bothering me."

Tina sighed. "Okay. I'll go, too. It'll probably be the last time I'll ever get to see the castle winery, anyway. And yes, before y'all ask, I am going home on Monday, with or without Jim."

"I'm also in," C.C. piped up. "That is, as long as we stay away from the Torture Chamber. I'm with Miranda on that topic."

Miranda stood. "Alright, then. Let's get it done." Looking at her watch, she smiled. "Just cracking the one o'clock hour. By the time we get back, it will be zero wine-thirty."

"Five o'clock somewhere?" Tina laughed.

"You bet. Now, come on."

They all followed Miranda into the lobby where Madison said, '*Later*,' and headed up to her room. Miranda waited for the others to grab their coats and bags before they all headed out to the van.

"I really wish we could have enjoyed our quasi-vacation without a murder investigation ruining our time here." C.C. sighed. "This is a really beautiful part of the country."

"It really is," Elise agreed.

"Although, I could go for a bit warmer on the weather," Tina muttered.

"Don't be such a wuss, Tina," Miranda said. "That's what stylish jackets are for."

"Whatever."

Barely fifteen minutes later, Miranda was pulling the van into the parking lot at Bella Luna.

"Huh, that's interesting," she said. "That's Cara's car, and I do believe that's Todd Griffin's Porsche parked next to it."

"Did the sheriff say anything about them coming out here?" Elise asked.

"He did not. Which begs the question, did they ask for permission?" Miranda parked the van on the other side of Cara's sedan and shut down the engine. "I wonder what those crazy kids are up to out here. Let's go find out, shall we?"

The three of them climbed out of the van and walked up the stone steps to the massive, carved doors of the castle winery. Inside, the lobby was silent. Eerily so, thought Elise as they crossed the atrium and climbed the steps to the second floor where the office was located.

"Why does it suddenly seem so ... weirdly quiet," Tina asked under her breath, as if someone or something might overhear.

"I know. Right?" Elise replied just as quietly. "I was just thinking the same thing."

"I don't remember it feeling so ... well, creepy in here," C.C. whispered with a shudder.

"Don't be ridiculous, C.C.," Miranda hissed. But Elise noticed that she, too, kept her voice low. "Let's just get what I need and get out, okay?"

As they started down the long hallway toward the office, they suddenly became aware of voices emanating from that end of the corridor, voices raised in what sounded like an argument. Elise grabbed Miranda's arm, stopping her just outside the slightly open office door with Tina and C.C. close behind. She put her finger to her lips.

Miranda mouthed *Todd and Cara* with eyes wide.

From where they stood in the hallway, they could clearly hear every word being said, or in Cara's case, now hysterically shouted.

And what was being shouted was shocking.

17

A fter the meeting at the morgue, Sheriff Masters and the team went back to the office and spent the next hour trying to decide on a path forward in either investigation. To Jackson, over the last week it seemed as if it was a 'one step forward and three steps back' sort of deal.

While Griffin's death had been confirmed as a homicide as opposed to the suicide it had been staged to be, like the Thompsen scene, there was almost zero forensic evidence for them to go on. Whoever had killed Rochelle Griffin and set the scene had left no prints, no DNA, nothing. The only prints in and around her body were hers.

In the Thompsen case, although they'd found a bloody print on the inside of the Iron Maiden's door, probably where the killer had held the door when they'd opened or closed it, that print was more or less a smear made by someone wearing gloves. And the blood was Thompsen's, so not helpful there, either. They'd also recovered one other partial from the door frame between the Armory and the Torture Chamber that had obviously been missed by whoever had wiped down both rooms. Unfortunately, there wasn't enough of it to even run through the system.

So, again, unhelpful.

Standing in front of his updated murder board, Sheriff Masters shook his head. "Alright, let's go through this mess one more time." He pointed to the side of the board that now housed Griffin's sparsely documented case. "Our theory now is that both of these murders are connected, agreed?"

"Big coincidence if they're not linked," Jackson murmured. "And in homicide, I don't believe in coincidence. Plus, obviously the suicide note found at the Griffin scene connects the two."

"Yeah, that's how it's running for me as well. So, let's drill down on it a bit. If we follow that theory, that these two murders are connected, what are the similarities? The differences?"

"Well, with both, there's almost no forensic evidence. That's a similarity, right?" Jesse asked.

Masters turned to him. "It is indeed. What, if anything, does that tell us, deputy?"

Jesse frowned. "That the killer was careful, thorough? Maybe both were planned ahead of time?"

"The killer? So, you're saying that the same person killed both Griffin and Thompsen? And that they planned out each murder?"

"Um, yeah ... no ... well, maybe." The deputy sighed. "I don't know."

The sheriff shook his head. "We can't assume anything at this point, can we?"

"The lack of evidence at both scenes may be a similarity, but the differences show something else as well," Jim said.

Masters nodded at him. "Go on."

"At the Thompsen scene, we found the murder weapon and it was clear how the man died. The scene wasn't staged to look any certain way. The body was hidden inside the Iron Maiden and the area hastily wiped down, which says to me that the murder was unplanned with the killer or killers covering their tracks on the fly. Also, even with Thompsen's stature, to my mind, it's doubtful that one person could've wrestled him into that Iron Maiden by themselves, at least not without some difficulty." Jim pointed at the board. "The Griffin scene was staged to look like a suicide—and elaborately so—with Phenobarbital scattered around the body to suggest that it was the cause of death. Then we got the autopsy results telling us that cause of death was not the Pheno but fentanyl-laced heroin. No murder weapon—syringe or heroin—was found at the scene. The staging, including a suicide note conveniently printed on the vic's printer, says to me that the Griffin murder was planned out in advance and executed to that plan."

"Good." Masters looked around the room. "What else?"

"The vineyard clearly connects both victims," Jackson said. "Griffin, from what we've learned, was the architect of the original sale by shares and also the real estate agent for that sale. She and Thompsen worked together on Miller Hensen's behalf. Then, funded by Hensen, Thompsen bought the last eighteen percent of the shares available. Yet Hensen's company is the lien holder for those shares."

"Meaning?"

"Meaning that I think you were right all along, Sheriff," Jackson replied. "I think the vineyard is the lynch pin and may have been the catalyst for both homicides. Plus, as the suicide note left at the Griffin scene suggested, there's a possibility of the third murder attempt with Gene Rollins' car crash."

"Good point."

Jim shook his head and said out loud what Jackson had been thinking at the start of the conversation. "It just seems like we catch a break and move forward a step or two, then we stall out and lose ground." He waved his hand at the board again. "At this point, we've gathered all this information, have a good working theory, but can't prove any of it in any concrete way. And we still really have no idea how it all fits together or who killed either of the two vics. On top of that, we've pretty much run out of suspects."

"It does seem that way, doesn't it?" Jackson agreed.

Masters turned back to his board and the room went silent for a moment, a depressing pall settling over them. Jackson thought everyone was probably thinking the same thing. Where did they go from here?

"Maybe we go back, recheck those alibis and cross check them with whereabouts for the Griffin murder?" Jesse suggested in a hopeful tone.

"We could do that, but—" The sheriff's cell phone went off before he could complete his thought. He pulled it out of his pocket and answered. "Masters. Hey, Molly. What's up?"

Jackson watched the sheriff's expression go from a frown to raised eyebrows to a half-smile to a grin. Something was definitely up.

"Thanks, Molly," he said. "We'll be right down to the lab."

The sheriff hung up and stepped over to the conference table. Looking around at each of them, his grin widened. "What were you saying about catching a break and moving forward, Jim? That was Molly in IT. Seems that her specialist has recovered most of the video from the winery's security system hard drive. Anybody feel like taking a walk down to the IT lab to see what we have?"

Jesse whistled.

"Hell, yes!" Jim shouted, pumping a fist in the air. "Hopefully, this is the smoking gun we've been looking for, at least with the Thompsen case."

"Amen, brother," Jackson agreed with a smile.

Masters laughed out loud and pointed at Jim. "Yeah, buddy. One step at a time. Let's go."

The IT lab was located in an annex of the building that housed the Sheriff's Department, so it was only a short walk away. As the team followed Masters into the lab's outer office, Jackson tried not to get his hopes up, but couldn't help feeling like they might be about to get the big break they'd been waiting for.

The lab itself was separated from the office by a wall with large windows through which they could see a warren of cubicles and computer stations. Molly was standing next to a man working on one of the computers, and when she saw Masters and the group, she waved them in.

The computer tech was almost giddy as she greeted them. "Hey, Sheriff. This is Stanley Wallis, computer tech extraordinaire." The tech nodded over his shoulder, but his fingers kept moving over the keyboard. "Stan's just doing some last minute clean-up and fine tuning on the video, but he's gotten almost the whole thing back. It's amazing."

"Some of it isn't as clear as it would've originally been," Stanley said, his eyes never leaving the screen in front of him. "But I think it'll be plenty good for what you're looking for. Just give me a sec, and I'll cue it up for you."

The team waited in silence, tensions riding high, as Stanley's fingers flew over the keys. Finally, he hit enter ... and the video began to roll. Jackson could see that the tech had been right, the video was a little grainy. However, the fact that they had anything at all was a miracle.

"Okay, now there are eight cameras in total around the castle's perimeter, but I figured the two out front would be what you needed, so I worked those first. This feed is from the camera above the entrance. You can see a good portion of the parking lot and anyone coming or going through the main entrance area."

Jackson could see the timestamp at the bottom of the screen. "So, we're starting at ten fifty-five on the Friday night of the homicide?"

The tech nodded. "Nothing happens until eleven-eighteen, so I cued it up to that point." He fast-forwarded a few moments, and then returned to regular play as soon as a vehicle came into view in the parking lot. "And we have lift-off."

They watched as the small sedan crossed the lot and then pulled up in front of the castle and parked. After a moment, the driver climbed out of the car and stood looking around the darkened lot, as if making sure he was alone before heading for the castle entrance.

"Roger Thompsen," Jackson murmured.

"Yeah. Looking a mite skittish, too, like maybe he's up to no good?" Jim commented.

"He's in there for about thirty before the next arrival," Stanley said, fast forwarding again. He switched the feed to play as soon as the next vehicle, another small sedan, came into view in the lot.

"Well, well, well. Cara Thompsen," Masters said. "Come to find out what daddy's up to perhaps?"

On the video, the woman climbed out of her car with her phone to her ear and hurried to the building, disappearing inside.

"Yeah, and maybe calling for backup on her way?" Jackson added.

"Okay, another fast forward here. There's forty minutes or so before our next visitor," Stanley said, speeding up the feed to where a Porsche Boxster raced into the lot at a good clip and slid into the spot next to Cara's car.

They watched as Todd Griffin jumped out of his sports car and ran toward the castle entrance.

"Looks like we know who Cara was calling," Jim commented.

"Looks like. He's in a hurry, for sure," Jackson frowned. "Too bad there's no video inside the building, but the time stamp here is twelve thirty-two. That's within the window of Thompsen's TOD."

"There's nothing now until almost two." Stanley said, and skipped forward one last time to where two people emerged from the winery. Todd Griffin seemed to be steering, as well as half-carrying, a hysterical-looking Cara Thompsen toward her car.

As she turned to get into the vehicle, the sheriff said, "Freeze it there." As soon as Stanley obliged, the sheriff leaned in. "Is it possible to zoom in on her?"

"Yeah, some. Probably not a lot and it won't be crystal but let's see." Stanley did some fiddling, and the view did indeed zoom in closer.

"What does that look like to you?" The sheriff asked, pointing at the light-colored blouse Cara Thompsen was wearing. "Those dark patches?"

"Could be blood." Jim replied. "Hard to tell."

"Run it forward slowly," Masters said to Stanley, who complied.

As the video progressed at a crawl, Todd watched for a moment as Cara's little car zoomed away, and then he turned toward the building.

"Yeah, stop right there."

In the frozen frame, Griffin was caught clearly in the winery's flood lights as he was coming up the walkway, and he looked to have some of the same dark splotches on the front of his shirt as well.

"Okay, run it out."

Stanley returned the video to play as Todd continued into the building, and then he hit pause. Swiveling around in his chair, he looked at the sheriff. "There's nothing else, and the feed's done about fifteen minutes later."

"So, our buddy Todd is the one who wiped the video," Jackson said, then grinned at Stanley. "Or thought he had."

"Yeah, you can't be too careful when it comes to hard drives. So much stuff can be teased out of them when you least expect it," Stanley agreed with a grin of his own.

"Good work, Stanley," Masters said, clapping the man on the shoulder. "Thanks for your assist."

"You bet, Sheriff. My pleasure." He hooked a thumb in Molly's direction. "Plus, my pal Molly here roped me in with a bottle of twelve year old scotch as a bribe." The tech waggled his eyebrows at her.

Molly laughed. "A bribe well played, my dude."

"That it was."

The sheriff chuckled. "Good thinking, Molly. Stanley, do me a favor and make a second copy of that whole sequence ... just in case. Don't want to take a chance of losing it again."

"Way ahead of you, Sheriff. I'll send a copy to your office as well."

Jackson turned to the sheriff as a thought struck him. "Sheriff, do you think maybe we should tell Miranda to wait on her visit out to the winery until we can get a bead on both Todd and Cara? You know, just to be on the safe side? Hopefully, she hasn't left yet, but you never know how things are gonna play out, right?"

The sheriff nodded. "That's a good idea. I'll contact Judge Hawkins for the warrant when we get back to the office, but that will take some time. While we wait for that to come through, I'll have a couple of deputies work on running down the current locations for both Thompsen and Griffin. So, yeah, we should tell Mrs. Rollins to hold off."

"I'll give Elise a call and have her give Miranda a heads up." Pulling out his phone, he punched in Elise's number.

STANDING in the hallway outside the winery office, Elise couldn't believe what she was hearing. The argument had escalated, at least on Cara's side, and Todd seemed to desperately be trying to talk her down off the ledge.

"Babe, you have got to calm down. We're gonna get through this. I promise."

"But *how*?" the woman yelled. "They're digging, Todd."

"Yeah, that's their job, but they've got nothing. We scrubbed down both the Armory and the Torture Chamber, remember? And I wiped the security video right after I sent you home, so there's no way they can connect us to your dad's death."

"Really? You sure about that, ace?" Cara asked, her voice dripping with sarcasm.

The door to the office was slightly open, and though Elise itched to sneak a peek, she didn't dare.

"Look for yourself, Todd. They've taken the damn hard drive."

"So what? There's no way to restore the video."

Cara's harsh laughter rang out. "Don't be stupid, lover. They get some digital expert in to look at that hard drive, and you never know. But the terrifying specter of that possibility aside, you want to tell me how that bitch found out about what we did? I mean, if your ex dug it out, then what's to stop that country bumpkin of a sheriff from doing the same thing?"

"Cara, Rochelle didn't find out anything. I told you, in her snide way, she suggested that perhaps our alibi of being at my place all night was bogus and then accused me of maybe somehow being involved. But that didn't mean anything, babe, she was just guessing. Looking for something to trip me up, but I swear, she didn't get it from me."

"Okay, she may have been just guessing, but how did she figure that our alibi was bogus?"

"Who knows? I wouldn't put it past her to have been spying on me and just waiting to catch me on something, anything."

"But Todd, she threatened to go to the sheriff with what she knew," Cara shouted. "That doesn't say bluff to me."

"Calm down. Yes, she threatened with what she *supposedly* knew but, trust me, it *was* all just a bluff. She didn't know anything for sure. She had no proof. She'd been looking for payback since the divorce. Anyway, it's not an issue now, babe. I took care of it."

"Oh, yeah, right. You took care of it … with another murder. And why did you feel the need to do that if she didn't have any proof?"

"Look, I'm telling you that we don't have anything to worry about. I planned it all out. Actually, I'd been thinking about it for a while now. I wore gloves, and again, carefully wiped the office down after staging it to look like a suicide. And I printed out the note. Dear Rochelle took responsibility for everything, even Rollins' so-called accident."

At that little tidbit, Elise glanced at Miranda, who was staring at the door with a face drained of color. She could only imagine what her friend was thinking, but hoped she would hold it together for a few more minutes. She laid a hand on Miranda's arm. The woman looked over with fury in her eyes, but shook her head.

In the room, Cara was angry again. "That was just overkill, Todd. You just added more fuel to the fire in bringing the Rollins crash into it. And do you think they won't snap to the fact that Rochelle's death was murder and not a suicide? That's just ridiculous and cocky."

Todd laughed at that. "Of course they're going to snap to it once the autopsy results come back showing that it was a nasty cocktail of heroin and fentanyl and not her Phenobarbital that killed her. I would have loved to have left the syringe and the heroin, made it look like a real suicide, but that would have taken more time and been too risky. Too hard to make sure there were no prints or DNA other than hers. Plus, they may have been able to trace the dope, so yeah, too risky."

"And what happens when they get the autopsy results back, when they confirm it was murder? It will just compound this nightmare. I don't want to have to look over my shoulder waiting for someone to come knocking on my door for the rest of my days. I'll go insane."

"Like I said, they have nothing to go on, nothing to connect me … to connect *us* to either murder. As long as we keep our stories straight and stick to them, we're golden."

There was a pause in the conversation, and Rochelle looked at Miranda again. She mouthed, *They killed them both.*

Miranda nodded and mouthed back, *And possibly Gene. What now?*

Elise shrugged and then looked back at the terrified faces of Tina and C.C. as they stood frozen behind her and Miranda. She mimed that the three of them should go get help and waved them toward the stairs at the other end of the hallway, but Miranda shook her head again.

If you're staying, I'm staying, she mouthed just as Todd moved on to another subject.

"So, any luck with the vineyard deed for your dad's shares? Brian and Gabe don't have much interest in the vineyard, so you know your mom will turn the deed over to you if you ask for it."

"I haven't found anything yet, but I'm not so sure that Brian won't want a cut. You're right, Gabe has no interest, and he'll be heading back to L.A. as soon as he can. Right now, I have to be careful when I'm at the house. You know, I also worry about Hensen. He put up the money for the shares, so he or his company may have some claim. We won't know that until we find the deed."

"Well, we'll deal with that when we get to it."

Elise turned to the others and gestured that they should probably get out while they could, but it was bad timing, as rock and roll began to blare from her handbag. It was her cell phone ring tone. She dug for the phone like a maniac as she pointed to C.C. and Tina to get out fast.

They both turned and immediately headed for the stairs as fast and quietly as they could.

"Hey, who's out there," Cara yelled from inside the office.

Elise found her phone, and when she looked at the readout, saw Jackson's name. She hit answer and dropped the phone into her sweater pocket just as Cara Thompsen jerked the door open.

Hoping that Jackson was listening, Elise swallowed hard as Miranda stepped forward with a bright smile. "Hey, Cara. Bad timing?"

18

"Hello? El?" Jackson frowned. Though the call had stopped ringing, it hadn't gone to voicemail. He also knew that the line hadn't dropped because he could hear rustling sounds, but Elise hadn't said a word. Then he heard Miranda's voice.

And his blood ran cold.

"Hey, Cara. Bad timing?"

"What's the matter, Jax?" Jim asked.

Jackson put a finger to his lips before putting his phone on speaker and then muting their end. "I think Elise must have gone out to the winery with Miranda, and Cara's there."

"Uh-oh," Jim said. "That's not good." He put up a hand. "But then again, they can't know that the video's been recovered, and neither can Cara. So, let's not panic."

They all gathered around Jackson to listen to the conversation taking place on the other end of the call.

"Miranda? What are you doing here?" Cara asked; her surprise—and something more—evident in her tone.

Jackson thought that Miranda's answer came through smoothly enough with not even a hint of anything wrong. But if nothing was wrong, why was Elise's cell phone still live? And why wasn't she talking to him?

"Oh, you know," Miranda was saying. *"I have to put together a shareholder update and need last month's statistics. With everything that's happened, I'm behind."* She gave a throaty laugh. *"Shocking, I know. Sheriff Masters said that I could stop by and pick up what I needed, but I thought the winery was off limits. What are you doing out here? Oh, and with ... Todd Griffin, isn't it?"*

Jackson's eyes met Jim's. "Oh, no. Both Cara and Todd are out there. Elise and Miranda are in the line of fire, and they don't even know it."

Todd Griffin's deep voice came through the line.

"Yeah. That's me. I've heard your name a few times as well, but don't think that we've ever actually met."

"No." Miranda answered in a slow, southern drawl. *"I'm sure that I would have remembered."*

Jackson looked over at the sheriff. "We need to get out there now, before things go south. I mean, all it would take is one wrong word and this could be really bad."

"Absolutely." Masters nodded. "Keep that line open so we can monitor the situation. I'll call Judge Hawkins for the warrants on the way. Let's go." He turned to Molly and Stanley. "Good work, you two," he said before heading out to the cruiser with Jackson, Jim, and Jesse.

"*So, how long were you out there in the hallway?*" Cara was asking on the speaker, as Masters and the team hurried down the corridor toward the lobby and the parking lot beyond. "*And who is this with you?*"

Jackson's heart was racing. If something happened to Elise and Miranda before they could get out there, he would never forgive himself.

Another smooth answer came from Miranda. "*What do you mean? We just got here. And this is my friend Elise Beckett. Oh, geez, or are you going by Landry now? Elise Beckett Landry?*" Her deep, smoky laughter rang out again, and Jackson could hear Elise laughing with her in the background.

"*I think that I'm gonna hyphenate for now,*" Elise said.

"*Anyway,*" Miranda continued, but Cara cut in.

"*Wait, are you related to that Deputy Landry who's working with Sheriff Masters on my dad's murder?*"

"*Am now,*" Elise answered. "*We just got married. We're actually on our honeymoon.*"

"*Isn't that sweet. I bet you've heard all sorts of things about the investigation.*" Cara said.

"*Lord, no. I don't listen to half of what Jackson says about any of his investigations,*" Elisa replied in a vacant tone, the southern in her accent pronounced. "*Mostly, I find it all so distressing. The murders, the robberies, all that criminal activity. I don't want to hear about any of that. I mean, this is supposed to be my honeymoon, for the love of mud.*"

Jim laughed out loud as the team climbed into the cruiser. "Okay, now if that's not a sign that Elise knows exactly what's goin' on, I don't know what is. She's just playing for time, buddy. 'Cause that there was a bunch of hooey, if I've ever heard it. And she sounds like an airhead, which she most definitely is not."

"I just want them to get what they came for and get the hell out of there," Jackson replied.

"Let's just breathe, gentlemen," Masters said from the front of the cruiser with his phone to his ear before turning back to his call. "Judge Hawkins, this is Sheriff Masters."

Jesse was behind the wheel so that the sheriff could make his calls and then get the backup set in place, and he peeled out of the parking lot without the siren but with the cruiser's lights flashing. Jackson and Jim continued to monitor the conversation taking place in the winery office from the backseat of the cruiser.

"So, what are y'all doing out here, Cara?" Miranda asked again. *"You never said. Winery business for you, too?"*

"Mmm, this and that," Cara replied in a vague tone. *"The police made a major mess dusting for prints, so I thought I'd clean up a bit. Of course, they were probably only ever gonna find my prints anyway, since I'm the office manager. They took the hard drive for the security system, too, but they left the office laptop, so you can download or print last month's numbers for your reports. Anything else you think that you'll need?"*

"Nope, I think that's about it."

"I suppose you've both been interviewed by the sheriff over Cara's dad's homicide." Todd commented, out of the blue. *"I mean, because you were both part of the group that found him, right?"*

"Well, sure." Miranda replied. *"From what I know, they're not only investigating the homicide, but are also looking into the orig-*

inal sale of the vineyard. They seem to think that may have played a part in what's happening now. Did the sheriff tell you that too, Cara?"

"Oh, crap, Miranda," Jackson murmured. "Don't shake the hornet's nest until we can get there."

"Take it easy, buddy," Jim said. "Almost there."

"Less than ten minutes out," Jesse called from the driver's seat.

Jackson blew out a breath and tried to stay calm. "A lot can happen in ten minutes. Drive faster."

"Uh … yeah," Cara said over the speaker. "The sheriff mentioned to me that they were looking into the sale. I think he told Todd that as well."

"What? Why were you interviewed, Todd?" Miranda asked. *"Oh, wait, of course. Wasn't your wife the real estate agent for the original sale?"*

There was a momentary pause before Todd spoke.

"My ex-wife," he corrected in a terse tone.

"Well, then, that would make perfect sense that they would want to talk to you both, right?"

"I suppose, though I didn't have anything to do with the original sale. That was all Rochelle's gig."

Cara spoke up. *"Well, I just can't imagine how the sale could possibly have had any bearing on these recent events. I mean, that was so long ago."*

"Hold up. Did y'all say Rochelle? As in Rochelle Griffin?" Elise asked, sounding shocked. *"The woman that they just found a few days ago who'd committed suicide was your ex-wife? That whole thing sounded*

just awful. And the poor woman who found her? Why, I can't even imagine finding something like that."

From the tone of her voice, Jackson could almost see his wife's innocent, wide-eyed look in his mind. He'd seen it in person on more than one occasion. And it didn't bode well.

"Yes, she was my ex," Todd was saying. *"And yes, during my interview with the sheriff, we did discuss the vineyard. I didn't find out about Rochelle's suicide until later that afternoon. We had our differences, but it's still tragic when someone decides to take their own life."*

"It is, yes," Miranda agreed. *"When was the last time that you spoke with her? Was she troubled? Her suicide must have been a horrible surprise."*

"Again, Rochelle was my ex, and we didn't split on great terms, so I hadn't spoken with her for quite a while. Anyhow, I don't understand how life could get so bad that a person feels that suicide is the only way out, but then, I guess that everyone has their own demons to fight. Rochelle did have more than her share. That I can tell you for sure." There was another pause. *"So, why are you asking all these questions about Rochelle?"*

"Oh, no reason, really. Like you said, I just find it tragic when someone dies by their own hand."

"Come on, come on," Jackson muttered. "Quit yammering and get your damn numbers, Miranda, and then you and Elise need to get the hell out of there while you still can."

As if Miranda had heard him, she echoed his words.

"Anyhoo, I suppose I should get the numbers for last month, and then we can get out of y'all's hair so you can get back to doing ... whatever y'all were doing."

"No kidding," Jackson muttered as Jesse pulled the cruiser into the winery parking lot. "Get a move on, already."

"We're here, Jax. Not long now." Jim frowned. "Hey, look. There's Tina and C.C.."

The two women were standing next to Miranda's rented van and began frantically waving their arms in the air when they saw the cruiser pulling into the lot. Both Jackson and Jim were out of the vehicle almost before it came to a stop next to the van.

"Sweet Baby Jesus!" Tina cried and flung herself at Jim. "I am so glad to see you guys."

"You can say that again," C.C. added. "Miranda and Elise are still in there with two murderers!"

"Why didn't you call me?" Jim asked Tina.

Tina rolled her eyes and hooked a thumb toward the van. "C.C. and I both left our bags in the van because we weren't gonna be here long, and my cell is in my bag. Miranda locked the van when we headed into the winery, so when we came running out to call, I could see my damn bag but couldn't get to it."

"Oh, geez," Jim muttered.

"We're kinda in a hurry here, ladies, so could one of you please give us a brief rundown?" the sheriff asked. "Jackson is monitoring what's happening in there, and the warrants for Griffin and Thompsen just came through. Backup is on its way, but we need to know all the particulars before we head in there."

"Well, we rode out here with Miranda and Elise and overheard a crazy conversation from the hallway outside the winery office when we got upstairs," C.C. began. "Cara Thompsen and Todd Griffin were arguing. They were both involved with the murders of Roger Thompsen and Rochelle Griffin. Anyway, then Elise's cell phone went off and all hell broke loose." C.C. proceeded to give the sheriff a quick, succinct account of what they'd witnessed.

Then Jackson heard Todd Griffin's voice loud and clear over the cell phone speaker, and the man's question for Elise had Jackson's breath backing up in his chest.

"YOU KNOW WHAT, HANG ON A MINUTE," Todd said, and his eyes narrowed. "Mrs. Landry ... Elise ... I thought you said that you didn't pay much attention to your new husband's investigations."

"What?" Elise's pulse sped up, and she took a calming breath as she eased closer to the open doorway. "I-I don't. Why?"

"Well, you seem to know a bit about Rochelle's suicide, even that a 'woman' found her." Todd looked back and forth at her and Miranda, then wagged his finger at them. "In fact, this whole conversation feels just a little contrived, if you ask me. Exactly how long were you standing out there in the hallway eavesdropping on our conversation?"

"Eavesdropping? Don't be ridiculous." Miranda stepped around the desk, opened the office laptop, and fired it up. "I told you, Todd," she said nonchalantly. "We'd just gotten here when Elise's cell phone went off. Cara opened the door right after that, remember?"

"Sure, I remember," Todd said before turning back to Elise. "So, who was on the phone?"

"I beg your pardon?"

"Well, Cara and I heard the phone ring—excellent ringtone, by the way—but you weren't talking to anyone when she opened the door. In fact, you didn't even have a phone in your hand."

"Todd?" Cara began, but he put up a finger to silence her.

"Hang on a minute, babe. Elise?" he prompted. "Care to explain?"

Elise blinked a couple of times, her mind whirling. "I-I sent it to voicemail and put the phone in my bag right before she came to the door."

"Really? Show me."

"Todd, come on. What's this all about?" Miranda asked. "We just came up here to get—"

"Numbers for your shareholder reports, I know. And that may be what you intended, but I'd like Elise to show me her phone."

"This is just absurd." Miranda shook her head. "You know, you're beginning to sound a little paranoid."

"Maybe. And I will apologize for my paranoia once Elise shows me her phone."

Elise swallowed hard and opened her bag. She made a show of digging around, then looked up at Todd, watched the slow, evil smile that spread across his face.

"Aw, that is such a shame," he said and pulled a small handgun out of his jacket pocket. "But unfortunately, it's exactly what I was afraid of. You're both pretty good, I'll give you that."

"Todd! What are you doing?" Cara cried. "Don't make this worse than it already is."

"Yeah, what she said," Miranda murmured, the southern in her voice underscoring her disdain for the man. "What are you gonna do with that? Put down the damn gun before someone gets hurt. What do they say in those old movies? The jig is up?" She glanced at Elise as she discreetly slipped something into her coat pocket. "You know, I've never understood that phrase. What jig? Up where?"

"Shut up, both of you." Todd turned to Cara. "You know, if you wouldn't have been such a basket case that night, we wouldn't be in this mess at all."

When Miranda took a few steps around the end of the desk, Todd immediately swung the gun back in her direction. He gestured for her to move away from the desk and join Elise near the door.

"So, Elise, about your phone? Maybe in your pocket?" he asked. "Let's see, shall we?"

Elise slipped her hand into her sweater pocket and pulled out her cell phone.

"Ah, there it is. And oh, look. It seems to be connected." He frowned. "Slide it over here, please."

Elise bent over and slid the phone across the stone floor to him. She watched as he picked it up, and with a grin, hung up on Jackson.

"You know, that phone has been on and connected this whole time," Miranda said with a sigh. "Deputy Landry has heard every word."

Todd tilted his head. "So what?"

"So what?" Miranda asked with surprise. "Jackson has heard everything you've said."

"And what *everything* was that?"

"Well ... you and Cara admitted to killing her dad and your ex-wife."

"So, you were listening out there in the hallway before the phone rang," Cara said.

"Of course they were." Todd shook his head. "But let's clear up a few details. Cara killed her dad."

"Todd!" Cara shouted. "What the hell? It was practically self-defense, and at least it wasn't planned. You killed Rochelle, and it was premeditated. You planned out the whole damn thing, had been thinking about it for a while. Isn't that what you said?"

"And what about Gene's accident," Miranda asked quietly. "Did you kill my husband too? Mess with his car somehow?"

"Nah, that wasn't either one of us. I'm pretty sure that was orchestrated by Rochelle. Maybe it wasn't meant to kill him, but I really don't have any proof one way or the other. It may have been just another weird accident. Who knows? I just tagged it onto the suicide note for added confusion."

Cara grabbed Todd's arm. "What are you doing? You're telling them everything."

"Oh, chill out. They have no physical proof. It's our word against theirs." He grinned and waved Elise's phone. "Besides, our earlier conversation happened before Elise's phone even rang, so there's no record of it."

"However, Jackson would have definitely heard the part about you pulling that gun out of your pocket," Elise pointed out. "Just how stupid are you?"

"I'd say pretty dang stupid," Miranda drawled. "And what on earth are you going to do with that gun? You gonna add two more murders to your repertoire?"

"Shut up. What do you know?" Todd growled. "Just like Rochelle. Think you know everything. Well, I showed her in the end, just like I'll show you two."

"Seems like you just couldn't let go of the fact that your ex-wife shut you out of the vineyard deal," Elise murmured. "All that money she was going to rake in that she hadn't said a word about to you. Blackmailing her into a sweet divorce settlement wasn't the blow to her that you'd expected it to be, which was not enough for you, right? She needed to be completely destroyed for her sins?"

"I said shut up. She thought she was so smart. Greedy, manipulating bitch. She got hers, didn't she?"

Slowly, Miranda took Elise's arm and stepped back toward the open doorway, but Todd waved the gun at them. "Ah, ah, ah. We're not done here, ladies."

Miranda smiled. "Oh, I think that we just about are, considering that Sheriff Masters and his team recovered the video from the night of the murder and should probably be hitting the parking lot any time now."

"*What?*" Cara cried, her eyes going wide.

Todd frowned and shook off Cara's hand. "Again, chill, Cara. She's bluffing. I deleted the whole thing, remember?"

Miranda *tsked*. "You really should have just taken the security hard drive with you that night, you know? Leaving it for the techs to go through was a rookie move. It's amazing what they can recover these days."

"Todd, we have to go before the police get here," Cara shouted and grabbed his arm again.

And then everything seemed to happen at once. Distracted by Cara, Todd turned slightly, and Miranda pulled what looked like a large, round paperweight out of her pocket and, to Elise's amazement, did an incredible imitation of a pitcher on a baseball mound. She hurled the thing at Todd so fast that he had no time to react. Her aim just about perfect, it struck him smack dab in the middle of his forehead, the force of the impact knocking him backward. A shot rang out, and Elise literally felt something whistle by her left shoulder. The gun flew from Todd's hand as he went down over the small step stool that was right behind him, taking a stunned Cara down with him.

Miranda, moving at lightning speed, didn't waste any time. She grabbed Elise's hand and the two of them raced out into the corridor. However, instead of turning to the left and toward the way they'd come in, Elise was surprised when Miranda tugged her farther down the hall to the right.

"Where are we going?" Elise whispered.

"There's a back stairwell this way. It'll take us down to the fermentation room and then down another floor to the cellar. There are so many places to hide down there that he'll never find us."

They slipped down the back stairs as quickly and quietly as they could, listening for any sound of pursuit. When they got to the fermentation room, Elise stopped Miranda for a moment.

"Miranda, are you sure about this? Why don't we head out to the van? We could just drive away, right?"

Miranda shook her head. "My bag is sitting on the desk in the office. My keys are in the damn bag. Plus, that moron has got to know that the cavalry is on the way. If he has any brains at all, which at this point I find doubtful, he'll get into that fancy sports car of his and run."

"But what about Tina and C.C.? We can't just leave them."

"Hopefully, they've called for help by now, but we can't worry about that right now. I just hope that that paperweight did some damage. It had some pretty good weight to it."

"I gotta say, that was an amazing shot. Where did you learn to throw like that?"

"I played my share of softball in my younger years, and I was pretty good."

"And how did you know that the guys have recovered the wiped security video? Jax didn't say anything to me about it."

Miranda grinned. "I didn't. I was bluffin', but it bought me some time to throw my fast ball." She grabbed Elise's hand again and headed for another flight of stone steps. "Now, come on. No more yammering. I know where there's another phone downstairs. We can do our own calling, but we need to be quick about it."

19

B ackup arrived before C.C. and Tina had finished their harrowing tale of events, and Sheriff Masters quickly barked out orders to the entire team. With the immense size of the castle and its numerous entrances, along with the group of just fifteen extra officers, there was no way they could cover every contingency. So, the team was split up into two groups, the smaller of which was positioned in the parking lot to keep an eye on both Griffin's and Thompsen's vehicles in case they tried to run. The sheriff had one of the officers take C.C. and Tina back to the station to wait and to keep them out of harm's way.

"Now, remember, stealth and vigilance, people," Masters told the rest of the officers. "We don't know what's going on in there, but what we do know is that there are not only the two murder suspects but at least two innocent civilians inside. We proceed as quietly as possible until details of the situation we're dealing with can be determined."

Almost to punctuate the uncertainty and possible danger the

situation presented, the sound of a distant *crack* caught their attention.

"What was that?" Jim shouted. "Was that a backfire? Or a gun shot?"

"Not a backfire," Jackson said, his heart beginning to pound. "And that sounded like it came from the winery."

Masters put up a hand to stem the rising speculative chatter from the group. "That's enough. Quiet down now. Let's not get ahead of ourselves. Like I said, we don't know exactly what we're dealing with here, so the plan doesn't change. We're going into that winery using our heads and common sense. Now, let's go."

With weapons drawn, the sheriff then led the rest of the team up the stone steps of the main entrance and through the massive oak doors. The last bit of conversation they'd heard from Elise's cell phone before the line had gone dead played over and over in Jackson's mind as they entered the lobby. Griffin, holding Elise and Miranda at gunpoint and demanding that Elise slide her cell phone to him. The helpless feeling of hearing the deafening click of disconnection from his only lifeline to his wife had made his stomach churn as they'd sped toward the winery. Now, with possible gunfire being heard, Jackson anxiously listened for any sounds that would indicate where Elise and Miranda were located and if they were unharmed.

When they crossed the lobby to the staircase leading to the second floor where the office was situated, Masters motioned with hand signals toward the corridor to the left, and several officers broke off, advancing in that direction on high alert.

"Okay, we're going up," Masters said softly to the rest of the team. "Again, quiet. With eyes wide open. Got it?"

As they followed Masters up to the second floor, the eerie silence only served to increase Jackson's concern for Elise and Miranda. Where were they? And on the heels of that thought, something new caught his attention. It was coming from somewhere up ahead. Was that an urgent voice? And ... moaning?

Masters turned to him and nodded toward the end of the corridor. "Sounds like it's coming from the office."

All sorts of scenarios ran through Jackson's mind but he worked to stifle his panic. Though his instinct was to race down the hall and find Elise, Jackson held onto his impatience as they cautiously made their way to the office door at the other end, checking every nook and cranny of the hallway as they went. When they reached the open door of the office, the sheriff put up a fist to halt the group where they stood. From there, they could clearly hear Cara Thompsen's hysterical voice.

"Please, Todd. You have to get up. We have to go."

There was more moaning before, "What's going on? What happened?" Griffin asked in a groggy voice.

"The Rollins woman threw that paperweight at you, hit you in the forehead, remember? I think it knocked you out for a few minutes."

There was another moan. "That bitch. Where did they go?"

"Who knows. They just ran out of here. God, you're bleeding all over the place, but we have to go. The police may be here any minute. Come on, *get up.*"

"You have to help me, babe. My vision is blurry and my head is throbbing, but we have to find those women before they get away."

At that, Masters stepped into the room, his weapon trained at the two people on the floor. "I wouldn't bother getting up, Mr. Griffin. You have bigger problems right now, so you probably should just stay right where you are ... and I'd appreciate it if you'd show me your hands."

"Don't shoot," Cara begged. "Please. Todd's hurt. Please don't shoot."

"Where's the gun?"

"What?"

"The gun, Ms. Thompsen? He was holding Mrs. Landry and Mrs. Rollins at gunpoint. What did he do with the gun?"

"I-I don't know." Cara looked around in confusion. "It was an accident. Really. He didn't mean it."

"Shut up, Cara," Griffin mumbled.

"Look, it just went off and flew out of his hand when he got hit with *that*." Cara pointed to the fist-sized, glass paperweight laying beneath the desk to her right. "The gunshot was so loud, my ears are still ringing, but it was an accident. He wasn't shooting at anybody."

Jackson stepped around Masters. "Was anyone hit when the gun went off? Where are Elise and Miranda?"

"I don't *know*. They just ran." Cara cried. "The bullet went wild. I don't think it hit either of them. Please, Todd needs help, an ambulance ... or maybe the hospital. He may have a concussion or worse. He doesn't sound right."

"I'm fine, dammit. Don't be so melodramatic," Griffin assured her, slapping away her hands and smearing the blood running down his face. But his words were slightly slurred.

The sheriff nodded. "We'll get him assistance, but until we locate the gun, both of you need to stay right where you are," the sheriff told her as Jesse moved cautiously around the room to find the weapon.

"Got it, Sheriff," the deputy called out after a few moments, as he bagged the hand gun from where it had landed in the corner next to a filing cabinet. He did the same with the paperweight he retrieved from underneath the desk.

Since he wasn't sure what Griffin had done with Elises's cell phone, Jackson pulled out his own phone and dialed Miranda's number. In the next moment, there was ringing from the desk area. Crossing to it, he realized that the ringing was coming from inside the purse sitting on the desk next to the computer. He hung up and looked at Masters.

"This must be Miranda's purse. So, neither she nor Elise has a phone on them."

"We'll find them, Jackson," the sheriff replied. "We can surmise that they're unharmed because they ran. So, they're probably hiding somewhere in this labyrinth of a castle. It may take us a while, but we'll find them, so just hang tight."

With that, Masters pulled out his phone and called for an ambulance. While they waited, he also executed the warrants and read both Griffin and Thompsen their rights. Thompsen was handcuffed and taken, sobbing, to a cruiser for transport to the station for booking, and Elise's cell phone was retrieved from Griffin, who'd stuck it in his jacket pocket when he'd pulled out the gun. Ten minutes later, the ambulance arrived. The EMTs checked Griffin out and felt that he should be taken to the hospital for further testing. The sheriff sent two deputies along with them with orders to keep a close eye on the man, and once released from the emergency room, to transfer him directly to the station to be booked as well.

They followed the EMTs—with Griffin on a gurney—out into the hallway, and once they'd disappeared from sight, the sheriff took out his radio. "Attention all teams. Suspects have been apprehended and are being removed from the building. All teams report to the parking lot. I repeat, all teams stand down and report to the parking lot." He turned to Jackson. "Okay, that was more anti-climactic then I thought it might be, not that I'm complaining. So, now let's go find your wife and Mrs. Rollins."

However, the moment the words were out of his mouth, his cell phone began to ring. "Masters," he answered. As a smile spread across his face, he glanced at Jackson. "Is that right? Well, put her through." There was a brief pause, then the sheriff continued. "This is Sheriff Masters. Yes, Mrs. Rollins, I can hear you loud and clear. We were just coming to look for you. Are you and Mrs. Landry alright? Unharmed?" There was another pause before, "That's good to hear." Then his smile grew into a grin, and he winked at Jackson. "Yes, ma'am, *that crazy SOB* has been apprehended and is now in custody. So, you and Mrs. Landry come on out of your hiding place. We'll meet you in the lobby. What was that? Yes, Ma'am, we'll bring your bag and Mrs. Landry's cell phone with us."

When Masters hung up, he clapped Jackson on the back. "Well, that didn't take long at all, either. Seems that Mrs. Rollins found another phone in the building somewhere and called 911. So, an uneventful arrest of suspects, and civilians found quickly and unharmed. Just how I like it. What's that old saying? All's well that ends well?"

"Works for me, Sheriff," Jackson said as they headed for the stairs. "Uneventful definitely works for me."

They only had to wait in the lobby a couple of minutes before Elise and Miranda came hurrying out of the corridor to the left from the other side of the winery. Elise made a beeline to Jackson the minute their eyes met, and she practically launched herself at him. He held on tight for a moment letting the fear and anxiety finally melt away, and giving a silent thank you to the Big Guy upstairs that she was in his arms and unharmed.

When he leaned back, he smiled down at her. "Hey, pal. How ya doin'?"

She smiled back, blew out a breath, and raised a shaky hand to his cheek. "Much better now, though it was pretty dicey for a few minutes there. So, y'all were listening, right?"

He took her hand and kissed her palm. "Yes, darlin', we were listening. That is, right up to the point when the line went dead and my heart just about stopped. That was just after we'd gotten to the parking lot and heard from C.C. and Tina what had happened prior to my phone call. I couldn't wait to get in here to find you. By the way, leaving that line open was smart thinking on your part, love."

"Yeah, well, it was a close thing. One minute the four of us were standing in the hallway listening to the unbelievable conversation that Cara and Todd were having inside the office, and the next, my cell phone was blaring from my bag. I had maybe ten seconds to shoo C.C. and Tina back downstairs and dig in my purse for the damn thing. I'd barely switched it on and shoved it into my sweater pocket when Cara jerked open the door." She shook her head. "I just wish you could've heard the conversation they were having before you called, wish we had a recording of that."

"No worries, like I said, we got the highlights of it from Tina and C.C., and we'll get everyone's statements when we get back to the station. Besides, we'd just finished watching the recovered security video incriminating both Cara and Todd in Roger Thompsen's death. That's when I thought to call you to have Miranda wait to come out to the winery until we could nail down a location on them both."

"Wait—*what*? You recovered the video?" Elise laughed out loud. "Hey, Miranda, did you hear that? They actually did recover the security video."

"What can I say?" Miranda replied with a shrug. "I guess I'm just that good. Now, can we get the hell out of here. I've had just about enough of all this craziness. I don't think I can take anymore today."

The sheriff handed Miranda her bag and nodded. "We can indeed. Unfortunately, we'll need to get everyone's statements at the station first. Your friends are already there and waiting for us."

"I don't care where we go, Sheriff," Miranda murmured. "I'm just done bein' here."

THEY SPENT the next couple of hours at the Sheriff's Department, going over the events at the winery. Tina and C.C. had already given statements by the time they'd arrived, so Elise and Miranda added theirs to the mix. Elise had gone into the interview room first, going over everything that they'd heard from the hallway before her cell phone had given away their presence, and then everything that had happened afterward.

"So, Cara Thompsen killed her father, and Todd Griffin killed his ex-wife?" Masters asked.

"Yes, Todd confirmed it all," she replied. "But the way Cara told it, killing her dad was self-defense and hadn't been planned. It sounded like it had happened in the heat of the moment, but that's just my take on what I heard. However, Todd admitted to planning out Rochelle Griffin's murder in advance, said that he'd been thinking about it for some time. He'd always intended to make it look like a suicide, even lamented the fact that he'd been unable to leave the heroin and syringe at the scene because it would have been too risky, too easy to trace."

"So, he used her prescription of Phenobarbital instead, knowing that we would eventually find out from the autopsy that it wasn't actually the cause of death, and that we would know at that point that it wasn't a suicide."

"Correct, but that didn't seem to bother him at all. He was almost cocky about it, so sure that he'd executed the perfect murder, that there was nothing to connect him to the scene."

"And the Thompsen homicide? We know from the recovered security video that Cara followed her father into the winery. It looked like she may have been calling Todd when she got there, but he didn't show up until about forty minutes later. They were inside for almost an hour and a half before they emerged and he sent her on her way. After she was gone, he went back inside. Fifteen minutes later, the video went black. So he had to have been the one to wipe the video ... or at least, thought that he had."

"That tracks," Elise said. "Todd did say that they had wiped down both the Armory and the Torture Chamber before he'd sent Cara home. Then he'd gone back in to take care of the security video. He was pretty shocked when Miranda told him that y'all had recovered the video, thought she was bluffing. So did she, for that matter. But as it turns out, though she didn't know it at the time, it wasn't actually the bluff that she thought it was."

"Yeah, that was some coincidence. It'll be another shock for him when it's introduced as evidence at trial."

"It's all just so awful." Elise frowned and shook her head. "You know, Rochelle Griffin's murder was obviously Todd's retribution for perceived wrongs, but even though Roger Thompsen's death was unplanned, I think Todd and Cara were hoping to get their hands on the vineyard shares that her dad had been able to purchase. I know that they were actively looking for the deed." She shook her head again. "Poor thing. Cara knew that Miller Henson had put up the money for the purchase but didn't realize that Henson's company was the lien holder for those shares."

"Yes, that would have been another shock for them both, had they gotten wind of it."

Elise leaned back in her chair and sighed. "Anyway, like I said, Todd had been planning to kill his ex-wife since the divorce. Besting her with blackmail for a sweet divorce settlement evidently wasn't enough for him."

Masters made a few more notes on his pad. "He definitely does not seem like the type to enjoy being bested by anyone, let alone an ex-wife."

"No, sir. I told Jackson that very thing the night before Todd's interview with you. Everything I'd heard about the man suggested that he was not a nice person, that he was vindictive and mean. So, I'm not surprised that this is how it all ended. However, I am a bit surprised that it ended without more drama and violence." Elise paused before carefully bringing up a sensitive subject. "Sheriff ... I know that you'd also looked into Gene Rollins' death and found some anomalies."

Masters nodded. "I looked. Unfortunately, while I found ... more unanswered questions, there is no proof to support any theories or changes to the final conclusions about the accident."

"The suicide note that Todd left suggested that Rochelle had orchestrated Gene's crash."

"Yes."

"Well, Todd did confirm that, while it definitely had been his theory, he had no evidence one way or another, that it just could have been the accident that it was determined to be."

The sheriff made a few more notes. "That is good to know. For Mrs. Rollins' sake, I do wish that we could say conclusively one way or another. Unfortunately, with so much time passing and any physical evidence no longer available, we'll just never know for sure."

Elise smiled. "I'm aware of that, and though Miranda was standing next to me in the hallway and heard what Todd said, she understands that too. She's aware that there's really nothing else you can do."

"I wish there was something. I really do." The sheriff checked his notes and then closed the folder. He gave her a brief nod. "So, I think we're done here unless there's anything else you want to add."

"No, that's about it. If you have any other questions, please let me know."

Masters laid his pen on top of the folder and leaned in. "I will definitely do that, but you do realize that there's a very good chance the you'll be called on to testify at some point in the future ... when this goes to trial, right? You may all be called."

"Absolutely. Guess there may be another trip to the northwest in our futures."

They stood, and the sheriff came around to her side of the table and held out his hand. When she took it, he gave her a warm look.

"Elise, I would just like to say what a pleasure it's been to meet you. Jackson is a fine law enforcement officer, but he is damn lucky to have snagged a sharp, intelligent, and beautiful partner in you."

She laughed out loud. "I will not disagree with that statement, Sheriff."

"I'm grateful for all the information you passed on and your assistance, however covert, in closing these cases. If you and Jackson ever decide to try someplace new, there's a position on my team awaiting him, and I would consider offering you a civilian consultant employment opportunity as well."

The last part of his statement was said tongue-in-cheek, but Elise found the sentiment lovely.

"That's very kind of you, Sheriff. However, I'm ready to go home to River Bend and get back to minding my grapes. It was a pleasure to meet you."

"Jesse will show you out to the lobby and bring Mrs. Rollins in for her statement."

Out in the lobby, Elise sat down in the hard, plastic chair next to Jackson and watched Miranda saunter down the hallway toward Interview Room A.

Elise reached over and took Jackson's hand for the warmth, for the simple comforting touch, for the connection.

He looked down at their entwined fingers, then his deep green eyes found hers. "You okay?"

She nodded. "I am now. It has been a day, hasn't it? However, I gotta tell you, I am so ready to go home."

Jackson laughed. "I have to say that I agree. Miranda's gonna put in a call to her travel agent once we get back to the Manor. She's gonna get us all on a plane back to Delphine pronto."

"That sounds good. Real good."

"Did the sheriff bring up the possibility of coming back to testify?"

She glanced over at him. "He did, but I am not gonna dwell on that until it actually happens. We need to call Mom when we get back to the room, let her know that we're finally done here and will coming be home in a day or two."

"You bet. I'm looking forward to some peace and quiet."

"Jackson Landry, what is wrong with you? Don't go puttin' that out there. The universe is a snarky thing, my friend, and that's a sure-fire way to bring on trouble."

He laughed again. "Sorry, love. I'll keep that in mind."

They only had to wait another twenty minutes or so before Miranda came strolling back out to the lobby with her arm through Jesse's and a megawatt grin for the young deputy.

"Are y'all ready to go?" she asked in a sultry drawl as she turned to the group. "I'm ready. I can definitely tell ya that, so this van is heading out. I need a drink, and I am not talking about a girly glass of wine. I want something with a little more juice. Who's with me? Can I get an amen?"

As if on cue, Jim, Tina, C.C., Elise, and Jackson all nearly shouted the affirmation as one.

"I am all in. Let's go back to the cubby bar and regale Maddy with our harrowing tale of all the fun that she missed out on this afternoon," C.C. suggested.

With another round of amens, the group headed out to the parking lot where the van waited.

With Miranda driving at break-neck speed, it was just going on five o'clock when they finally got back to Riverside Manor where Madison was waiting in the parlor.

"What the heck took you guys so long?" She complained when they all trouped into the room. "I thought you were just going out to the winery to pick up some paperwork."

"That was the plan," Miranda said, pulling Madison up out of her chair and slinging an arm around her shoulder as she herded her toward the cubby bar with the rest of the group following along. "Unfortunately, a couple of murdering numb-skulls interrupted those plans."

"What?" Madison gave Miranda a wide-eyed stare.

But Miranda shook her head. "I need a drink first, so the expla-nation is going to have to wait until I have one in my hand."

When they'd gotten seated with drinks all around, Madison

finally turned to Miranda. "Okay, let's hear it. What was this about murderers?"

Miranda took a sip of her bourbon and then pointed at Elise. "You tell her the tale of how we solved two murders this afternoon."

"Now, that's not exactly true," Jim began, but Miranda cut him off.

"Zip it, Lawman. Y'all may have figured out the first murder at the eleventh hour with the help of the recovered security video, but *we* got the goods on both murders in about forty-five minutes." She turned back to Elise with a nod. "Proceed."

Elise giggled at the look on Jim's face, but started at the beginning and walked her sister through the crazy events of their afternoon. When she'd finished, Madison just stared at her for a moment, then shook her head.

"You know, I don't get it, El. Are you simply incapable of staying out of trouble? I mean, it's like murder just follows you around like a black cloud."

"That is so not true." Elise frowned at her sister. "And this had nothing to do with me."

However, Madison wasn't having it and pointed at Jackson. "And you? What were you doing during this whole debacle?"

Jackson gave Madison a lazy grin and, sitting back, laid his arm around Elise's shoulders. "Along with the team, I was being an incredibly handsome, amazingly smart lawman. Did you not hear how we swooped in at the end and saved the day?"

"Oh, brother," Madison muttered.

The entire group erupted in laughter, and after a few moments, Madison joined in with another shake of her head. "Well, all I know is that Gram is gonna have a few things to say about this, for sure. I can't wait for that."

"I will agree that it has been a helluva way to spend our honeymoon," Jackson replied. "I'm looking forward to getting home."

Miranda stretched and stood. "And speaking of, I'm with you, Jax. I'm gonna go up to my room right now and give my travel agent a shout. I won't be able to go home with y'all quite yet, as I still have a few loose threads to tie up here, but we'll see if we can get the rest of you on a plane home PDQ."

Elise watched her friend leave the bar, then turned to the group. "Knowing Miranda, she'll have us on a flight back home by tomorrow. So, how about one last dinner together in the dining room here at the Manor to celebrate before making an early night of it?"

"I'm up for it," C.C. agreed.

"Me too," Madison chimed in.

Tina nodded. "Jim and I are all for it. What about Miranda?"

Elise smiled. "I'll let her know. Meet in the dining room in an hour or so?"

With the plan set, the group left the little cubby bar for the last time and started up to their rooms to prepare for a final dinner.

20

The next morning, Elise rolled over and found the other side of the bed empty. A glance at the digital clock on the nightstand told her that it was just shy of seven o'clock. Though early for her, Jackson was always an early riser whether he was working or not, but as she often thought, she preferred waking up with him.

Just as she sat up in bed and looked around the room, the door to the bathroom opened and Jackson came out wearing a pair of jeans and shrugging into a pale green, button-down shirt. His hair was damp from his shower and he was barefoot. The very sight of him made Elise's pulse jump.

Mmm, Mmm, Mmm, she thought, and gave him a sleepy grin.

"Mornin', darlin'," he greeted her and came around the bed for a kiss. "It's still early. You ready to get some breakfast? Jim and I have to go over to the office for a bit. Masters wants us to sit in for the interview when he talks to Cara Thompsen later this morning."

Elise frowned. "Does she have representation? I mean, I know she killed her dad and all, but it sounded like it was in the heat of a nasty fight. You know, spur of the moment? And Miranda did say that she and her dad had a terrible relationship for most of her life, which after seeing the man with my own eyes, I can understand why."

"That all may be true, darlin', but don't forget, no matter how it happened, she called Griffin and together they stuffed her daddy's body into that Iron Maiden. Then they wiped the place down, and Griffin tried to destroy the security video."

"I know, I know. It's just ... well, I can't help feeling bad for her. She's smart and ambitious. She was on a good path, right? She had everything going for her, and then she threw it all away in a moment of rage. It's just sad, you know?"

"It is that," Jackson agreed.

"Are y'all gonna talk with Todd as well?"

Jackson shrugged. "I don't know. Griffin has a concussion. They gave him a scan but don't think there's anything to worry about there. Guess Miranda's paperweight hardball scrambled his noggin pretty good, though. They kept him overnight at the hospital for observation, just to be on the safe side. He lawyered up almost immediately, so I don't know if the sheriff will talk to him or not. More than likely, it won't be until after we're long gone, if he does."

Elise shook her head. "While I feel bad for Cara and the decisions she made that brought her to this point, I have zero sympathy for Todd Griffin and hope they throw the proverbial book at him."

"Oh, there's no doubt about that. The man was an accessory to murder, helped to hide that murder, and then planned and implemented the murder of his ex-wife on top of it all. I think that constitutes throwing said book."

Elise laughed and pulled him in for another kiss. "I just love it when you talk that way."

"Well, there's more where that came from, darlin'." He slipped a stray lock of hair behind her ear. "You gonna come down with me? Or are you gonna lounge around and come down later? Miranda's travel gal got us all booked out on a red-eye flight late tonight. And first class into Austin to boot."

"Oooh, first class? All of us?"

"Yeah, well, I think Miranda was just grateful that we were all here when this whole thing went sideways. I guess the flight makes a couple of stops and gets into Austin at, like, six a.m. So, I'll take first class for that as I intend to sleep the whole way."

She stifled a yawn. "Yeah, I agree, but I think I'll hang back here this morning and lounge for a bit longer, then give mom a call with a heads up about our travel plans. I'll get around after that, get us mostly packed up and ready to go. We can pack up the car later when you're done at the office."

"Sounds good." He got up and rounded the bed, grabbing his boots as he went. "I'm thinkin' that maybe we all head over to the valley early and find us a really good restaurant somewhere near the airport for dinner."

"I think we could drop off the rental car and find a good restaurant *at* the airport. These days there's always one or two," she replied, watching him don his boots and then grab his wallet and keys from the dresser.

"Maybe so."

"But we can figure that out later. We've got time."

"I will leave that up to y'all." He came back over and gave her another quick kiss. "Take care of you," he murmured against her lips. And then he was gone.

Elise stretched and thought briefly about laying back down for an hour or so, but in the end got up and hit the shower. It was just clearing the ten o'clock hour when she got down to the dining room where she found Madison and Miranda sitting at a big, round table for five at the window. Madison had her humongous event binder open on the table in front of her and looked to be working on some kind of party theme. Miranda had papers strewn over a quarter of her space and was furiously working on her laptop.

"Hey, y'all. Whatcha up to?" Elise asked as she sat down with her coffee on the other side of the table.

Miranda growled. "I ran over to the winery at the crack of dawn this morning to retrieve those stats that we went over there to get yesterday. I need to get these shareholder reports out to the Morans. I wasn't kidding when I told Cara that I was late with them."

"And you, dear sister? What are you cooking up over there?"

Madison looked up. "The Grundy's fiftieth wedding anniversary party. Their daughter, Mena, is the one in charge, and boy, is she a piece of work. I swear, she has something that she wants to change almost daily, and we're just about two months out. We need to lock it all down within the next week or so, and I'm putting my foot down if she makes one more noise about changes." She sighed. "I'm just finishing up the template for the third, and *final* revision for the invitations as they have to be in the mail within the next two weeks. People make plans these days so far out that invitations for these kinds of events need at least a month's lead time."

"Well, looks like you're on it, Maddy," Elise said with a wink. "You always are."

"Saw Jax and Jim earlier," Miranda said drinking down the last of her coffee and giving the coffee station a glance filled with longing. Then she shook her head and set the mug down on the table. "Guess they had to go back over to the Sheriff's Office one more time, huh?."

Elise nodded. "Yeah, Sheriff Masters asked them to sit in for the interview with Cara Thompsen, so they shouldn't be gone all that long."

"I would imagine not, since she and Todd confessed to their respectively committed homicides," Miranda drawled.

"They took Todd to the hospital and held him overnight for observation after your fast ball just about knocked his block off." Elise laughed.

Miranda finally cracked a grin. "Yeah, Jax told me. Warmed the cockles of my frozen heart to hear that."

"Unfortunately, he lawyered up directly after, so Jax said he wasn't sure if Sheriff Masters will interview him before we leave, which is fine by me."

"That lame brain can stonewall and grandstand all he wants, but it won't change the facts, and it'll be a harsh reality for him once it goes to trial." Miranda shook her head. "And though I'm not looking forward to it, I hear that we all may be called back to testify at some point."

"True. But I'm hoping he'll finally just take a plea and put us all out of our misery before that happens." Elise gestured with her mug. "And I refuse to worry about that prospect until we get the call sayin' it's a go."

"Well, I seriously hope that creep doesn't find a way to weasel out of it in the end," Madison grumbled. "I hope they put him away for a very long time."

"Amen, Maddy," Miranda said with a nod.

"As for today," Elise began, changing the depressing subject. "Since we don't fly out until late tonight, there's plenty of time for us to get ready to go. I'm just sorry that you aren't coming home with us, Miranda."

"I know," Miranda muttered. "But I've got some things with the winery that I have to take care of before I can head back to Texas. I also need to get with the Morans about finding an office manager to take over Cara's job. They live in Eugene and so aren't close enough to handle day-to-day operations, either. We need someone in the area."

Madison frowned. "What about Brian Thompsen? He works for the vineyard, right? Or maybe Adrianna Santoro, since her daddy was the original winemaker."

"Adrianna seems like a perfect solution, especially since she's marrying the current winemaker in a few months," Elise agreed. "And since they are also gonna receive the majority share of the vineyard at that time."

"Wait—*what?*" Madison turned to Miranda with a surprised look. "Are you giving them your shares?"

Elise winced. "Oh, sorry, Miranda. I didn't mean to spill the beans."

Miranda waved away her concern. "Don't worry about it, El. It's not public knowledge yet, but I've already told the happy couple that I was passing it on to them as a wedding gift."

"Well, I think that's just lovely, Miranda," Madison said.

Miranda shrugged. "It's the right thing to do and what Gene would have wanted. Besides, I don't have the energy or the bandwidth for the damn thing. And you're right, El. Nico and Adrianna love the vineyard and will take good care of it. It's a nice legacy for both Gene and Dario."

"It is that."

"So, what's on your agenda today? C.C. and Tina went over to Murphey shopping, for God's sake." Miranda shook her head. "Shopping," she repeated with disgust. "In *Murphey*."

Elise laughed at the look on her friend's face. "Well, to each her own, I guess."

"Whatever."

"I don't have any specific plans for today. I did call mom to let her know we'll be heading home tonight." She glanced at Madison. "Family dinner tomorrow afternoon. Gram's cooking her world famous pot roast."

"Oooh, yummy." Madison waggled her eyebrows.

"Anyway, we'll have time to unpack and rest up beforehand. I'm gonna head back upstairs in a bit and get us packed up, so that when Jax gets back, we can take off. He wants us all to have a nice dinner somewhere close to the airport. Can you come with, Miranda?"

With a sigh, Miranda nodded. "I suppose. Don't have anything else to do tonight. I know a pretty good steak house in the area, so I can make reservations for us."

Elise grinned. "Excellent. One more thing off of my plate. So, I should grab a quick bite now and then go get the packing up started."

THE INTERVIEW with Cara Thompsen was a fairly short and terribly sad affair. In the space of thirty minutes, she's gone from wild-eyed denial to weepy admission of guilt to full-on hysterical regret. She swore that though the confrontation with her father that night had started as an argument, he'd pursued her into the Torture Chamber and physically attacked her, as evidenced by the residual bruising at her throat and upper arms. In the heat of the moment, she'd grabbed the dagger off the wall and stabbed him with it. By the end of the interview, her attorney was negotiating for a plea of diminished capacity due to the years of trauma she'd suffered under her father's abuse in exchange for her cooperation.

And cooperate she did. She gave them everything they needed to close the cell door tight on Todd Griffin. However, her life would never be the same. A life lived with abuse by a man that should have protected her and instead died by her hand in a fit of rage. It would cost her in so many ways and add to the damage already done.

Jackson figured nobody really escaped unscathed in these kinds of situations. In Cara's case, she was brought to justice, but again, there were no winners.

As Jim and Jackson were getting ready to head back to the

Manor, Sheriff Masters and Deputy Navaro met them in the lobby.

Masters shook both their hands in turn. "Gentlemen, I want to thank you both for your time and effort, your expertise, and for sticking with it ... with us," he said, indicating himself and Jesse. "You're both as solid as they come, and should you ever want to make a change in location, as long as I'm top lawman here, there will always be a place for you in Shiloh County."

"That's very kind of you to say, Sheriff," Jackson said.

"Bull. There's nothing kind about it, Jackson. It would be an honor to have either one of you on my team." Masters looked back and forth between them. "Now, when do you leave? Do you need anything before you go?"

Jackson looked at Jim, who shook his head. "Nope. I think we're good. Miranda got us all on a red-eye tonight. It pushes off the gate at eleven forty-five."

"And gets into Austin at the damn crack of dawn," Jim complained with a grin. "But we're goin' home, so I'll suck it up in first class."

"First class?" Jesse whistled. "Nice."

"Well, I wrapped things up with Sheriff Halbrook in Bastrop this morning, so everything is handled on that front. He'd like a call for a quick rundown tomorrow afternoon. I'm thinking you'll both be back on the job there by Monday, but he can give you the details. In the meantime, safe travels home and keep in touch."

They headed out to the rental car, and Jackson turned to look back as he opened the driver's side door. Both Sheriff Masters and Deputy Navaro were standing in the office doorway. Jackson raised a hand one last time and climbed in behind the wheel.

It was just after one o'clock by the time they got back to Riverside Manor, and Jackson found that Elise had them packed up and ready to go just like she'd said she would. Everyone else seemed to be on the same page with the exception of Miranda, who would be staying on into the next week.

By three, they'd checked out of their room, packed up the rental car, and were ready to hit the road. It was a good two-hour drive over to the airport in the valley on the east side of the city. Miranda had made reservations for dinner at a steak house near the airport, and Madison, C.C., Tina, and Jim rode along with her in the van with Jackson and Elise following in their rental car. After dropping off the car, they made their six-thirty dinner reservation with time to spare.

"Well, that was an interesting honeymoon side trip," C.C. said as they got seated at their table and the waiter took their drink orders.

"I'm not sure that interesting is a word I would use," Madison replied. "I'm just glad that it's all over."

Tina laughed. "Well, I'm not sure that it's *all* over yet. Remember, we may be making an appearance in court sometime in the future."

"Speak for yourself," Madison replied. "I won't be taking part in that, as I didn't participate in y'all's crazy afternoon. Anyway, at least we're on our way home right now. Geez, I miss my own bed."

"Me, too," C.C. agreed. "I used to be able to sleep anywhere, but not anymore."

"I may sleep for a week when we get home," Tina muttered.

"Doubtful, darlin'," Jim replied. "By the time you wake up on Monday morning, you'll be itching to get to the shop, if for no reason other than to check to see if your assistant took proper care of your baby while you were gone."

Tina slapped at him playfully. "That isn't true ... exactly. The jewelry shop pretty much runs itself. However, I am hoping that Bindy has some good sales numbers to report when I get back."

Elise glanced at Miranda. "How soon will you be able to come home, Miranda? I hate leaving you here by yourself."

"While that is a very nice sentiment, El, I am an adult and have traveled all over the world by myself over the last ten years. I think I can handle a few more days alone at the Riverside Manor."

"Well, you do have Nico and Adrianna there in Meadowview, so you won't really be alone, right?" Madison pointed out.

"That is true. Anyway, I hope to have everything wrapped up and ready to catch a flight home by no later than Wednesday."

The waiter came back with their drinks, then took their dinner orders. When he walked away, Miranda lifted her champagne glass and stood, looking around the table at each of them.

"Close your mouths, y'all. I am fixin' to make a toast."

They all picked up their glasses and waited for her to continue.

"First, I would like to thank each and every one of you at this table for accompanying me here," she began.

"Well, you did pay our way," Jim murmured with a grin.

Tina elbowed him and rolled her eyes. "Jim Stockton, for the love of ..."

At Miranda's narrow-eyed glare, Jim's grin disappeared and he pressed his lips together. Jackson struggled to keep a straight face at the look on his partner's face.

Obviously feeling that Jim had been sufficiently cowed, Miranda turned to Elise and Jackson and continued in a soft voice. "I am especially grateful for the two of you. I don't really know how I would have coped with the recent horrific events on my own, but your presence and support was very much appreciated."

Jackson cleared his throat. "I have a feeling that you would have done just fine, Mrs. Rollins. And I think Gene would have been so very proud of his wife."

Clearly caught off guard, Miranda blinked a few times, and momentarily overcome by Jackson's comment, put up a finger for a moment. Then, in pure Miranda fashion and with a voice steeped with emotion, she scolded him. "Thank you very much for that lovely compliment, Jackson. However, this is my toast, so zip it."

Everyone laughed, but then Miranda sobered and finished her toast. "I don't have many close friends, y'all. However, I am extremely fortunate to be able to call each and every one of you my good friends. So, I thank you for coming with me to Bella Luna, and I wish you safe travels home." She took a deep breath, raised her glass, and then took a sip of her champagne as everyone followed suit. "Now, enough with the mush. Let's eat."

ABOUT THE AUTHOR

A native of Oregon, Joni Sauer-Folger spent twenty-two years with an airline traveling and moving around the country before settling down near the beautiful Pacific Ocean with her three very spoiled cats. When she's not spending quality time with the characters she creates, she enjoys gardening, crafting, and working in local theater.

For more information, visit:
www.jonisauerfolger.com

 X

ALSO BY JONI FOLGER

Written as Joni Folger

River Bend Vineyard Cozy Mystery series

Grapes of Death

Of Merlot and Murder

Performance of a Deadly Vintage

Champagne Toast, Murder Chaser

Enchanted Affairs Cozy Mystery series

Monkshood, Tea, & Murder

Written as J. G. Sauer

Immortal Series

Immortal Reckoning – Novella Prequel

Immortal Obsession

Immortal Savior

Immortal Ascending

Guardian Series:

Tarnished Guardian – Novella Prequel

Search for the Mystic Stone

Looking Glass Series:

New Years Through the Looking Glass

Madness Through the Looking Glass

Written as Joni Sauer-Folger

Hidden Treasures, a romantic suspense novel

www.ingramcontent.com/pod-product-compliance
Lightning Source LLC
Chambersburg PA
CBHW020359110726
47899CB00006B/1779